THE
STARTUP
WIFE

Also by Tahmima Anam

A Golden Age
The Good Muslim
The Bones of Grace

THE STARTUP WIFE

Tahmima Anam

CANONGATE

First published in Great Britain in 2021 by Canongate Books Ltd,
14 High Street, Edinburgh EH1 1TE

canongate.co.uk

1

Copyright © Tahmima Anam, 2021

First published in the United States of America by Scribner, an imprint of
Simon & Schuster, Inc. 1230 Avenue of the Americas, New York, NY 10020

British Library Cataloguing-in-Publication Data
A catalogue record for this book is available on
request from the British Library

ISBN 978 1 83885 248 1
Export ISBN: 978 1 83885 249 8

Text design by Wendy Blum

Printed and bound in Great Britain by Clays Ltd, Elcograf S.p.A.

For Sarah Chalfant,
with love

Prologue

NO SUCH THING

People say there's no such thing as Utopia, but they're wrong.

I've seen it myself, and it's on the corner of Tenth Avenue and Fifteenth Street.

Jules and I are summoned on an unseasonably hot day in April. We sneak out of the house, and six hours later we're standing in front of a wide industrial building. Across the street is the High Line, then the West Side Highway, and beyond that, the joggers and the piers and the flat expanse of the Hudson. There's no sign and no doorbell, just an enormous metal door, so we mill around and check the address. Minutes pass. I tell Jules we shouldn't have lied to Cyrus, and Jules reminds me of all the ways Cyrus would have made this trip impossible. Finally, after what feels like an eternity, the door sighs open and we cross the threshold into a pool of biscuity sunlight.

The reception area is magnificent, the square angles of the

1

warehouse tamed into undulating curves. Everything gleams, from the polished wooden floorboards to the metal-framed windows that soar upward. "I love it," Jules sighs, collapsing into a chair. "Please can we have it?"

I look up and see a giant hourglass suspended from the ceiling. "We are never going to get in."

Jules is relaxed, like he walks into this sort of place every day. "But our platform is amazing. No one in the history of the world has ever built anything like it."

I laugh. "It looks expensive. Are you sure we don't have to pay anything?"

"Nope."

We've been called for an audition. If we pass, we get to come here every day and call ourselves Utopians.

Someone comes over to tell us it's time. We go up a flight of stairs, and then another, the light getting paler and brighter as we climb. On the third floor we are led through a corridor festooned with hanging plants. The air is cool but not too cold. There are repeating patterns in bright colors on the walls; there are paintings in frames and jagged sculptures bolted to the ceiling.

In the boardroom, we are greeted by the selection committee. A woman with long straight hair and the most beautiful neck I have ever seen approaches us. "I'm Li Ann," she says. She gleams from every angle and I have to resist the urge to lean in and smell her perfume.

We shake hands. My grip is overly firm and sweaty.

Li Ann invites us to sit. "You've heard of us, I imagine." She smiles, managing to appear confident but not mean.

Of course. Who hasn't heard of Utopia? There are the BuzzFeed stories, *What is the secretive tech incubator that boasts support from Nobel laureates, past presidents, and the elite of the startup world?* The hidden camera shots taken from inside. The outlandish claims by people pretending to be Utopians who say that the labs have successfully cloned a chimpanzee and invented a pocket-size carbon capture machine that cleans the air faster than you can take a selfie.

"It's like winning the lottery," Jules had said on the bus ride over. "It's like getting into the Olympics. It's like turning on your computer and finding a secret cache of cryptocurrency."

"Why don't we introduce ourselves," Li Ann says. "I'm the head of innovation here at Utopia."

"Hey, I'm Marco," says a man with deep-set eyes and a sharply trimmed beard. "I created Obit.ly, a platform that manages all the social and public aspects of death."

A woman with bright pink hair waves hello. "I'm Destiny. I'm the founder of Consentify, a way to make every sexual encounter safe, traceable, and consensual."

A thin, stern man in a lab coat leans against the table. "My name is Rory. I run LoneStar." He speaks with a clipped Scandinavian accent. "I want every single person in the world to stop eating animals."

We would never fit in. First of all, it would be impossible to find a cute, vitamin-gummy way to describe the platform. And then the rest of it, the confidence, the hair, the way they all look as if they slid into place like a synchronized swim team—I cannot imagine ever being that comfortable in my skin. Cyrus likes to call me the Coding Queen of Brattle Street, but right now Cambridge and my graduate school lab seem totally irrelevant. For the last six years I've been working on an algorithm designed to unlock the empathetic brain for artificial intelligence. After a drunken night with Cyrus (more on that later), I had the idea of turning the tiny fragment of code I'd written into something else—*this*—and that is why Jules and I are here.

"We're ready when you are," Li Ann says.

That's my cue to start the presentation. I fiddle with my laptop. Jules passes me his cable, and the sight of his hand, steady and unshaking, is reassuring. Whatever happens, we'll go home and laugh about it with Cyrus.

"It doesn't have a name," I begin, explaining the blank title page.

"We'll come up with something great," Jules says.

There's an image of the landing page, with the Three Questions. "This is our new social media platform. We have devised a way of getting people to form connections with others on the basis of what gives their life meaning, instead of what they like or don't like. It does this by providing rituals for people based on their interests, beliefs, and passions."

"Like custom-made religion?" asks Rory, the Scandi vegan.

"Sort of. But imagine if you could integrate your belief system with everything else in your life. A system that embraces the whole you."

"Maybe you should call it Whole You," Destiny suggests.

"How it works is, you answer a short questionnaire about things that are important to you. Not just the traditions you've inherited but the things you've picked up along the way. The life you've earned, as it were."

Marco nods. "Cool. So, if I were about to die, would it be able to come up with a way for me to have a special funeral?"

"Yes, it would. Would you like to give it a try?"

Jules passes his laptop to Marco. Marco types for a few seconds. "*Game of Thrones, The Great British Baking Show*, and Ancient Egypt," Marco says. "Let's see what it does with that."

We wait the 2.3 seconds it takes the algorithm to go through its calculations. Then Marco starts to read from the screen: "'I would propose that you be buried, in the style of the Ancient Egyptians, with your most precious possessions. Then, if you wanted, you could have your loved ones perform the Opening of the Mouth ceremony.'" He looks up from the screen. "There's an Opening of the Mouth ceremony? Is this real?"

"Yes," I reply. "All the suggestions are based on real texts: religious scripture, ancient rites and traditions, myths. Here it gives you an option—sometimes the algorithm does that—you could choose to be cremated, like the Dothraki and the Valyrians, but if you wanted your family to perform the Opening of the Mouth ceremony, you might choose to have your body displayed, your hands clasped over a sword, as was the tradition in Westeros. In that case, you could also have stones placed over your eyes."

"Yeah." Marco smiles, rubbing his hands together. "I sometimes fancy myself a Dothraki, but I'm more of a Seven Kingdoms guy." He keeps reading. "'The Opening of the Mouth ceremony is a symbolic ritual in which the body's mouth is opened so that it can speak and eat in the afterlife. This would enable you to integrate any number of baked goods into the ritual.'"

Jules and I exchange a glance. How did we manage to make the platform so goddamn awesome, is what I'm thinking.

"I can't believe it," Marco says.

Jules leans over and reads the end of the ritual. "'Someone in your family might recite the following incantation . . . *I have opened your mouth. I have opened your two eyes.*'"

Marco grins. "I'm totally going to put that in my advance-directives Dropbox."

We walk them through the platform, the target audience, the growth plan. I describe the tech behind it.

There's a pause when no one says anything. I turn to the others, and it's hard to look at them all at once. Sunlight pours in from the large window behind them and they are encased in a giant gold halo.

Rory puts his palms on the table. "Nothing good has ever come from religion," he announces.

"My father would agree with you," I say. "But it's a powerful institution—imagine if we could change it somehow."

Rory glances away, and I can almost feel him rolling his eyes.

Jules pipes up. "Look, we're here to restore something to people who have grown up in the shadow of social media—those who are living their entire lives in public. We want to address the thirty-seven percent who say they don't believe in God because their politics or their sexuality excludes them from organized religion. We believe that even the nonreligious among us deserve our own communities, our own belief systems, whatever they may be based in. Ritual, community, that's what religion offers that no other human construct has been able to replace. Until now. We are here to give meaning back to people, to restore and amplify faith—not in a higher power but in humanity."

I catch Li Ann smiling to herself. Jules has nailed it. Maybe he's right, maybe no one in the history of the world has ever built anything like it.

"I like what we've seen so far. Right, everyone?" Destiny and Marco nod, and Rory manages a tiny head tilt. Li Ann leans in and lowers her voice. "We're especially interested in projects that will support human community in the afterworld."

"The afterworld?"

"The future when there will be nothing left," Destiny says.

"You're planning for the apocalypse?" Jules asks.

"We want to be prepared," Rory explains. "In the next fifty years, things will change in ways we cannot yet imagine."

Marco reels off a list of ways the world might end. "Famine, deadly pandemic, mass antibiotic resistance, climate collapse, insect collapse, world war." He ends with a flourish: "Asteroid."

"We are not connected to any major public utilities," Li Ann explains. "We get our water from an underground aquifer. The servers are disconnected from the major fiber-optic lines. All waste is recycled. We are funding research into last-resort antibiotics and antivirals, building an army of robotic bees, and turning electricity into food. We believe that technology has a role to play in the post-world world."

I realize where we fit in. "You're going to need faith?" I say, trying not to start singing the George Michael song.

"Well, that's what we've been debating," Li Ann says. "I think it would be great to offer people something to help frame their existence. Rory wants to do away with all that, but some of us still think it's important."

"If we are going to imagine a better world, I would prefer it to be based on science, not superstition," Rory says.

I ask the question that's been on my mind since the call came: "How do you pay for all of this?"

"I've been given a mandate," Li Ann says. "On the one hand, we operate like any other startup incubator. But our mission is also to find solutions to the inevitable demise of the world as we know it. Our endowment is made up of tech companies, high-net-worth individuals, even some government pension funds. I think there's a general sense that we are going to face unprecedented challenges in the future, and everyone wants to be prepared."

What will Cyrus say? I haven't thought about him for at least half an hour, which is the longest I've not thought about him since our reunion. The doomsday cult thing is definitely going to put him off.

Or is it? Cyrus is full of surprises. I would never have guessed, nine months ago, that he was going to be the sort of person who would get married on a whim. I wouldn't have thought that about myself either, but there you have it. Love. Mysterious ways.

Li Ann promises to send us her decision before the end of the day, and Jules and I are returned to the ordinary, imperfect world.

One

CYRUS JONES AND THE MAGIC FUNERAL

Cyrus and I got married exactly two months after we met the second time, which was thirteen years after we met the first time.

The first time, I was in ninth grade and Cyrus was in eleventh. I knew his middle name, what classes he took, when he had free period, and which afternoons he stayed late for swim team or jazz band practice. In other words, I was in love with him. Cyrus did not know any of my names or that I had recently moved to Merrick, Long Island, from Queens, that I had skipped fourth grade and was in possession of one friend, a girl called Huong who occasionally sat beside me at lunch, that my parents were immigrants from Bangladesh and that was why my lunchbox contained rice and curry, something I was perpetually ashamed of, not just because of the curry smell that stuck to my clothes but also because my mother never closed the Tupperware properly, so there were always little bits of chicken and rice plastered to the insides of my backpack.

For fifteen years my parents lived above the Health Beats pharmacy in a one-bedroom apartment with two narrow windows and a view of Roosevelt Avenue in Jackson Heights. My sister, Mira, came along, and then me. They worked long hours and sent regular Western Union payments to Bangladesh, but because we ate dal and rice most nights and never went on vacation and I only got to wear hand-me-downs, they managed to save a little every year, until they could put a down payment on the pharmacy, then on another one in Woodside. By the time I met Cyrus, my parents owned a mini-chain of three Health Beats, and we had moved out of the old neighborhood and into a shiny new housing development on Long Island.

After a summer of unpacking boxes and sticking stars to the ceiling of my room in the pattern of the Messier 81 galaxy, I arrived at our new school, Washington High. Mira was a freshman at Columbia, already busy finding her new tribe, the climate activists and the radical new leftists and the Students for Yemen. I was left to fend for myself with my smelly lunches and my complete inability to engage in small talk. My only refuge was math class, where I skipped two grades and landed in AP Geometry, with Cyrus.

I spent the year gazing at the back of Cyrus's head and wishing he'd turn around and say something to me, but he never did. I just stared and stared at that glorious blond hair, so wavy it was actively greeting me. At the end of May, when we were supposed to take our final exam, Cyrus didn't show up for class. A week later, he handed our teacher, Mr. Ruben, a large folder, and in that folder was a graphic novel titled *How to Teach Geometry*. Mr. Ruben was shown standing in front of the chalkboard completing the final angle of an isosceles triangle. Chapter by chapter, the book went through every lesson Mr. Ruben had taught us that year, starting with angles and ending with architectural puzzles. There were equations and formulas, drawn-to-scale buildings with intricate detail: the Chrysler with its scalloped exterior, the columns of the Parthenon, the triangles of Egyptian tombs. Mr. Ruben displayed the pages on the walls of our classroom, and we all stared in wonder. "Freak," someone whispered under their breath. Freak was right. Mr. Ruben didn't know what to do, so he gave Cyrus a zero for failing to show up for his exam.

The rumor was that Cyrus failed all his classes—the AP Lit class in which he'd written a story without using the letter E, the European history class in which he made a 3D diorama of the battle of Algiers, even Drama, where he submitted a short film. Everyone in school knew Cyrus, but no one could claim to be his friend; he was always alone, and he never stayed after school or turned up in the cafeteria at lunchtime, so the mystery of his final exams remained just that.

Cyrus disappeared. He didn't come back for senior year and he didn't graduate. Eventually I went to college and forgot about him. I blossomed. I was miles from Merrick, a world away from high school, and I stepped into my brain like I was putting on a really great pair of sneakers for the first time. My brain-sneakers and I sprinted through courses and seminars and got me summa-cum-lauded. I cut my hair very short and got the first six digits of Pi tattooed on my left shoulder. In the meantime, I made a friend—a girl called Lynn—and I had a handful of casual hookups and lost my virginity in my dorm room while Constance, my roommate, was at a double feature of *Blade Runner* and *The Big Sleep*.

Lynn was an actress who was cast as the only woman in the drama department's all-male production of *Macbeth*. We bonded over our late blooming. Lynn had spent the summer before college at fat camp and emerged nymphlike just weeks before orientation, but the high school scars were still raw, and over kale chips, which she dehydrated in a toaster oven that she kept illegally in her dorm room, we put Band-Aids over all the slights, sneers, and total invisibleness we had managed to escape. I told her about Cyrus—possibly the first time I had ever said his name aloud outside of my bedroom walls—but even then I downplayed my attraction to him, noting him as just another piece of flotsam from the shark tank that was high school.

I can't remember when I came up with the idea of the Empathy Module, only that it had been lurking somewhere in the back of my mind for as long as I could remember. Maybe it was all the apocalyptic sci-fi I was reading that made me want to figure out a way to live without a fear of machines. They were going to be smarter than we were someday, we all knew that. They were going to beat us at chess and cook our meals and drive our cars. Someday they would paint and write operas and sing them back to us in perfect harmony. But what if they also had the one thing that humans possessed only on rare occasions? What if they had an intrinsic, automatic, unflinching, couldn't-be-switched-off understanding of other people? What if they had empathy? Then they wouldn't be our rivals, they would just be better versions of us. We wouldn't have to fear them, and we wouldn't have to subjugate them. We could just try to be more like them, because they'd be the best of humanity.

I went straight to grad school and started working in Dr. Melanie Stein's lab. Dr. Stein had pioneered the reverse engineering of the brain. She was one of those formidable women who seemed to flourish in academic departments, her awkwardness hardened into a kind of opaque, terrifying brilliance. She was not mean, she was just never nice, never talked to fill awkward silences, and always made me feel as if I had said the dumbest thing ever. Before I met Cyrus again, I wanted nothing more than to grow up and become her.

My first encounter with Dr. Stein was not terrible. It was the start of the year, and I had just moved to Cambridge and into my tiny apartment in Ashdown House. She asked to meet me at a bar on Mass Ave, and when I turned up—I couldn't believe how cold it was, I was already in my Michelin Man jacket—Dr. Stein was sporting a sexy poncho. She said, "I need to know right now that you're not going to drop out or slow down, because if that's anywhere near the horizon, you should go and join Dr. Li's lab, which is full of the well-intentioned but only moderately ambitious."

"I'm fully ambitious," I said.

She ordered a vodka martini, extra dirty, and I was so nervous I ordered a Diet Coke even though I hate Diet Coke.

"So tell me about this Empathy Module."

I shrugged out of my giant coat. "You know far better than I do that the last parts of the brain to be mapped are the ones that control our emotions."

"I do know better than you do," she said. The blue of her eyes was so light, I felt like I was looking into a church window. I couldn't help staring. "I'm a cyborg," she said, taking off her glasses and inviting me to look deeper.

"What do you mean?"

"My eyes. They're transplants. I would've gone blind without them."

"Wow."

"His name was Hans Eikelheimer. His wife sometimes emails me."

We raised our glasses to Hans, and I thought at that moment that she had decided to make me her friend.

"I don't think we can get to the ultimate reaches of the brain by mapping," I said. "I mean, I don't think that's the only way. It needs to be paired with other types of modeling, especially when it comes to emotional intelligence."

"We already know that."

"But how do we reach empathy? If we want our robots to be like us, we need to get beyond the algorithmic layers of intelligence and ensure that the AI of the future has the ability to imagine what it's like to be someone else. It's not just a way to make them more human. We should focus on making them better than us, not like us."

"Okay, that's novel. You think that's how we're going to survive the Singularity?"

"Yes, by making them greater—not smarter but kinder. More affected by the pain of others."

"You want to save the world."

"Why else would I be here?" I said, beaming.

I pranced home in my enormous coat, smug in the conviction that she was, in some tiny way, going to reciprocate my crush.

But after that evening, Dr. Stein and I did not, in fact, become friends. She avoided eye contact when we bumped into each other, and during our advisory meetings she picked on tiny aspects of the module, telling me it would never work to map the neural pathways the way I was proposing because we didn't know how emotional information traveled, insisting that, until the entire brain had been reverse-engineered, we wouldn't know how the limbic system truly worked. I always spent hours rewinding through our brief exchanges and coming up with better arguments which I would practice later, when it was too late.

Four years into my PhD, at the start of another summer of research in my overly air-conditioned lab, I was informed that my high school English teacher, Mrs. Butterfield, had died. When I got the message—a text from an unknown number—I was reminded of all the times I'd meant to write to her but never had. The message said, **Please bring a sentence from a favorite novel to Mrs. Butterfield's service**. An invitation followed.

I'd never been to a white person's funeral, but I knew I was supposed to wear black, so I put on a turtleneck and spent the ride down from Boston rolling my chosen sentence around in my mind. Mrs. Butterfield always knew I was more devoted to science than literature, but she didn't hold it against me—she believed that I deserved novels as much as the students who went around quoting David Foster Wallace. I should have kept in touch.

When I entered the auditorium, I saw some familiar faces—a few teachers; the principal, Mr. Gatney; Iris and Ruby, the twins who formed a band my senior year called One Placenta; and even some of the boys who were never seen without their shiny varsity jackets. I said some awkward hellos, silently judging everyone yet annoyed when they didn't remember me. We shuffled into our seats; the lights went down and up again, and standing in the middle of the stage was Cyrus Jones.

His head was bent over a microphone. "Mrs. Butterfield's family—her niece Elizabeth and her nephew Constantine—were, sadly, not able to travel from California to be here, and they asked me to conduct today's celebration in their stead." He spoke slowly, and it sounded like he had a slight English accent, and I was going to have a stroke.

"You will remember Mrs. Butterfield as the teacher who impressed Shakespeare and Hemingway upon you. You will remember that she drove to school every morning in her pristine Volkswagen

Beetle. You will remember her kindness and her solitude. As she passes, we celebrate all of this, but it also gives us an opportunity to celebrate what we didn't know.

"There are people we are familiar with only in certain contexts—ministers, therapists, doctors. Teachers are our most intimate acquaintances for a period of our lives, but the relationship is tilted toward us; they mute themselves in order to act as a conduit for our growth. No one played this role more seriously than Mrs. Butterfield. There are the things we knew about her—you will remember, no doubt, the fondness with which she spoke of her dog, Harold—but the rest of her remains an enigma. Death gives us the opportunity not to complete the picture, necessarily, but to contemplate the unknowability, the strangeness, of others, even our most intimate friends. And what better way to do that than through fiction, the human endeavor that cleaves itself most closely to the mysteries of our lived experience?"

Cyrus gestured, inviting us all onto the stage. The lights changed; he faced each of us in turn and moved us around into a circle. When he reached me and looked into my eyes and whispered, "Asha Ray," all of the blood pooled in my legs.

"Hello," I breathed.

Finally, we were assembled. Cyrus asked the person on his left to begin.

"'Do not go gentle into that good night,'" they said. Cyrus nodded to the next person in the circle.

"'Good night, good night, parting is such sweet sorrow.'"

Then: "'I'd rather learn from one bird how to sing than teach ten thousand stars how not to dance.'"

And: "'People coming and putting a bunch of flowers on your stomach on Sunday and all that crap. Who wants flowers when you're dead? Nobody.'"

There was laughter. Cyrus gave it a moment. The next person read: "'When lilacs last in the dooryard bloomed, and the great star early drooped in the western sky in the night, I mourned, and yet shall mourn with ever-returning spring.'"

"'And I will look down and see my murmuring bones and the deep water like wind, like a roof of wind, and after a long time they cannot distinguish even bones upon the lonely and inviolate sand.'"

I was last. "'Hope is the thing with feathers that perches in the soul, and sings the tune without the words and never stops at all.'"

The lights went down, and in the darkness Cyrus whispered, "Jana—Mrs. Butterfield to most of us—and I spent a lot of time talking about death. Her final words to me were 'The Prince of Darkness is a gentleman!' and I knew, when she said it, that her pain was coming to an end."

I couldn't believe he was right there, being a real person. And while I had no reason to hope this was true, I felt like maybe he was thinking the same thing about me. He looked so different than when I saw him last—the basic facts of him were still the same, the lanky, long torso, the angle of his jaw, his wavy, calligraphic blond hair—but everything had slowed down. He was beautiful and older and completely perfect.

Afterward, he found me in the cafeteria nibbling through a sandwich. "We kept in touch," he said. "After I dropped out. She would call me and check that I was reading enough Shakespeare. She told me everything else was optional."

I wasn't thinking about Mrs. Butterfield. "How did you do that?"

"You mean the service?"

"Getting all those people to have a moment."

"That's kind of my thing," he said. "I create rituals."

"But do you do that to all the grieving people?" I asked.

"What?"

"Look into their eyes and cause mayhem? Internal organ damage?"

He smiled. "I hear you live in Cambridge."

"How did you know?"

"Mrs. Butterfield gave me a list of people to invite. Turns out we're neighbors."

"No."

"Streets away."

"All this time?"

"All this time. Do you want to take the bus back up with me?"

"My sister is driving me. She has a meeting with the Boston chapter of Planned Parenthood."

"Mira, right? Is she . . . ?"

"Exactly as she always was. How about dinner tomorrow night?"

"Great. I'll pick you up at your lab."

"You know my building?"

"I've been paying attention," he said. And then he leaned over and kissed me on the cheek and burned a hole right through my face.

The next day, the first thing Cyrus said to me was "What did you do today?" as if the gap between what he knew and what he didn't know about my life was only twenty-four hours long. This put me at ease, even though when he folded himself into the seat across from me I caught a glimpse of his pale pink nipple and almost fainted.

I told him I'd been to a lecture on lifespan.

"I'm down with extending lifespan."

"You want to live forever?"

"Maybe not forever," he said, "but I may not be done by the time I'm a hundred."

This was typical, I came to understand, from Cyrus. That he never wanted things to end. "You're not afraid of being old?"

"Under the right circumstances, no."

"How old are your parents?" I asked. "Lifespan is mostly genetic."

"I never knew my father," he replied. "And my mother died after eleventh grade."

All those years ago, I'd been obsessed with him and never known anything about him, not even the very basic facts. "That's why you did those crazy projects?"

"We did them together—she gave me ideas from her hospital bed. Right down to the last days."

We talked about the intervening years. After his mother died, he had gone to live with an aunt. He didn't finish high school. He backpacked around Mexico, and then he helped to organize a copper miners' union in Chile, and after that he had taught English in Ecuador before returning to America. He met Julian, his best friend, while hiking the Presidential mountain range in New Hampshire (they had met on Madison and started talking on Jefferson, and by the time they had done the Washington traverse, they were inseparable). Days before I'd moved to Cambridge, Jules had convinced Cyrus to move into his house, just streets away from my dorm. By now I was over being shy; I decided it would be best to just tell him.

"This is a strange and wonderful coincidence," I said, smiling. "That the you I was so smitten with all those years ago is the same you who moved around the corner from me at the very moment when I am about to complete my metamorphosis."

"You were smitten with me?"

"Oh, don't act like you didn't know. I could've written it on my forehead with a Sharpie and it would've been less obvious."

He laughed. Then he said, "Into what have you metamorphosed?"

"That's for you to figure out," I said.

"Well then, that *is* a wonderful coincidence."

"You're really Cyrus Jones," I said, shaking my head.

"You're really Asha Ray," he replied.

The metamorphosis was this: I was no longer the awkward new kid at school with the smelly lunchbox. I had taken the heaviness of my childhood—the story of my parents and their exile and those years above the pharmacy and all the striving I had to swallow—and I had turned it into fire-breathing. I was clever and awesome and, despite my less than stellar performance in Dr. Stein's lab, beginning to understand my powers. This is the me that Cyrus met for the second time. In his mind, the person sitting in front of him and the person who gazed adoringly at the back of his head for nine months were one and the same, and for me, the boy with the long wavy hair who made magic out of homework and the man sitting in front of me who made magic out of a funeral were also one and the same person, and suddenly every novel Mrs. Butterfield had me read made perfect sense, because all the great love stories are about two people bringing the story of their yesterdays and the story of their todays into one epic sewn-together poem, and that is what they mean when they say lightning strikes. It's not when it strikes the first time, it's when it strikes twice, which hardly ever happens, except, I think, when you fall in love.

Cyrus didn't seem to mind that I sometimes went on and on about brain modeling. In fact, it seemed like he had been waiting to talk at length and in detail about various things himself, and that for the first time, he had the right audience. Me. When I wondered out loud if the Empathy Module was ahead of its time, he told me that in the third century, an engineer called Ma Jun invented an entire mechanical puppet theater powered by a waterwheel for the emperor Cao Rui. What happed to Ma Jun? Nothing. Just that there were no water-powered mechanical puppet theaters for at least three hundred years after that.

We were together all the time. We talked and talked. We talked while walking the baking streets of Cambridge. We talked while eating. We read the same book, a Korean novel about a woman whose family freaks out when she stops eating meat, and then we talked about meat, and about Korea, and about our families. Cyrus had none, so I did most of the talking that afternoon, telling him how my parents existed in a halfway world between Long Island and Bangladesh, too comfortable to go home, never comfortable enough to stop longing for it.

In the middle of July, a heatwave made it impossible to go any-where, so we stayed inside and watched the entire five-year run of *Babylon 5*. We followed the fan as it rotated on its pedestal. Julian was spending the summer in Hong Kong, so we had the place all to ourselves. We found a thumb of pot in a kitchen drawer, and after we got high, we stood on chairs and made Oscar speeches.

Cyrus lived with Julian, and Julian, or rather, his family, owned the house. It was gray with red trim and a steeply pitched roof. It was enormous. There were rooms crammed with heavy furniture and the kind of curtains you wanted to call drapes. There was a library, a glass conservatory, and two dining rooms. This was Julian's father's way of showing his disapproval—saddling him with the family home in the fancy part of Cambridge, where he received letters from the neigh-borhood society requesting that he mow the lawn and please take his mail out of the overflowing box on the curb.

When the heatwave passed and the evenings were cool again, Cyrus invited me to a wedding.

"Who's getting married?"

"I haven't actually met them," he said. They were friends of friends and they'd asked him to come up with a ceremony.

"So you gave them a theme?"

"Sort of. You'll see."

Cyrus wanted to do something—many things—with his life. He wanted to travel and paint murals and get a law degree so he could run for office. But another part of him was already tired, and maybe that was why Julian had been able to convince him to move in. He held on to a lot of those old plans, but in the meantime, he continued to earn his living by conducting baptisms and cremations and writing little prayers for people to say at the bedside of a sick relative. There were so many others out there, he explained, for whom God served as a placeholder for what they really wanted— something that was greater than they were. He just helped them find that meaning without the baggage of religion. Released from compulsion, they were free to build whatever kinds of scaffolding they chose around their lives. I dubbed him a humanist spirit guide, and this made him happy.

The wedding was two hours outside of Boston in a bookshop that used to be a sawmill. We rented a car and Cyrus drove and we listened to Jeff Buckley singing "Hallelujah," which put me in a very somber mood even though I was wearing my most cheerful outfit, a red tunic which was one half of a matching set my mother's cousin had sent from Bangladesh. Cyrus was dressed in a not dissimilar shaped shirt with a small round collar and a navy waistcoat.

We pulled over at a rest stop and Cyrus unpacked two triangular-shaped rice balls he called Onigiri. He was always making me taste things—mostly Japanese things—I'd never heard of. He unwrapped one and showed me how to put the seaweed around it so it looked like a large samosa. It was delicious, filled with pickles and sour plums. As I plucked off a piece of rice that had stuck to the corner of my mouth, I felt his hand cradling the back of my neck, and then he was hovering over me, and I can't remember which of us leaned in first, but soon we were kissing, and a little sound escaped from my mouth, a noise that appeared to originate elsewhere, deep down inside where my brain couldn't reach.

He tasted like rice and vinegar and his lips were very soft. I tried not to count the number of years I had been waiting for this moment. Until this morning, we had hardly touched. A few days before, we had run into someone Cyrus knew on the corner of Harvard Avenue and he had introduced me to her—it was a girl—as "my friend Asha. Asha, this is Ling, my Chinese tutor." Being called his friend nearly killed me, but then last night he had called me and said he had booked a room in a small hotel and would I consider spending the night with him? And that is how I knew for sure that we weren't just friends.

The kiss lasted a long time and lingered on my mouth for a while after that. We arrived in Montague; the mill was perched by the side of a river and there was a long driveway leading down to a cluster of buildings. Strings of lights decorated the path like a tangle of fireflies. We were early; Cyrus deposited me inside and went to attend to the bride and groom. I found myself in a large rectangular room with wooden beams holding up a low ceiling. The shelves were built along the walls and over the windows, which looked out onto the river below. People were unfolding chairs and moving large vases of flowers, and over the bustle you could hear the sound of the water as it rushed by. I tried to make myself useful by carrying in a case of wine.

Cyrus returned with a small purple wildflower in the pocket of his waistcoat. There was a little time before the ceremony, he said, so we went to an adjacent building where, in a nook, we found two small stools next to a bookcase.

"Do you remember, in high school, there was a talent show called Lip Synch Battle?" Cyrus said.

Until that point, we had both resisted starting too many sentences with "Do you remember, in high school?"

"Yes, of course I remember." I'd sneaked out of the house because I didn't have the words to explain the importance of Lip Synch Battle to my parents.

"Well, one year I signed up."

I was so surprised I slapped his knee. "Serious?"

"Yup. I think it was before your time."

"All by yourself?"

"I didn't have any friends."

This I knew. "That's because you never bothered talking to anyone."

"I was going to do 'Bohemian Rhapsody.'"

"No."

"I bought the outfit, practiced the hell out of it. I think I was pretty good. But then, at the last minute, I choked. I had to beg Mrs. Stanley not to announce my name, and I went home and cried myself to sleep."

"I would have really liked to see that. 'Bohemian Rhapsody,' I mean, not the crying. What did you do with the outfit?"

"I went home and put it in the trash."

"I am super turned on by the thought of you in sequins."

"You should be. I was so hot."

We kissed again. He circled his arms around my waist and I leaned toward him. Suddenly I couldn't wait for the wedding to be over.

A man in a gray suit came and waved to us. "It's time," he said.

The hall was full and I took a seat at the very back. I was struggling to recall the names of the bride and groom—Cyrus had told me, but right now all I could remember was the way he had run his finger along the rim of my collar.

The groom was standing at the front of the room, and the light from the window made a halo around him. There was no music, only the soft roar of the water being turned by the mill. Cyrus stood beside him and gestured to the audience, and together we all sat down. I heard a rustling sound behind me, and when I turned around, I saw a woman in a puffy dress and a thick veil. As she walked past me, I noticed that the dress and the veil were made entirely from long strips of paper. "It's *The Iliad*," an older man beside me whispered. "Charlie and Bethan are classicists."

Bethan joined Charlie and they turned to face each other.

"Penelope," Cyrus began in a voice that was both soft and loud, "waited for Odysseus for twenty-two years. She knitted, and she waited.

"Some of us search for a lifetime to find our soulmate. We scour the earth and journey to distant shores. Charlie and Bethan, born in the same hospital on exactly the same day, appear to have been soulmates from the start—the way Plato imagined soulmates, as two bodies that were once joined together. This marriage is not just a union but a *re*union of mates who have been known to each other in another realm."

Charlie and Bethan, holding hands, leaned toward each other. Cyrus was looking at them, but he was speaking to me.

"We will now conduct the Anakalupteria, the ancient Greek ritual of the removal of the veil."

Charlie stepped toward Bethan. With great tenderness, he tore the first strip of paper from her veil. He held it up and read: "'Bethan, I pledge my love, my body, my life to you.'"

Bethan reached up and tore another strip of paper from the veil. "'Charlie, I pledge my love, my body, my life to you.'"

Another strip: "'...like that star of the waning summer who beyond all stars rises bathed in the ocean stream to glitter in brilliance.'"

Charlie pulled a ring from his pocket and placed it on her outstretched hand. "Wishing to marry you, I honor you with this."

"Wishing to marry you, I honor you with this," she echoed, doing the same.

"In the tradition of Ancient Greece, and sanctioned by the state of Massachusetts, and in remembrance of your mothers, who could not be here today, and surrounded by these beloved texts, I pronounce you bound together by the love you share and the promise you have made."

To the sounds of laughter and clapping, Charlie and Bethan kissed.

After the party, the dinner, the toasts, dancing, champagne, the bride pulling away pieces of her dress until she was left in shorts and a T-shirt that had I HEART HOMER written across the front, Cyrus and I drove to the B&B he had booked. We greeted the owners, a sunburned couple called Sam and Sam, and their orange cat, then we took our things to the top floor and closed the door behind us.

Sex with Cyrus. Was it everything I'd dreamed it would be? I could say no, but I would be lying. It was. Was I Goldilocks with my perfect bowl of porridge, my not too soft chair, my excellently firm bed? Yes, yes, and yes. Did he make me do things I'd always wanted to do but was too much of a repressed nerd to ever admit to wanting? Mm-hm. Did it make me question everything I had ever done before in the name of sex? Absolutely. Did my stomach do somersaults when I thought about it afterward? Constantly.

Did I worry it was too good to be true?

No.

Because I had made a promise to myself that I would no longer waste time doubting the greatness of a thing that was right in front of me.

In the morning I casually suggested to Cyrus that we should start a platform that allowed people without religion to practice a form of faith. I said I would customize the Empathy Module algorithm to create rituals around the things that people loved: their hobbies, their obsessions, their favorite characters in their favorite books. It would pull from history, from novels, from poetry and witchcraft. People could form micro-communities around their interests, and in this age of emptiness, it would give them a kind of virtual parish.

"You can do that?"

"I have magic hands." I giggled. "Just like you."

"You want to start our own religion?"

"Something like that."

"How about we just worship each other forever?"

He pulled the covers away and leaned over to face me. We were on the top floor of the B&B, and the ceiling sloped down above our heads. The white paint reflected the bright light outside, and Cyrus was so, so lovely. I felt his imprint all over my body. I would never forget, now, the smell of maple syrup and old wood and the things he had said to me after and the way he had delicately pulled a strand of hair from my forehead. "Seriously, though. How many of these rituals have you done?" I asked him.

"I don't know, dozens."

"And were any two the same?"

"I get a lot of requests for *Harry Potter*. But no, they're all different."

"Imagine if we could use AI to give people exactly the kind of experiences they were looking for, things they shared but were never able to integrate into a faith-based system."

"How would we do that?"

"I don't know. But I can figure it out." I would need someone to help me design it, but I had a vague idea of how I might get started. It wouldn't work if the rituals were ever the same—there would have to be an infinite number of possibilities, and we would have to decide where the system would get its data, and there were a million other things to sort out. But I knew it was just a matter of time before I worked it all out.

One of the Sams knocked on the door to announce breakfast, and at their kitchen table Cyrus and I held hands and struggled to cut our waffles. After breakfast we went back to bed and stayed there until it was time to leave. On the ride home we talked about other things, and then he dropped me off at my apartment, and when we said goodbye, I wanted to cry and tell him we should never spend another minute apart, but of course I didn't, because even though there was little pretense between us, I had some sense of preserving my dignity. Twenty minutes later he called me, and instead of going to the lab, as I'd planned, I met him for tea and then we went back to Julian's house. "Did you mean it when you said you just wanted to worship each other forever?" I asked.

"Yes," he said. "I want to get married."

"I was just thinking the same thing," I confessed.

"I don't actually want to get married, I want to already be married."

I knew what he meant. The in-between stuff seemed unnecessary. I had loathed every minute of my sister's wedding. The thought of having to douse myself in gold jewelry and wear a sari safety-pinned to me so tightly I'd be doing Kegels without even trying made me want to throw up. But Cyrus was all about ceremony. "Are you sure?" I asked him. "You don't want to stand in a field of cornflowers or walk around a circle of fire?"

"Let's pretend we've done it already."

"Speeches and champagne and biryani?"

"Tents and drunk dancing and I do."

"Well then I do too."

I called my sister. "Mira, I need you to come to Cambridge."

"Now?"

"The day after tomorrow."

"Why?"

"I am marrying Cyrus Jones."

"Fuck off. Cyrus? Cyrus from high school? The guy with the hair?"

I was so happy that she understood the importance of Cyrus's past hotness. "Yes! I'm sorry I didn't tell you." And then I said, "You're wondering why he suddenly loves me back."

"Of course he loves you back. You morphed into a cross between Snow White and Iron Man."

"What was I before?"

"One of the Seven Dwarfs. Bashful, if I'm being generous."

"I can't wear a sari and get pinched by aunties. You have to come."

"I'm sorry. Ahmed and I are trying to get pregnant."

"Oh. Can't you just bring him and have sex in Cambridge?"

"It's not sex, it's IVF."

It was the first I'd heard of it, and I felt like a jerk. "I'm really sorry, I didn't know."

"I have a bicornuate uterus. It's shaped like a heart yet is totally inhospitable for babies. You should probably get yours scanned too, just in case."

"You want me to come over?"

"Oh God, no. I don't suppose you can wait?"

I knew I couldn't. "I'm on a high. I can't explain—I feel like it needs to happen right now, this very minute."

"I get it. Go—take selfies and tell me everything later."

"I love you."

"I love you too, baby."

Julian flew in from Hong Kong and came straight to city hall. When we arrived, he was already there, waiting under a small rectangle of shade in front of the bell tower. He and Cyrus greeted each other with excited cries like they'd been apart for years, even though it had been only the summer.

"Jules, this is Asha. Asha, Jules."

Jules turned to me and threw open his arms. I was wearing a yellow sleeveless dress, and he squashed my elbows against my ribs as he hugged me.

"What's this I hear about a wedding?" he boomed.

Cyrus said, "You're it, friend. You're the wedding party."

They could've been brothers. Their haircuts were different (in that Julian believed in haircuts and Cyrus didn't), but they were both tall and bore their bodies in similar ways, with a kind of casual swagger. That they had met on a mountaintop was fully apparent. But whereas I thought of Cyrus as big/small—a large person who often commanded an entire room just by walking into it, and yet could become almost invisible at will—Julian was just big in every way, as if he'd lost his volume control and settled on a kind of outside voice no matter where he found himself.

With a flourish, Julian reached into his front pocket and pulled out a hat—not a fedora or a beret but one of those cones that children wear at birthday parties. The cone said CONGRATULATIONS. We made our way merrily inside. On the second floor, a tiny seed of doubt took hold. What was I doing? It had been a summer—not even that—and here I was in a plain dress and flip-flops. I went over the arguments that Cyrus and I had rehearsed with each other. We both hated weddings. It would save us months of dating, which neither of us had ever liked.

But really, it was none of those things. There was both a very good reason and no reason at all for Cyrus and me to get married within a few weeks of meeting again. The good reason was that we were in love, or at least we believed ourselves to be in love, and for me the feeling was so strong that it felt like the first time I had ever believed in anything. But also, doing something so irrational both fit into who I wanted to be—a person who chooses her own destiny—and yet told me something entirely new about the world, which is that things that seemed impossible and out of my reach, like marrying a man I had teenage dreams about—were actually within my grasp, and all I had to do was stretch out my greedy little hands and take what was mine.

When we approached the town clerk who would marry us, I suddenly wished I were holding a purse, one of those things people call a clutch. I would've liked to be clutching something—flowers! God, why didn't we have flowers? We had nothing but a giant friend in a paper hat.

The clerk, a woman in a blue pantsuit that was perhaps one size too small, was stationed behind a podium. Cyrus handed her the marriage license. Julian pulled out his phone and started recording. The clerk asked us how to pronounce our names. SIGH-RUS and AH-SHAH, we said. She examined each one of us in turn and, seemingly satisfied, turned to her podium. Cyrus and I held hands and waited.

"We are gathered here at this hour to join Asha Ray and Cyrus Jones in marriage," she began.

Upon hearing my name, tears came to my eyes.

"Today is the day you have chosen to formally and legally declare your commitment to each other. Marriage is among the most serious of all decisions. You are willingly entering into an intimate pact of trust and love."

Since we had decided against a ceremony, I hadn't expected so many words. The words moved inside me and I started to sob. Cyrus squeezed my hand.

"As equal partners, you will share the privileges, sacrifices, and responsibilities that come with the union. As your relationship continues to grow, you will face the challenge of being true to each other while remaining true to your individual selves.

"Asha, do you take Cyrus to be your lawful wedded spouse?"

"I do," I said.

"And Cyrus, do you take Asha to be your lawful wedded spouse?"

"I do," he said. Julian changed positions and pointed his phone at me. Then the clerk said—was that a crack in her voice? yes, with a crack in her voice—"By the power vested in me as a justice of the peace, and most important of all, by the power of your own love, I now pronounce you legally married." And we kissed, a short, melting kiss mixed with the salt of our tears, the particular flavor of which I knew I would remember forever.

And so it was, without ritual, in the most ordinary of ways, that we were married. I moved into Jules's house and put my clothes into Cyrus's closet. I put my electric toothbrush in the bathroom and plugged in my phone charger, and that was it. I was ready to start a life with Cyrus, who was everything he had been all those years ago when I first met him: mostly human, a little bit cartoon, a tiny bit ghost.

Two

LOVE AND MARRIAGE

Once the semester started, I was in class all day and at the lab late into the evening. Cyrus packed lunches for me in a metal bento box, and we walked together up to the T. At the lab, I thought about telling a few people, but then I didn't. Would being married take away from my persona as a futurist soothsayer? Definitely. And Dr. Stein would not approve. I kept my head down and acted like nothing had happened.

But everything was different. I hadn't changed my name, but sometimes I woke up in the morning and heard myself saying, "Good morning, Mrs. Jones." Or when I was putting our clothes in the dryer, I heard, "Doing laundry for your husband, Mrs. Jones?" Mrs. Jones kept me up at night. She was my shadow self, a laundry-doing, husband-pleasing ordinary person who wanted nothing more than to be an excellent wife. I had vivid fantasies about murdering

Mrs. Jones and burying her in the tangle of weeds that passed for Julian's garden.

Despite my fear of becoming Mrs. Jones, my work changed for the better. Being with Cyrus made me feel powerful, as if I had somehow conjured him out of my dreams. All the ambitions I had around the Empathy Module suddenly felt within my reach, because if the two of us, after all these years, could find each other again, then surely I was capable of taking some of that magic and putting it into my human replica. I plunged into my work with new ambition, and though Dr. Stein continued to ignore me, it mattered less. I hummed through my days, and when I was finished, I went home to Julian's.

Julian's house was grand, but as the days grew colder, I discovered it had a major flaw: it was freezing. The windows were too big and the wood was all warped, so even if we stuffed towels under the doors, it was still drafty. I tried to use the toilet in the lab as much as possible, because peeing in that house was like attempting an arctic expedition.

Aside from this small inconvenience, Jules was an excellent host, in that he treated the house as if he, too, were a temporary inhabitant. He didn't care about it, so it really didn't matter who else lived there. He was an easy housemate—if quick to get irritated, even quicker to forget what was bothering him. A parade of people came through: friends, lovers, loud laughing guys from his lacrosse team, distant cousins who also hated being Cabots. Jules was in an a cappella group called Pitch Slapped, and they regularly rehearsed and got high in the living room, their songs floating up the stairs and getting stuck in our heads.

One day I was in the library, a room on the northern side of the house that never got any sun, when Jules came in. I wasn't sure what he did all day—he didn't seem to have a job, and Cyrus had told me he was touchy about being asked what his plans were. After college, he'd started a website called Sellyourshit.com, which seemed for a while like it might compete with eBay, but eventually it crashed, taking some of his father's money with it. After that his parents gave him the house and a small allowance, which was their way of cutting him off. Cyrus had met Jules's parents a few times, been to their house in the Hamptons and in Savannah, Georgia, where they spent the winter. It's not that they weren't nice to Jules, just that they had no expectations of him. "They smile in this creepy way," Cyrus said, "and nod as if Jules is slightly, you know, not quite there and they have to humor him. It drives him crazy."

I had just been through another soul-killing seminar with Dr. Stein, and to make myself feel better, I was deep in an armchair with three scratchy blankets over my legs, reading *2001: A Space Odyssey*.

"Oh, there you are, I've been looking everywhere," Jules said. "It's Cyrus."

"Did something happen?"

He sat down beside me. "No, we just— It's the anniversary of his mom's death next week. I think we should do something."

I felt like an imposter for not knowing the date. "I had no idea."

"He doesn't like to talk about it. But he can't be alone."

"I can take the day off. Does she have—is she buried somewhere?"

"He scattered her ashes in Port Townsend, that's where she was from." Before I could ask, he said, "It's on the West Coast, near Seattle. He hitchhiked all the way there when he was sixteen."

"Is there anything I can do?"

Jules was staring into the cold fireplace. "I came out to my parents right around the time that Cyrus's mother died. It was late— I'd known for years, but I was afraid to tell them."

I didn't know what to say, so I asked, "Do you have brothers and sisters?"

"One of each. They make bank and play golf. I'm the youngest, the runt."

"Oh."

"Sometimes I think of a world where my parents died in an accident so I would never have had to tell them."

"What happened when you did?"

"Everything changed. It was like they disappeared, like they were right in front of me but they were ghosts."

"I saw Cyrus's mother at school sometimes."

"What was she like?"

"She was beautiful. It looked like she'd had him when she was very young." Something came to me. "She loved Ella Fitzgerald. I remember that about her—she sang at the parents' talent show."

"You guys had a parents' talent show?"

"The school needed money, so the parents put on a show where they paid to see each other do stuff. The teachers did it too—I'm still haunted by the sight of my algebra teacher singing Cat Stevens."

"Hippie Cat Stevens or Muslim Cat Stevens?"

"Hippie." I looked over at Jules. "So should we practice a song?"

"I don't know—are you any good at singing? Because we all know that I am awesome."

"I'm Bengali," I said. "It's in my blood."

The following week, on the twelfth anniversary of the death of Poppy Jones, Cyrus disappeared. I woke up in the morning and found that he was not on the other side of the bed. He was not downstairs in the kitchen and he was not outside in the garden and he was not in any of the rooms on any of the floors of the house. He did not answer his phone. He did not reply to text messages or emails.

Jules was eating peanut butter out of the jar when I gave him this news. "How long has he been gone?"

I checked my phone. It was eleven thirty. "I don't know what time he left, but I haven't seen him all morning."

Jules nodded. "He'll be back in a few days."

"A few days? Are you kidding me?"

Jules took a gallon of milk out of the fridge and gulped straight from the carton. "I told you, his mom's death is still raw."

"You are the only person I know who consumes real dairy," I said. "And why the fuck didn't you say anything to me sooner?"

"What, that Cyrus likes to do a runner? It's his thing."

"His *thing*? And you never thought to warn me?"

"You got married before I even learned your name."

He was right. "A few days? Do you try to get in touch with him in the meantime?"

"Nope. You just leave the door open, and he comes back when he's ready."

Early the next morning, Cyrus slipped into bed beside me. I'd fallen asleep after hours of staying awake and checking my phone every few minutes, so I thought I heard him say he was sorry, but I might've just been imagining it. I took my cue from Jules and didn't ask where he'd been. That night we put Poppy's photograph in a frame and surrounded it with candles. In the piano room, where there was a decaying concert grand, we arranged small bunches of poppies in coffee mugs. And then Jules and I did a duet of Ella Fitzgerald's "A Sunday Kind of Love." Jules had an excellent baritone, and I didn't completely embarrass myself either, because I'd practiced nonstop while Cyrus was away.

Afterward, Cyrus lay down on the carpet. I sat beside him and he rested his head on my lap. He cried and cried. "Mama," I heard him whisper. I felt pulled toward him, drawn to what he sometimes called the dark behind his eyes, and I was also a little afraid, because I saw now that this man walked around with a hole in his heart, and I thought about how hard I would have to work to fill that hole, and I was worried that I wouldn't ever be able to.

And after that, the three of us—Julian, Cyrus, and I—definitively and permanently became a tribe.

At Thanksgiving, I went home to tell my parents everything. I was going to wait until Thursday, when Mira could be there to cushion the blow, but while we were unloading the groceries the day before, it all came out in one breath: Mrs. Butterfield's funeral, meeting Cyrus again, moving in with him. I left out city hall, but I said I was in love and that Cyrus made me want to be married, which wasn't completely true but at least wasn't an outright lie.

"Who is Cyrus?" my mother asked.

"He went to high school with me. But then he dropped out." Why? Why did I say that?

My mother pointed a sweet potato at me. "A dropout?"

I turned to my father, hoping to find an ally. "He's actually very smart," I said. "Reads a lot." Inside I was thinking, *Reads a lot*, that's the best you can do?

My mother stood up and hovered behind my father's chair. "Explain this to us so we can understand. You're telling us about a boy, fine. We are okay with boyfriends, you're old enough to make your own decisions now. If you wanted to go out with a girl, that might be different."

"Don't be homophobic, Ammoo," I said.

"But what's this about getting married? Why do you have to marry him?"

"I don't have to marry him, I want to marry him."

I didn't tell them that I'd already married him.

My parents didn't want to be pharmacists. My father had spent his entire life hoping to someday publish his novel, the details of which he had never revealed to any of us. All we knew was that every night after dinner, he would shut the study door behind him, and we would have to finish picking the rice from the place mats and do our homework on the dining table. And my mother, although she loved putting on that uniform every day and giving people advice about spider bites and hormone replacement therapy, really came alive during the annual performances of the Long Island Tagore Society, in which she would direct the Bengali writer's most famous work. Right now she was in rehearsals for *Chitrangoda*, a musical play about a warrior princess. I figured that's why she reacted to my news like I was challenging her to a dual.

"You're too young to get married. Full stop."

"Why don't you act like all the other aunties?"

"Don't insult me. I'm not like the other aunties. That's why you and Mira turned out to be such brilliant young women."

"Just be happy, throw me a party. Mira was married by the time she was my age."

"That was different," my father said. "Mira and Ahmed have known each other for many years. Ahmed's father is my oldest friend."

"We did not come to this country so you could be a child bride."

"I'm in graduate school."

"That's right, school. Finish school."

"I promise you'll like him."

"Of course we will like him, that doesn't mean you have to marry him."

"What's his profession?" my father asked.

I couldn't say humanist spirit guide, so I said, "He studies world religions."

"Is he a priest?"

My mother gasped. "A Catholic priest?"

"He's not a priest, he just studies religion. In a nonreligious way."

"Religion is poison," my father said. "The entire history of humanity is littered with the bodies of people who have fallen afoul of religion."

"Just meet him," I said. "He's coming tomorrow."

Thanksgiving dinner was Auntie Lavinia and her son, Guy; Mira and her husband, Ahmed; the Hosseins from Manhasset; and Derek and Elsa Rosenberg, the elderly couple next door whose three daughters had all moved to Tel Aviv. My mother liked to stuff the turkey with rice and tiny koftas, and my father liked to put cardamom in the sweet-potato casserole. Other than that, we did Thanksgiving just like white people, eating dinner in the afternoon and falling asleep in front of the football.

Cyrus arrived early with his hair in a ponytail and handed a bouquet of white roses to my silent mother. "Hello, Mira," he said to my sister, who winked and squeezed his arm. "Don't worry," she whispered. "Our mother is all bark." Cyrus shook Ahmed's hand, and Ahmed looked him up and down and nodded.

At the table, my mother was scrupulously polite to Cyrus. "Please, eat," she said, piling stuffing onto his plate.

Auntie Lavinia was arguing with Guy about his homework, which she tried to convince him to start right away instead of waiting for Sunday night. "You'll be at your father's over the weekend, I can't be sure he'll make you do it."

Guy rolled his eyes. "He will."

"Is there even a desk in that little apartment, and who knows if you have the peace and quiet to do your studies?"

"There's a table, Mom."

"I told him at least get a two-bedroom place. But he makes you sleep on the sofa. How's a boy to learn anything sleeping on the sofa?"

"It's not rocket science," Guy said. "It's Norse mythology."

"Don't know what they're teaching kids these days," Auntie Lavinia said. "Horse mythology?"

"I've always been fascinated by the Norse gods," Mr. Hossein said. "What do you think of Loki?"

"You mean the bad guy in *Thor*?" Guy asked.

"We saw that movie," Elsa Rosenberg said. "Didn't we, Derek. It was ridiculous."

My mother passed Cyrus the gravy. "His plate looks dry," she said to me. I instructed Cyrus to douse his turkey.

"He wasn't just a bad guy," Cyrus said. "Loki. He was a complex character who shape-shifted between the gods and the giants."

"That's not what my book says," Guy mumbled.

"Pie?" my mother asked Cyrus.

And on it went. For a moment Cyrus sparked my mother's interest when he explained that Loki also shifted between genders, bearing children both as a father and as a mother. But that lasted only a few minutes, and soon we were clearing plates, and then we ate pumpkin cheesecake and everyone sighed about how full they were, and before we knew it, we were kissing each other on the cheek and saying goodbye to Auntie Lavinia and I still wasn't sure where my parents were going to fall on the whole married thing. Finally, when it was just the six of us arranged awkwardly on the L-shaped sofa in front of the football, my father broached the subject.

"We hear you're interested in marriage," he said.

Cyrus looked up from the photo book of the Taj Mahal that had been sitting on our coffee table for two decades and fixed my father with an earnest smile. "I am, sir," he said.

"We are a bit surprised," my father said.

"I can understand that," Cyrus replied.

"Asha has never even talked about you."

Do something, I mouthed to my sister, but I could tell that even though she had my back, she was also kind of enjoying the spectacle.

"Sometimes," Cyrus said, "you meet someone and it's like you've always known them."

"Asha always knew you," Mira said, attempting to lighten the mood. "You just never paid attention to her."

"That was my loss," Cyrus said. "But when I met Asha again after all this time, it seemed inevitable that we would end up together. She's the most extraordinary person I've ever known. I can't imagine spending my life with anyone else. She is smart, kind, wise, funny, beautiful, and I feel incredibly fortunate to have married her."

"What did you just say?" my mother said, gasping.

"We got married in August," I confessed.

"You've been married since August?"

"Vah Vah!" My father stood up and applauded. "This is wonderful!"

Mira was surprised. "You're happy?"

"Your wedding was wonderful, darling, but we just can't afford the Marriott again."

Cyrus shifted from the edge of the sofa and knelt in front of me. "Thank you for marrying me, Asha Ray," he said, and to my surprise he pulled a box from his pocket, and inside the box was a small circle of gold that fit my finger perfectly.

A little burst of sound came from the TV; the Patriots must have scored. I glanced over at my mother, and she had this stunned look on her face like she didn't watch Bollywood films with Auntie Lavinia every other Sunday at the Roosevelt mall.

The week after Thanksgiving we were trapped in Julian's house during the year's first real snowstorm; the lab was closed and the roads were rivers of powdery white. Jules lit a fire and we played Old Before My Time, a game I'd made up with Mira where we confessed things that made us sound old.

"Okay," I started. "Describing people as 'chill' as if it's a compliment. Like 'Yeah, I'm so into that guy, he's so chill.' How? How is being super-relaxed a quality one seeks in a partner? The only people I really need to be super-chilled out are pilots."

"Or air traffic controllers."

"Yeah, but in a focused and uptight way."

"I don't understand TikTok," Cyrus said.

"I don't understand Reels," Jules said. "What is the point if everything keeps disappearing?"

"Reels don't disappear. Stories do. Keep up." I said.

"So I got a letter today from some people in Missouri," Cyrus said.

I gathered the game was over. Cyrus started reading the letter aloud: "'My wife and I grew up watching *Little House on the Prairie* and we both have this yearning to kneel beside our bed at night and say some kind of prayer. Wouldn't it be nice if we could do that without questioning the viability of a higher power? What if we could put our palms together, look up at the sky, and do some real talking about the day, about the things that had gone wrong, the things that we were okay with, the things we hoped might happen tomorrow? Could we do that, could we just do that and enjoy it? We don't want to cheat on our atheism.'"

"Jeez, Cy, if only you could give every skeptic what they wanted, some kind of believable replacement for God," Jules said.

"Well," I said, "I did propose that to Cyrus, but he wasn't sure."

"I didn't say I wasn't sure, I said I didn't want to be a priest."

Jules looked back and forth between me and Cyrus. "You want to give this man his own religion?"

"I just said I could code an algorithm that would allow people to get a kind of Cyrus ritual, you know, a combination of all their things, wrapped up in a little modern package, without the sexism, homophobia, and burning in the fires of hell of actual religion."

"You know," Jules agreed, "that's not a bad idea. People might actually go for that."

I shrugged. "It's up to Cyrus."

"What's wrong, Cy, you don't want to be the new messiah?"

Outside, the snow continued to fall. Everything was blurry and quiet.

"We need marshmallows," Cyrus said.

"Why don't we do a little experiment," I suggested. "I can code a mini version of the algorithm, and Cyrus, you can decide if you like it."

"You know what I don't like about s'mores?" Cyrus said. "The chocolate should be melted. Otherwise it's just the marshmallow that's warm, and they're never hot enough to take the chocolate down."

"Fine," Jules said, sighing dramatically. He leaped up, darted into the kitchen, slammed a few cabinet doors, and came back with marshmallows, chocolate, graham crackers, and metal skewers.

"Why are you so well prepared?" I asked.

"It's the white man's dessert. Every household comes fully equipped."

We made the s'mores. Cyrus repeated his opinion about the chocolate. Jules suggested Cyrus squeeze a little Hershey's syrup over his. "That's another staple of the Caucasian larder." He winked.

"I'll do it," Cyrus said.

I was surprised. "Really?"

"Anything for you." He smiled.

"Hallelujah!" Jules said, slamming his hand on his armrest. "I always knew we were meant for great things."

We toasted with our skewers. I promised to get to work immediately. Jules asked how long it would take to do a small release. He said we should try to get it out to a few people as soon as possible. You know, just to see what happened.

What happened was this: I started coding the platform, and Jules became maniacally attached to it. Not half an hour would go by before he'd barge into the dining room and ask how far I'd gotten, what would the features be, and should we think about beta-launching soon, and did I need a coffee? "This is genius," he kept saying, pacing back and forth along the room, running his hands over the patterned wallpaper. "It could be huge."

I wasn't sure what he meant by "huge," but even though I stayed super-cool and casual about the whole thing, I found myself getting a little excited too. I was sneaking away between classes and cutting into my lab time thinking about the idea. Essentially it was a giant library. But I didn't want to pull the information off Wikipedia or some other obviously amateur site, so after I got the scaffolding up, Cyrus had to lend us his brain. Late at night and on weekends, the three of us gathered around the twelve-seater dining table and went through the categories, trying to find ways of combining them. "You have here that it's called *The Tibetan Book of the Dead*, but that's actually a Western construct because the translator, Evans-Wentz, decided to give it that title."

"So what's the Tibetan book called?" Jules asked.

"*Bardo Thödol, Liberation Through Hearing During the Intermediate State.*"

Jules tapped on his keyboard.

"The thing is," Cyrus went on, "if someone told me they were interested in *The Tibetan Book of the Dead*, or Tibetan Buddhism, I would first tell them about the *Bardo Thödol*, and then I would direct them to read the larger body of work that it's based on, which is *Profound Dharma of Self-Liberation Through the Intention of the Peaceful and Wrathful Ones*, and then I would tell them to read George Saunders."

"Who is George Saunders?"

"He's a novelist."

"A Tibetan novelist?"

"American. He wrote *Lincoln in the Bardo*, which is about Abraham Lincoln mourning his dead son, who is in the Bardo, the transitional state. So if someone were mourning, say, a child, they might read Lingpa, but they might also read the novel."

"Who's Lingpa?"

"He wrote the *Bardo Thödol*."

This was the kind of conversation we were constantly having with Cyrus. Cyrus doubted whether the AI could replicate the ways his mind worked. "It's going to be too linear," he said.

Cyrus was consistently, encyclopedically brilliant. He made connections that no other person could ever make, between texts—religious tradition, history, fiction—and the world—movies, pop songs, memes. This was why he was the perfect test case for the Empathy Module. If it could mimic the workings of Cyrus's mind, it would definitely be more human than any other AI platform ever made. I thought of Cyrus as Prototype 1, the subject after which all of my work would someday be modeled.

I wondered sometimes if this was part of my attraction to Cyrus. Was I in love with the whole him, or mostly his mind as a challenge for my algorithm? No, it was definitely the whole him. Either way, we were high on all of it, all three of us feeding off Cyrus's big brain, his appetite for just about everything, and how it seemed to be making its way into zeros and ones, all with the little tap-tap-tapping of my fingers.

By the time the snow had melted and the apple blossoms had turned everything pink and yellow, I was ready to start testing the prototype. There was no design, no interface—it was just a series of questions on a blank page.

Name three things you love or that define you, it asked.

"Jules, you go first."

"Chess, singing, and Kirk Douglas in *20,000 Leagues Under the Sea*."

"I didn't know you played chess," I said.

"You want me to be the first guinea pig or not?"

The second question was *Name the experience that has most shaped you as a person.*

"I tried to dive into my swimming pool, but it was too shallow and I gave myself a concussion."

Cyrus and I both knew this was not the experience that had most shaped Jules as a person, but we kept silent.

Are you drawn to any particular religious tradition?

Silence from Jules.

And finally: *What occasion/important life event is this ritual intended for?*

"I want a baptism," he said.

I typed his replies into my laptop. We waited. The system took fifteen seconds, which felt like a long time.

I started to read the reply on the screen. "'Your body will be washed from head to toe, this time avoiding the injury that was caused the last time you tried to baptize yourself.'"

"I was just trying to dive," Jules interrupted. "I wasn't baptizing myself."

"'Your friends and family will gather around and sing "A Whale of a Tale," just as Kirk Douglas did in *20,000 Leagues Under the Sea.*'"

"I totally forgot about that song."

"'You will dip your head below the water, angled at forty-five degrees, the way a knight on a chess board might approach his opponent. You will be reborn into whatever faith you have chosen to guide you, or if you choose not to follow a faith, perhaps this moment will give you pause to reflect inward, to think about what you want to believe in for the rest of your life.'"

"Asha, is this thing looking into my soul?" He laughed. And then, for about ten days, he sang "A Whale of a Tale" until we had to beg him, for the love of God, to stop.

> *Got a whale of a tale to tell ya, lads*
> *A whale of a tale or two*

My spring semester coughed on like a pre-penicillin illness. Terrifyingly, Dr. Stein said nothing to me about how I'd been slacking off, she just lost interest in me at a greater rate than I was losing interest in her lab. I told Jules and Cyrus that once we beta-launched the platform, I really had to make up for all the idling I'd been doing. On the first day of May, we sent a link to a curated group of people we had cobbled together from friends of friends, random Facebook groups, and a site called Find Your User Testers. We sent an email with lots of exclamation marks. *This will be fun! Help us A/B test our product!* We asked them to send us anonymous feedback, tell us if they liked it, if it spoke to them in some way. Our initial outreach was to about three hundred people.

It was Friday. We barricaded ourselves in the house with the TV on a continuous screening of *The Expanse* and spent the whole weekend waiting for something to happen. Every few minutes, I checked the stats. By Sunday night, about a hundred people had opened the email. About fifty had received rituals from the platform. Eighteen sent their feedback.

> *This was fun! Thanks for the distraction from my Insta.*
> *Thanks! Except I accidentally drowned my cat while try-*
> *ing to baptize him. Just Kidding! LMAO.*

Whoever invented this thing, I don't know you personally, but I am writing to say that I've just had a life-changing experience. It sounds stupid to claim this from just a few minutes on your site, but my mother died last year and honestly I've been to every priest, therapist, grief counselor, and shaman in greater New York and this is the first time I started to feel alive again. I put my palms together for you.

This sucked.

Blowing my mind, incredible tech.

"Well, that's that," Cyrus said, dusting his trousers as if he'd just finished off a croissant.

On Monday, determined to make up with Dr. Stein, I spent twenty-three straight hours at the lab. Finally, toward the end when I was standing in front of the water fountain for several minutes without appearing to drink anything, she tapped me on the shoulder and told me to go home immediately. *Oh!* I thought, *she loves me again!* And I stumbled home and fell into a deep sleep.

When I woke up, Jules was waiting for me in the dining room with a cup of coffee that had been made disgusting by the addition of grass-fed butter.

"We have a decision to make," he said. "But it's up to you, Asha. We'll only do it if you say yes."

I took a sip. The butter clung to my lips. "You and Cy want to have a baby, and you want me to be the surrogate? The answer is no. I'm not giving birth to a white-on-white mash-up."

"We've been invited to audition for a spot in an incubator. There isn't any money—but it's a space to get ourselves set up."

I paused for a moment and let his words sink in. "You mean the platform? I thought we were just messing around."

"We were, but you saw the demo. We could give it more time, find out what it can really do."

"Why is this on me?"

"Because the incubator is called Utopia and it's in New York."

He let that sink in for a minute. Utopia. The holy grail of incubators.

"You've got the most to lose, Asha."

"How did they hear about us?"

"I don't know. But they want us to go down there and show it to them."

I wasn't sure. "Don't we have everything we need right here, thanks to a generous donation from the Cabot family?" I swept my arm across the gleaming oak dining table. "And anyway, no one really liked it."

"The sample size was too small," Jules said. "And the UX was shit."

"Aw, Jules, you're hurting my feelings, calling my code all brains and no beauty."

"Do you want to maybe just meet them, check it out, see if we like it?"

It was all happening too quickly. "I don't know." Then something occurred to me. "Why are you having this conversation with me and not Cyrus too?"

Jules rubbed his hand up the side of his cheek as if grating a wedge of Parmesan. "Because he would totally not let us do it."

He was right. Cyrus would laugh, and then he would talk us out of it. "Well, you know what they say—hubs before grubs."

"No one in the history of sayings has ever said that."

"It means I am not crossing your picket line."

"Oh, come on, Asha, you know you want to. I'll even splurge on Greyhound instead of the Chinatown bus. And maybe we'll hate it and it won't even matter."

"Or maybe we'll love it and you'll put me in some kind of moral dilemma where I have to choose between the forces of Cyrus and Jules."

"Call it whatever you want. I know you're flattered. I know you're curious."

I was both of those things. We went back and forth a few more times. Finally, I agreed, and we made up a story for Cyrus about how I was visiting my sister and Jules was going to sign some paperwork at his dad's law firm.

And that is how we ended up auditioning for Li Ann and her band of merry Doomsayers.

Three

I AM WHAT I AM

Cyrus has been sitting in the house with his legs crossed all day, taking deep breaths with a little chime app on his phone. When the chime goes off, he stands up, walks around the room seven times to stretch his legs, then gets back on his mat, faces the wall, and sits there until the bell rings again. I might find this extremely irritating if it weren't for the fact that after one of these sessions, he is always twice as everything I love about him. He's tender and thoughtful and even somehow smarter. I call it Zen Face. Zen Face is my favorite of Cyrus's faces, even better than Gazing over a Candle at Dinner Face, or another—close to the top—Freshly Shaved and Smelling like Grass Face.

When we get home, Jules and I pad around the kitchen and make sandwiches out of whatever isn't moldy. I think of Rory and his vegan startup. Already I'm a little fond of the people we met that morning, and I'm trying not to spend too much time imagining what it might be like, walking into that building every day and calling myself a Utopian. Being surrounded by all that shiny promise and making plans for the end of the world. But then there are all the things I thought I was going to do with my life. I try not to think about my student loans and the postdoc at Stanford, which, until yesterday, was my dream job. Can I do it? Can I drop everything to chase a dream?

Eventually, Jules and I stop waiting for Cyrus and start eating our sandwiches. Outside, the night is dense and quiet. I'm picturing all the people strolling home after a late-night movie or a pizza, all the youth and the cavalier confidence of just starting out in life. I could be those things too, I suppose, but I was born with a tendency to think and overthink, a habit of picking everything apart until it came out tasting like burnt toast.

My sister, Mira, is the opposite. She knows exactly what she wants, and she makes no apologies. She also has an ability to be serious and completely nonchalant at the same time. When she decided at the age of fifteen that she was going to start wearing a hijab, my parents freaked. "Go out in a bikini!" my mother begged. "That's what America is for."

Mira tried to explain that she was protesting, among other things, the bombing of children in Yemen, the hypersexualization of young women in Western society, and frankly, the way our parents had somehow given us the illusion that we could do anything we wanted. Then she rocked that hijab like you wouldn't believe, told all the well-meaning people who wanted to whitesplain the importance of modesty in Muslim culture to fuck off because she was in no way intending to be modest, told the brown boys in the schoolyard to fuck off and stop calling her sister, and told the racist shop assistant at Best Buy to fuck off when he suggested all that fabric would make an excellent guise for shoplifting headphones. I know exactly what Mira would do at a moment like this. She would not hesitate. She would not wait for anyone's permission. She would grab it with both hands and fly like a girl on a dragon's back.

The bells. Cyrus rounds the corner and makes his way toward me, and just from the way he does this, I can tell it's no ordinary Zen Face. "Nice trip?" he asks, dreamy and unfocused. He leans over and takes a giant bite of my sandwich.

I blurt everything out at once. "Jules and I went to New York to check out this amazing place called Utopia and we want to move down there and turn the platform into a startup. I'm sorry we didn't tell you but we were so sure you were going to say no that we were afraid to ask."

Because of the meditation, everything Cyrus does is slow and deliberate, including shifting facial expressions. Right now he's somewhere between "Am I awake?" and "What the fuck?"

"If we're accepted, we'll only have twenty-four hours to decide," Jules says.

Cyrus makes tea. The kettle takes about a thousand years to boil, and while it's boiling, we do some eye-contact Ping-Pong where we all look at each other and glance away multiple times. Finally, the tea is in front of us. "I understand why you didn't tell me," Cyrus says.

Jules mumbles something about how he wasn't actually afraid of Cyrus.

"So, just to be clear—you both want to do this? Asha, you're going to, what, drop out of grad school?"

"I don't know," I say. "The place is so cool. Everyone looks like they came out of a gene-editing experiment. And they are making plans—actual plans—to save humanity from the apocalypse."

"And what happens to the platform?"

"We figure out how to make it faster and smarter and prettier, and then we send it out into the world." Jules pushes his arms out like he's freeing a pair of doves.

"A startup," Cyrus says. "Like social media?"

I know how Cyrus feels about social media. "We don't have to call it that."

"People are going to sign up and make connections with each other and we are going to somehow profit from it. What else would you call it?"

"You can take a bad thing and make it better," Jules says.

"This is all moving too fast."

"Look," I say, "we'll try it out, see what happens—give it six months. If it doesn't work, we'll come back. Not like we have major things going on right now."

"PhD not major enough for you?"

"People drop out of their PhDs all the time. I'll get back to it at some point."

"Well, if you want my blessing, the answer is no."

"Aw, Cy, man, you're being such a downer."

"Technology is grotesque, you two both understand that, right?"

"Don't patronize me," I say. "I know it's not perfect."

"It's not imperfect, it's evil."

"You sound like my sister."

"It spies on you. It mines you for data. It extracts your soul and then sells it back to you. It's designed to make you spend money so you're too busy shopping to notice the world is burning down. The only way I'm going to be a part of it is if we're doing something to fundamentally change it."

"You want to be Robin Hood," Jules says.

Cyrus leans against the counter, stares hard at Jules. "I am what I am."

He has the zeal of a Scientology pamphlet, but I can't totally disagree with him. Maybe the platform wasn't going to take over my life, maybe it wasn't all me, but it certainly was him. It was his person, his thoughts, all the things he'd read and learned, everything that meant something to him, and something even deeper, his ability to look into people and see what they needed, not what they said they needed but some kind of yearning inside them that they didn't even recognize in themselves. "Li Ann wants us in the incubator precisely because we're doing something new. That's why she's interested."

"We take you for granted, Cy. All your weird ideas could actually blow people's minds," Jules says.

Cyrus shakes his head. "It's just— We have to think about the impact. Most of the time I deal with people I have some connection to. If it's remote, I can't predict what's going to happen."

"What's going to happen is that we are going to move to New York, and we're going to launch the platform, and we're going to do something amazing, and everyone will be like 'Oh my God' and we're all going to live happily ever after."

Cyrus shakes his head. "I can think of a dozen ways this can go wrong."

"Be the change," Jules says.

"Shut up, Jules."

But Cyrus is considering it. He's holding his mug with both hands, and looking out across the long table that must have belonged to several generations of Cabots, and allowing himself to think the same thing that has been going around in my mind since yesterday. What if we did something unprecedented, something novel and possibly even revolutionary?

Cyrus shifts his weight, leaning on the table. "Okay," he says. "I'll do it. But only because you're promising me, right here and now, that we're not just going to rewrite some neoliberal script and put a bow on all the fucked-up shit that happens in the world."

"Totally." I nod.

"And I have conditions. I will come to New York, and I'll keep helping with the algorithm. But just as a researcher, nothing more. Don't drag me into the startup thing."

Cyrus wants to stay pure.

"Whatever you want, Cy," Jules says. Then he turns to me. "Asha, are you in?"

Here's my chance. I can say no, and I can return to Dr. Stein's lab, and we can forget this whole thing ever happened. I'm tempted, I really am. But then there are these two people right in front of me, and more than ever I'm feeling like we belong to one another, and that if we stick together, we can quit one life and start another. I'm thinking about the look on Li Ann's face, how she took our idea so seriously, as if it really could become one of the things that survive a major planetary event. It's the first time I've turned my lines of code into something tangible, and I can't deny that it made me feel something about my work that I've never felt before. "What the hell. I'm in," I say.

At this very moment, our phones beep with a message from Li Ann. *Congratulations! Welcome to Utopia.*

Jules says, "It's a sign."

And Cyrus says, "We need a manifesto."

There are people who may have marked this moment with a drink. But Cyrus wants to mark it with a manifesto, so that is what we do. We get a sheet of paper from the printer, and after about thirty seconds of back-and-forth, Cyrus writes it all down.

We are equal partners and make all decisions together.

We don't spy on anyone.

and

We don't sell our souls (we don't sell anything).

We consider spitting into our palms but settle for signing at the bottom of the page. Cyrus folds up the piece of paper and tucks it into his pocket, and we toast with our mugs of tea.

"Oh, and there's one more thing," Cyrus adds. "We need a name."

"True."

"I was thinking we could call it WHY. Except spelled W-A-I."

"What does it stand for?" Jules asks.

"We Are Infinite."

We Are Infinite. Trust Cyrus to come up with the perfect name.

The next day, we sign our agreement with Utopia and start packing.

Even though I have made up my mind, I want Dr. Stein to try to talk me out of it. To tell me that my brain is too valuable to waste on something as ordinary as a website. She will tell me how important my work is, commit to giving me more time, promise not to ridicule me in front of the third-years. Plead with me to stay.

But that is obviously not what happens.

I tiptoe into her office, and as usual when I am with her, my voice gets high, like I've just French-kissed a helium balloon.

"Dr. Stein, I've been thinking about the module, and it's just not going where I need it to go."

"Hm, yes. Your assumptions are all wrong."

Her office is bare. There are books arranged neatly on the shelves, but there is not a single piece of paper on her desk, as if someone just brushed off all the clutter and had table sex with her.

"In order for the module to work fully, I need to wait till the brain is reverse-engineered."

She fixes her eyes on me, and I can feel my heart beating in my throat. "That's what I told you: 2029."

"In the meantime, I was thinking I could make it do something a little more—achievable."

She tilts her head. "Like what?"

"Just a different application. I've been thinking it might be interesting to experiment with the module in a commercial setting."

"Oh? And what precisely would that be?"

"A platform that anticipates people's need for meaning and ritual," I mumble, then gave her a long, overly detailed explanation of the site.

"And you're going to do, what, raise money and move to the Valley?"

I start plucking at a piece of dry skin on my upper lip. "I don't know anyone in the Valley," I say lamely.

She pauses and her voice is half a degree softer when she says, "And you think this is a good way for you to spend your short time on earth?"

I feel like the shallowest person in the world when I say, "Yes."

"Then that's what you should do."

"Thank you, Dr. Stein."

Dr. Stein looks at her watch, a thick black band that tells her a number of things, including the time. "Well, good luck," she says, shuttering her little window of humanity.

"I want . . . I would love to return, when the time is right," I say. "I just thought I'd explore the option."

"Consider it explored," she says. "And I really do mean good luck. It's brutal out there."

"I didn't mean to offend you."

"This isn't about me, it's about you," she says. She takes off her glasses and her eyes get a little smaller. "I had high hopes."

"Well, you never said."

"I'm your adviser, not your therapist. Now go, I'll sign whatever paperwork you want me to sign. Surat Chowdhury wants to transfer to my lab and I can give him the good news. At least someone will end up happy."

And that is how I leave my coveted place in Dr. Stein's lab, with a stupid wave and a promise to keep in touch. When I tell my parents, I try to cast it in a better light—I tell them it's a little break, more like a sabbatical: a chance for technology to catch up with my ideas—and within weeks, Cyrus and I move to New York and, because there is nowhere else to go, into my parents' half-converted basement.

I had neglected to think about where we were going to live in New York, and Cyrus never thinks about things like that. It isn't that he doesn't care about where we are going to sleep, it's more that things always seem to work out for him. I feel like I'm living with Inspector Gadget. Most of the time it's less exhausting to just see what fate will throw his way—in this case, my parents and their basement. I don't want to return to Merrick, but the basement is free and takes some of the edge off my new status as a dropout. My mother and father can tell their friends how happy they are to have us at home. Like most Bengali parents, they're still surprised I ever left.

We have no savings and no income, so Jules is going to move in with an aunt, and the three of us are going to live off his allowance. The aunt lives in a co-op on the Upper East Side, but Jules is scrupulous about dividing his allowance equally, so we've committed to a regime of subways and lunchboxes for the foreseeable future.

We take a weekend to drive our things down, an afternoon to unpack our few possessions, and then we are ready for our adventure.

Four

I HEART NEW YORK

Li Ann greets us at the door, looking like she stepped straight off a magazine spread for super-smart yet totally hot women. When I see her I am immediately gripped by paranoia, imagining it'll only be a matter of time before she and Cy screw each other's brains out. Then I scold myself for a) doubting Cyrus, b) being unsisterly and assuming that all women are out to fuck each other over, c) making a kind of heteronormative assumption about Li Ann's sexuality, and d) ruining the first day of my exciting new life. I get a grip and try to enjoy the moment.

Li Ann, Marco, and Rory give us the drill. "We're happy to welcome you to the community," Li Ann says. "We just wanted to go over the ground rules and make sure you don't have any questions."

"We're glad to be here," Cyrus replies, following my explicit instructions to come with us on the first day, introduce himself, and be nice.

"We wanted to let you know that one of your obligations as members of the community is to sit on the admissions committee once a year. We all take turns. It's actually quite fun."

"Last week," Marco tells us, "we had a detailed pitch from an apocalypse-porn company." He raises his eyebrows, daring me to take the bait, but even though I'm itching to know how apocalypse porn is different from regular porn, I don't ask.

"The other rule is that you don't talk about Utopia to anyone. You don't talk about other people in the community, you don't post on socials, you don't give people tips on how to get in."

Jules and Cyrus and I look at each other. "Okay," we say, nodding, "sure."

Rory asks if we'd like a tour. He seems friendlier today, but it's hard to tell because his face moves so little.

We take the tour. The place is like a combination of laboratory, yoga studio, and toddler playroom. In some of the spaces, there are hardly any desks. People sit on the floor with their laptops or balance on giant balls or recline on squishy, unformed sofas. There is a gym, a swimming pool, and a meditation room. And then there is Rory's lab, which we are not allowed to enter. Through a small window we see two people in white lab coats hunched over long tables, surrounded by walls covered in plants.

"We're trying to grow vegetables without soil—just electricity and cell regeneration," Rory explains. "That way, when the bee population collapses and there are no more farms, humanity won't starve." I check to see if he's joking, but of course he's not.

Finally, we arrive in an open-plan space with big industrial windows and concrete floors. The arrangement in this room is more conventional, with two rows of sleek desks facing the large windows.

"This is you," Li Ann says, gesturing to the empty side of the room. "You're sharing the space with Consentify."

Destiny, of the pink hair, smiles to signal her welcome. Behind her on the wall is a framed poster of the girl from *Pulp Fiction*. NO MEANS NO, it says in red letters.

Li Ann leaves us to get settled. "If you need anything, come knock on my door."

And just like that, we are Utopians.

We don't have the faintest idea what to do next. We consider our row of desks and twelve pristine ergonomic chairs.

"So?"

"So."

"Here we are," I say.

Cyrus nods. "Living the dream."

Jules, who has taken in the tour without a word, erupts. "Oh my God, Cy, you look like you just stepped in dog shit. You're going to ruin this whole thing. Did you hear what she said? Free food! Free desks! Free yoga!"

"You hate yoga," Cyrus says.

"Not anymore, my friend, not anymore."

I had worried about the wrong thing. I didn't expect Cyrus to be won over by Utopia, but I thought he would at least be a little impressed with Li Ann and her doomsday prepping. But he had hated it on sight. I'm seeing it through his eyes now, everything shiny and engineered, the expensive artwork, the reminders that we are products of extreme privilege, solving problems that most people would be lucky to have. I feel bad, because of course he's right, but I also resent him for taking the air out of my moment.

"What do you think it will be like?" I ask, trying to change the subject. "I mean every day."

Cyrus doesn't care. "Do you know, Jules?"

"Not really. I ran Sellyourshit.com from my bedroom."

"It won't be like we're running a hamster wheel, right?"

"No, Asha, it totally won't be that," Jules assures me. "It'll be like it was before, except with other people."

"What other people?"

"The people we have to hire."

"Oh." I hadn't thought about that.

"We get to choose the people." It's becoming clear that none of us knows anything about starting a business. We've hardly even had jobs.

"Let's make a plan," I say brightly.

I spot a whiteboard on the wall, but if I stand up in front of it, Destiny and her Consentify team will see me writing down my inane thoughts, so I rustle around in my bag and take out a pen and a notebook.

"I need coffee," Jules says. "Let's go downstairs."

The cafe downstairs is vegan, nut-free, gluten-free, and actually free. All you have to do is fill out a survey on your way out. We get three coffee hemp mylkshakes with extra CBD shots and settle ourselves in a corner with a view of the Hudson.

Cyrus is gazing out the window at the pier. I can feel him silently judging me. He's here but he's not here—he's said yes, he's shown up at Utopia, he's moved into my parents' house, and now he sees the whole thing for what it is, a shallow and pointless adventure.

"I'm going to start working on v2 of the platform," I say, falling back onto what I know best. "That's obviously the next step."

"I'll get into the business plan and start thinking about fundraising," Jules says.

Cyrus breaks away from staring at the Hudson and turns to us. "I think we should take a step back and put everything on the table," he says.

"What do you mean?"

"I mean, I want us to talk about our deepest fears. Jules, can you take notes?"

I say, "I'm worried my parents will hear you and me having sex."

"I'm not going to write that down," Jules says, groaning.

"Please take it seriously, Asha."

"Okay, fine. I'm worried Li Ann is going to kick us out when she finds out how normal we are."

"I'm worried I'll embarrass myself again," Jules says.

"I'm worried we're going to become evil like everyone else."

"This is great," I say. "This is super productive."

"You don't just become evil," Jules says. "It's not contagious."

"I'm worried it will get away from us and we'll lose our moral compass."

"With you in charge? No way."

"I'm not in charge, remember?"

"Right."

Cyrus continues. "I'm worried people won't have anywhere to turn to if something goes wrong, if the ritual they get isn't right or they want to change something," Cyrus says.

At least he's trying. "Good idea," I agree. "We need some way for people to talk to us, and to each other, about how the ritual is working for them." I scribble *Messaging service* on a piece of paper to remind me later.

"Maybe they can upload photos," Jules suggests.

"I don't want to turn into Instagram," Cyrus says.

"It's not Instagram, it's insta-religion."

"It's not religion."

We have the debate all over again. The whole point is that we are giving people an alternative to religion, but we always have to skirt around religion in order to do that. And every time we mention it, talk about God or fate or creation, Cyrus freaks out, as if we're handing him a crown of thorns.

"People need to hold on to something," I tell him. I am thinking about my mother, how for years she had refused to enter a mosque, but lately, I've found her peppering her sentences with "Inshallah, God willing," and once I even caught her kneeling on the carpet in her bedroom, her body angled in a direction which I assumed was east, toward Mecca. "When they get old, or when something bad happens to them, people need belief systems."

"So we're just going to create one more thing for people to blindly follow."

"Think of it as a set of choices." I don't have to explain it to him— Cyrus knows exactly what we're doing.

"This is important," Jules says. "And only you can do it."

Cyrus nods. Once again, he is dragged off the fence. But just barely.

Destiny reads me the gym schedule. "Upside-down yoga at six a.m.," she says. "Water yoga at seven. Hot yoga at eight."

"What time is the Very Hot Yoga?"

Instead of saying "There is no very hot yoga" or, worse, "Should I put in a request to the Wellness Committee?," she says, "It's right before Unbearably Hot Yoga," and so we become friends. Around eleven, when I start to get hungry, she brings me an overpriced donut from the diner across the street.

"I love New York," I say every day after the last bite.

"I love bread," she says, nodding.

After a few weeks I get up the courage to ask her about Consentify. "So, what's your app going to do?"

"It's going to make you sign a contract every time you want to touch someone."

"Hm. Do you think, maybe—" I start to say.

"That we're killing sex?"

"Yes."

"That's the question everyone asks."

"Sorry."

"I really don't mind. It's good to get your fears out—it's the only way we remake the world. First of all, every sexual encounter should be consensual—agreed?"

"Agreed."

"But the very basis of our culture tells us that the gray zone, the space between what you know and what you don't know about your partner—that's the sexy part."

"Isn't it?"

She looks down at her hands, brushes an imaginary bread crumb from her leg. "No, it isn't. We have to unlearn the meaning of seduction. We think it's all about mystery, that it's about what we don't know, rather than sharing something we agree to beforehand." There are little patches of red climbing up her neck. "Feeling that bit of tension, where you don't know what the person is going to do, are they going to unbutton your shirt or put their hands on your crotch, what is that?"

"Anticipation?" I ask.

"Fuck no. I want to live in a world where women aren't afraid."

I can't disagree. "Tell me how it works."

"You list all the things you're consenting to, and then you both do a facial-recognition thing, and that's your signature."

"You write it all down?"

"No, you just swipe over the parts you consent to having touched."

I want to ask where the idea came from, but something about the way her voice seizes up tells me I should leave it there. She pulls out her phone and points to her screen, which has a diagram of a body. I roll my finger over the chest, the abdomen. Breasts pop up on the screen. Upper diaphragm. *Touching, kissing, fondling.* I press on all three words and they light up.

"Maybe you should give her a name."

"It's gender-neutral."

"Maybe you should give them a name."

"Maybe." She taps on her keyboard. Turns to a woman on her left with curly red hair. "What do you think, Maisie? Should we give the consent image a name?"

Maisie pulls the headphones from her ears. "Sorry, I was watching *The Sound of Music.* It relaxes me."

"The ditched baroness was the best character in that movie," Destiny says. "What was her name?"

Maisie Googles. "Baroness Elsa von Schraeder."

And that's how Von is born. A few days later Maisie brings an inflatable doll to the office. It leans against the *Pulp Fiction* poster and wears a sweatshirt that says BRAINY.

Sometimes Cyrus, Jules, and I take our packed lunches to Hudson Yards and judge the terrible people it has attracted. "One day we are going to be just like them," Jules predicts, watching the tourists with gilded shopping bags heave themselves up the metal spider-web.

"Cyrus won't let that happen, will you, Cy?"

"I won't, I promise." His hand is warm on my hand.

We gossip about the other people at Utopia. Jules was on the admissions committee for the first time last week. "You will not believe the crazy shit people are pitching."

"Did any of them get in?"

"Li Ann gets final call. But I voted for Buttery."

"Please say it's something to do with cultured milk."

"No, Asha. It's buttery as in Butt-ery."

"If I ask you not to tell me, you're going to tell me anyway, right?"

"Yup."

"Go on, Jules, just say it." Cyrus laughs.

"It's simple, really. First, there's a jet spray that cleans your asshole. Then there's this other squirty thing that moisturizes. Hence the buttery."

"That's it?"

"You subscribe to the moisturizer. Customized scents."

"Well, at least after the apocalypse, your people can aspire to have the clean buttholes that brown people have had for centuries."

"You're telling me your people have cleaner butts?"

"You're telling me you don't know about Muslims and ass-washing?"

"I can attest," Cyrus says. "She washes her butt. Now I do too."

"When I went to college, my mother was like, 'If I've taught you anything, it's to wash after you go to the toilet. Please don't just use paper, that's disgusting.' By then I was already indoctrinated."

"No wonder we're so afraid of you."

"Yeah, perfumed assholes. Imagine if everyone knew how superior we were."

Unfortunately, Buttery doesn't make it into Utopia. But it's summer in New York, and everything is sweet and light as whipped cream. Even living with my parents isn't so bad. My mother packs the freezer with enormous portions of curry, and when she's at rehearsals, we sit down at the table with my father and play cribbage using an old board he brought over from Bangladesh. Mira lives ten minutes away, and sometimes when Ahmed is working late, she and I curl up on the sofa while Cyrus talks to my father about his novel, and it's like being a kid again, except Cyrus is there, making everything better.

"I need your priest to talk to a friend of mine," Auntie Lavinia says. She has come to help my mother with her Fourth of July biryani. My parents insist that, unlike their neighbors who buy hot dogs from Costco, they celebrate American independence with an actual meal.

"Cyrus is not a priest."

"Your mother said."

"Ammoo thinks Cyrus can do no wrong."

"He's so clever he could have been anything!" my mother shouts from behind the biryani. "All he does is read."

That isn't true. Cyrus does more than read. On Mondays, he attends a meeting of the Dungeons and Dragons Ravencroft Holy Society. On Tuesdays, he goes to a weekly Al Anon meeting, although he has, as far as I know, never been affected by addiction. On Wednesdays, he attends the prayer circle of the local Gurudhwara specifically for the LGBTQ Sikh community. On Thursdays, he attends choir practice for St. Saviors Church, on Fridays, he goes to the Long Island Mosque for afternoon prayers, on Saturdays, he attends the East Ham Rabbinical Society Talmud study group, and on Sundays, not being one for rest, he attends, in turns, an Episcopalian sermon, a Catholic Sunday Eucharist, a Quaker meeting, and a Unitarian service. In between, he is in constant touch with friends who are Wiccan, Buddhist, Jain, or Greek Orthodox. He is interested in everyone and everything. He occasionally strays into Utopia, sometimes for a few hours in the afternoon, and then wanders off to some meeting or other in the name of research.

"My neighbor has cancer," Auntie Lavinia says. "He doesn't have long, maybe a few months, at most a year. He was a rabbi, you know, very respected, but after he got sick, he said he just wanted to be a Hindu. But you can't convert to Hinduism. The people at the temple won't have him. He isn't a Hindu and he isn't a Jew. How will we put the man to rest when his time comes? His wife died a few years ago, he doesn't really have anyone. I told him your husband here is a religious guy, he would know."

"He's not religious," I say. "He just studies religion."

"Yes, that's what I said." She starts chopping an onion and our eyes water. "Can he talk to him? Help him plan? He's restless, not knowing."

"I'll ask Cyrus."

"I was married for thirty years." Auntie Lavinia wipes her eye with the back of her hand.

I know what's coming.

"Then my husband runs off with the girl at the King Kullen checkout."

"Yes, Auntie Lavinia. It was terrible."

"King Kullen! Not even Whole Foods."

"Not even Whole Foods" is a repeated lament from Auntie Lavinia.

"I'll talk to Cyrus, okay?" And I pick up an onion, knowing my fingers will stink up the keyboard later.

"The thing is," Destiny says, "I don't actually mind if we kill sex." We are at the Utopia café drinking turmeric lattes. Rory and Marco and Jules are there too.

"Sex is natural, sex is good," Marco hums.

"It's time for men to start feeling some of the anxiety that we feel. Maybe it's all natural and fun for you, but we're thinking when we meet a man for the first time, where on the shit spectrum is this guy going to be?"

"I would put most men somewhere between a little handsy and sexual harassers," Jules says.

Marco tells Jules not to let the side down.

"I'm not on your side," Jules tells him. "Not if your side is protecting its own to the point where we don't acknowledge there's a problem."

"You're all missing the point," Rory argues. "Patriarchy defeats everyone, men and women alike. But more important—much more important—our rapacious greed is destroying everything that is human about us. Unless we start seeing nonhuman animals in a different light, we are going to self-destruct."

"Amen, brother," Marco says. "That's why I'm trying to disrupt the way we die."

I ask what he means.

"My app, Obit.ly—it's going to make the whole process of dying more intentional. You're going to get to curate your own death on social media."

"Do we really need to curate death?" Destiny asks.

"Do we really need to police our sex lives?" Marco counters.

"I know a lot of women would enjoy sex a hell of a lot more if they felt safe." Destiny chugs the last of her latte and leaves a line of pale yellow foam on her upper lip.

"None of this will matter when mass agriculture collapses," Rory says, trying to broker a truce. "We all have good intentions, but our efforts are futile."

"I know, let's get the priest in here, he can tell us what's kosher."

I've had it with Marco's smug Grim Reaper act. "Cyrus is not a priest. And anyway, why does a man have to adjudicate? We've stated our position, which is that consensual sex is what we need and deserve. If you're not into that, you can piss off."

Destiny leans over and squeezes my hand. Her fingers are cold, so I give the back of her hand a good rub and then I say, "He may be the priest, but Jules and I are the gods. Come on, Jules, let's get back to work."

While Cyrus is out getting to know every faith-based system in the greater New York area, Jules and I spend all our daylight hours at Utopia. When we leave, only Rory's lab is illuminated, and we can see him moving around in there, alone in a white coat, tending to his souped-up plants. By the time summer is over and autumn is starting to bite, I have finished coding v2 of the WAI platform.

"We have to raise money," Jules says. I knew this was coming—

we can't live on his allowance forever, and we don't have the money to launch—but neither of us knows how to do this, not even Jules, whose amniotic fluid was probably flecked with gold. I've gone as far as leafing through copies of *Harvard Business Review*, and sub-scribing to daily updates from various websites that promise to tell me how to do it, but all I can see is funding for self-driving cars, for putting stuff up in the cloud like it's one giant safe-deposit box in the sky, and subscriptions to everything from dye-free tampons to vegan protein powder. There's fintech, biotech, oiltech, real estate, bento boxes of skin care, and tiffin carriers of meat-free protein. There are no funds for quasi-religious platforms. We are not solving a problem, at least not one that anyone has identified as important or, crucially, an opportunity to get rich.

I ask Li Ann. She's launched apps before, and she knows how to raise money—after all, she's the one who got all those bigwigs to fund Utopia's endowment in the first place. Aside from running the selection committee, she spends her time on little side projects— "The afterworld is going to need a few frills," she tells us. Right now she's working on something she calls Spoken, a filter that scans emails to make sure the language isn't accidentally triggering or offensive. "Everyone can sound woke," she says. "No matter how old they are."

Li Ann's office faces west, with a full bank of windows over-looking the water. She sits behind a glass-topped desk looking like Nefertiti while two young men in identical polo shirts code furiously beside her.

When I knock on her door, she looks up and waves. "Please, come in, Asha. How's the platform?"

"Slow, but we're making progress."

"I hear you've been pulling some late nights."

"There's a lot to do," I begin. "We're a little overwhelmed by the whole fundraising thing."

"It's a dark art," she says, nodding.

"I think at some point we're going to need to hire a few people."

She claps. "Hiring! That's exciting. I love the process of finding the right fit." She looks over to her two manservants and beams.

"We just can't afford it right now."

"You know, there's really no price tag on the right talent. It's always worth it to get the very best." Her phone pings. She picks it up, glances at it, puts it back down. "I know a good exec recruiter, you'd love her."

"That's great, thanks, Li Ann."

"What does Cyrus say?"

"About the fundraising or the hiring?"

"Either." She shrugs.

"Not very much, to be honest." I laugh. "I'm still not sure he's into it."

I see her straighten. "Have you incorporated?" she asks, giving me a sideways glance.

"Excuse me?"

"Have you registered? Started an IP portfolio? Decided who owns what?"

"There's nothing to own," I say. "It's just numbers, zeros and ones."

"You're joking, right?" Little points of red flash behind her dark brown eyes.

"We're married," I say, digesting my own lameness in real time. "But you're right, of course. We should have a legal entity."

She scrolls through her phone, and a few seconds later, I feel mine buzz. "I've sent you the name of a good lawyer. He won't charge you— he'll just take a few points to start with. I suggest you stop coding and get your house in order." And then she waves me away with a flick of her hand, and she does it with such elegance that I don't even mind.

When the lawyer asks me for basic information, I realize we don't even have a website. I mean, I haven't even Googled THE WAI to figure out how many weird iterations it will take to find a domain name that fits. Jules, Cyrus, and I argue the relative merits of www.thewai-faith.com (hated by Cyrus), www.waiistheway.com (hated by me), and www.ourwai.com (hated by all of us). Finally, we settle on www.thewai.io, and Jules throws up a splash page, and Cyrus spends an inordinate amount of time writing copy that is both too long and utterly opaque. I send the address to the lawyer, whose name is Barry, and we set off to meet him.

The law firm is intimidatingly shiny, with polished floors and a buttonless elevator. We wait in a boardroom, and when Barry appears, we all jump in our plush leather chairs. "So," he booms, "you're one of Li Ann's companies. What's this I hear about some kind of new religion?"

"Don't you want some guarantee when the world ends?" Jules says. "A hedge of sorts?"

Barry nods. "I've got two hundred acres in New Zealand. That's where I'm going when the shit hits the fan."

"Well, we're here for everyone else," Cyrus says.

"What he means is, it's not a religion, and it's not a cult. It just occupies that space." I'm wondering how many times I'll have to explain this.

"Let me tell you how venture works," Barry says. "They make ten investments. One is in the home-run column. Three go into the win column—and that means acquisition, even if they lose their shirts. The rest hit a wall and turn to dust before anyone can say achoo. As far as I can tell, you're looking at option A or C."

"We don't care about the money," Cyrus says.

"Two months ago we were living in Cambridge and making s'mores in Julian's fireplace," I add.

"Startups are full of accidental entrepreneurs," Barry says. "The main thing is to figure out a way to make sure the band will always stay together."

I tell him we are married.

"All three of you?"

"I'm the wife, Cyrus is the husband, Julian is the other wife."

"Sounds about right," Jules says.

"So, what, you want to go thirds?"

We look at each other. "Yes," Cyrus says, "that's what we want."

"Okay!" Barry slams his hand against the table and rattles the whole city block. "I'll draw up the papers. Sign them and send them back. And you two," he says, pointing to Cyrus and me, "go get yourselves a post-nup. Your odds aren't good."

"What did he mean?" I ask as soon as we get back into the buttonless elevator.

"He means he thinks you and Cy are going to have trouble being married and working together," Jules says.

"But we're more than married. We are epic."

Cyrus pulls me into his arms. "We are infinite."

"He's just quoting the odds. Doing the math. Reading the tea leaves."

"Yeah, okay, we get it. But we're not going to be statistics. He doesn't even know us."

I see Cyrus and me reflected in the elevator mirror: long and short hair, tall and small, spirit guide and coder. Cyrus kisses the top of my head. "Let's get another lawyer," he says.

"Totally. This one's full of shit."

Five

KISSING FROGS

Li Ann tells us we have to start networking. She says words like "elevator pitch" and "investment thesis" and "seed funding," all while tapping her phone and sending me links. After every conversation with her, I Google things furiously until I have a handle on the lingo. Jules goes to fundraising events and then comes back and says he had some *conversations* but that they didn't lead to anything. We start preparing our three-year business plan and financial model. Finally, Jules signs us up for something called Entrepreneurs' Speed Dating, which he assures us bears only a passing resemblance to actual dating, and we turn up at the venue a week later, ready to be matched.

All I do these days is hang out in places with polished concrete and exposed brick. This one is no different, except it's dimly lit and smells like chocolate because it is called the Chocolate Factory—there must be a diffuser somewhere that aerates pure Dutch-processed cocoa into the perfect air freshener. Right now it's set up to resemble a restaurant on Valentine's Day, little two-person tables with chairs facing each other, a small vase of flowers in between. There is a bar along one side of the room, where Cyrus, Jules, and I perch uncomfortably, mingling only with one another.

Destiny and Li Ann arrive and we wave them over. Destiny is pitching for Consentify and Li Ann is just here to make everyone else look unkempt.

"I wish smoking would come back," Destiny announces.

"No, you don't. Smoking has probably led to a lot of nonconsensual sex," Li Ann says.

"You're right! Fuck smoking."

"Probably not as much as alcohol," I add.

"There's only one thing that leads to nonconsensual sex, and that's men."

"And patriarchy."

"Fuck patriarchy," Destiny says. "But seriously, though, why has no one invented something else we can do with our mouths that socially signifies that we are calming our nerves and makes us look super-cool while we're doing it?"

"Huge market opportunity," I agree. "What would you call it?"

"Poking?"

"Stroking."

"Let's figure out the business plan later. Now I have to fix this slide." And she marches off in search of the Wi-Fi password. Li Ann floats away to scan the room.

Jules and Cyrus have dressed up. They're wearing shirts with buttons. They have combed their hair.

"Who's going to do the pitch?"

Cyrus suggests it should be me.

"Why me?"

"Because it was your idea."

"It wasn't my idea. Jules and I thought of it together."

"Yeah," Jules says. "Bottling Cyrus. Eau de Cyrus, now in a convenient spray that will turn your ordinary life into a deep spiritual experience."

"Shut up, Jules."

"I can't do it alone," I complain. "What if no one likes it?"

"No one will like it," Jules says. "And then someone will, that's just how it goes."

"Fine, I'll do it if you come with."

"Sit at the bar and eat olives," Jules tells Cyrus. "We'll point at you so they know what they're bottling—I mean getting."

I disagree. "Not olives. Olives are messy. Nuts. And a short drink, like a whiskey."

"Go," Cyrus says, shooing us away.

The problem is, there is room for only two people at each table, so every time the buzzer rings, Jules has to carry an extra chair with him, and we spend a lot of time explaining that we are co-founders and that Cyrus, over there in the long hair with the martini, is also a co-founder but isn't really willing to talk to investors. We cycle through seven or eight white men in suits who appear interested for the first fifteen seconds and then start crossing their legs and leaning back in their chairs to discreetly yet clearly look over our shoulders at who might be next. Then we meet Harriet, who appears with a truly excellent blow-dry, and I'm crushing on her so hard I completely flub the pitch. Jules takes the next one, another man in a suit, somewhat older, with a weak chin and a thinning patch of blond hair. He speaks in a low, almost sweet voice when he asks Jules to repeat the name of the company.

"WAI," says Jules. "Pronounced 'why.'"

"Why is it called WAI?"

"Because we want people to ask something fundamentally different of their online experience. Not *what*—as in what can I get from this moment, what can I buy, sell, display, say about myself. Not *who*—as in who am I following and who is following me, and who likes me and who is indifferent. But *why*, as in why am I here, and what am I doing with the small amount of time left to me on Planet Earth?"

"Also," I chime in, "it stands for We Are Infinite. And it nods to the AI framework that's at the heart of the platform."

The man—I see from his tag that his name is Frank—turns to me and asks about the framework, and I start talking about the Empathy Module.

"You seem to know a lot about the engineering side."

"I coded it, so, yeah."

"Ah, I see."

"She's from MIT," Jules says.

"Media Lab? What year?"

Jules says, "When we realized the commercial possibilities of the platform, it seemed a shame not to monetize sooner rather than later." How does he do that, I wonder, how does he make being a dropout sound so desirable?

Frank nods. "What are you looking for?" he asks, and Jules launches into the valuation, the team size, and our expected launch date. I wonder if one of them might turn to me and ask what I think is a realistic timeline, given that I'm going to be the one to deliver it, but they don't, so I look over at Cyrus, who appears to be on his second martini. Then the buzzer rings, and we go through the rounds with two other people I wouldn't be able to distinguish in a lineup except that one has a slight paunch and the other boasts that he only eats in a two-hour window in the middle of the day and that it makes his head clearer than the bells chiming in St. Paul's Cathedral. That's in London, he says, as if I hadn't aced AP Geography.

"It was the martini," I say to Cyrus when it's all over. "I told you it had to be a highball, and you went off script."

"Such small things our fates depend on."

"Actually, it was me. I sucked."

"You were great," Jules says, patting me on the back.

We both know that isn't true. "You should do them yourself. I just don't have the charm."

"You'll get the hang of it."

Destiny bounds up to us. "I think I did it," she says, brandishing three business cards. "How'd you make out?"

"Zero."

"Oh, shit, did you fall flat?"

"Like a vegan pancake."

"It's not you," she says. "It's the system. It's rigged against you. Look at you, your fucking nose is pierced. And your name is Asha."

"I think I just bombed."

She turns to Jules. "What do you think?"

"I think we need to practice."

"Maybe Asha needs a little more white male privilege."

Jules shakes his head. "Don't make this about me."

"I'm not saying it's you, it's just that you have to face reality, which is that no one is going to bet on Asha running the show."

I agree. "Yeah, Jules, just do that 'See you on the golf course' thing and get the money, and we can worry about our souls later."

Cyrus isn't going for that. "We're worrying about our souls now, remember?"

"I don't mean it that way. I just mean let me out of the whole pitching thing. Cyrus, you and Jules do it."

"I'm the Researcher," Cyrus says.

"You're the one who lends credibility to the framework," Jules says to me. "Without you, I'm just a guy with a crazy idea."

"A white guy with a crazy idea," Destiny says.

I nod. "I'm with her."

I've set Jules off. "Shit, Asha get off your high horse and work with me, will you? Maybe try not to look so sarcastic next time someone asks about your engineering chops."

"Oh, so now you just want me to roll over when people assume I'm the window dressing?"

"It's just a game we have to play. Anyway, you could try practicing a little."

He's right. I totally crashed out with Lady Blow-dry. "Okay, you got me. I'll be rehearsing my speech in front of the mirror from now on."

"I'll be your mirror," Cyrus says.

"You, my friend, are in the doghouse. Talk about sipping cocktails while watching the house burn down."

Destiny buys me a consolation drink called a raspberry shrub, which tastes like raspberries that have been sitting around in the back of the refrigerator. I secretly wish Destiny had crashed out too, so we could moan about how terrible it is that the patriarchy makes the world go round, but I can't kill her mood now.

"Tell me how you did it."

"I told them I was at the cutting edge of the post-MeToo moment and that at some point, the culture was going to decide we needed better safeguarding tools, and men would be too ashamed to say no. It's the women we have to convince first, then there's a tipping point and it will become universal. I have graphs to back it all up."

"Maybe we need more graphs. But to prove what, that people are all feeling like they need a little non-God god around?"

"They probably don't do surveys for that."

"No. But maybe something related, like whether religion is seeing a resurgence—I'll get Jules to look into it." I wish I'd talked to Destiny before showing up here, and now I'm leaving with zero business cards and my hair smelling like a Mars bar. We part with Jules and Destiny on the sidewalk, and Cyrus and I make our way to Penn Station.

Cyrus falls asleep on the train while I keep cycling through the evening in my mind. I think about the parade of suits I just met, and the fact that from now on they are going to be my audience, the people I have to sell to, and this makes me sad and annoyed at myself. I start to feel a tickle of longing for Dr. Stein and her transplanted eyes. At least she bothered to be disappointed when I sold out. I had dragged a reluctant Cyrus along with me based on the notion that we were going to change something, yet what I saw tonight was more of the same, the same people with the same power to look straight through me as if I haven't spent my short life making myself uninvisible. "Fuck you, Frank," I whisper under my breath.

We get to the station and I nudge Cyrus awake. Our bikes are parked there, but I'm so tired I call us a cab, and soon we're unlocking the back door and throwing ourselves into bed.

Cyrus and I have maintained an Anglo-Bengali wall. At Utopia, I'm all about work, algorithms, funding, and building the platform. Every night, on the train ride home, through St. Albans, Lynbrook, and Baldwin, I dissect the day, remembering the lines of code I've written, the bug fixes, the tense conversations with Jules about money, and when I get to Merrick, I get on my bike and relive my childhood by speeding down Hewlett Avenue and turning in to my parents' driveway, and by the time I take the side door to the basement and jump into bed with Cyrus, we are all about the other things, books we are reading, the terrible state of the world, and sex, daily, necessary, like an insulin injection to maintain all of what is good and alive.

Still, minor irritations pop up. It bothers me that Cyrus is not more troubled by the fact that we live with my parents or that I had to get my dad to underwrite our credit extension. I want to say something to him, but it makes it harder that he doesn't have parents.

It has snowed—an early first snow—then rained, then snowed more, and my sister and I are clearing the driveway. As usual, she blurts out what I've been thinking. "He should at least help around the house more," she complains, attacking the hard surface of the snow with the end of her shovel.

"I don't want to make him feel like he's not pulling his weight," I say, defensive whenever the issue comes up. It's been a week since the speed-dating event.

"But he isn't," she counters. "Why am I over here when I could be shoveling my own damn driveway?"

"You know Ammoo hates it when he hangs around the kitchen asking if he can help."

She shakes her head. "Not super-psyched about freezing my ass off right now."

I want to confront Mira about the real reason she's in such a crap mood, but I know it's because she isn't pregnant yet. It's been over a year, and though she never talks about it, I can tell it's slowly breaking her heart. And she's right, of course, about Cyrus. I say I can't talk to him because he might be sensitive about the whole parents thing, but really it's because I'm too much of a coward to tell him to get his act together. I'm worried he's going to tell me that I'm the one who got us into this whole thing in the first place, and that if I don't like it, we should possibly just go back to Cambridge and forget it ever happened.

I know I can't do that. Despite everything, I'm thrilled by our life. I love Utopia, Destiny with her inflatable doll, Rory and his electrocuted vegetables, and the way it feels like at any moment our lives might be completely upended. I don't miss the hush of the lab, I don't miss the projections and the hypotheticals and the distant, untouchable future. This world is real even in its unrealness, perched on the edge of the city as if nudging something great, and that great thing could be us.

▸

A month later, Destiny is up to three donuts a day. Her business cards have not turned up any real leads, and neither have the two hundred emails she has sent to seed investors, angels, VC funds, and other people known to drop money on ideas. She's conspicuously reading every article and blog post available on raising funds as a woman, and proclaiming how the odds are against her.

"Only two percent of all VC money goes to female-founded companies, did you know that?" she bellows. I do know that, because she told me yesterday.

She is full of ideas to redress the imbalance. "Let's scan all the correspondence we get from VCs through the Spoken filter," she proposes to Li Ann. We are in the cafeteria trying Rory's new vegan dish, faux fish pie. It's weird, but also hard to stop eating. "That way we can get a snapshot of the problem."

"What do you mean?" Li Ann says.

"You know, we just scan it for sexism, and then we do a whole exposé on how impossible it is to get funding if you're a female founder. *The New York Times* will love it."

"Oh, I'm not doing Spoken anymore," Li Ann tells us, taking a delicate bite. "Is it me, or is this like baby food laced with heroin?"

Destiny puts her hand on her heart. "Why? It was such a good idea."

"With all the data privacy issues, we're not going to get anyone to buy a filter to read their emails."

"And tell them what assholes they are," Destiny says.

Li Ann nods, surprisingly upbeat. "I'm using the code to build something else, but in the meantime . . . ready? . . . cigarettes for asthmatics!"

"That was not how I thought you were going to end that sentence," Destiny says.

"I'm serious. You guys gave me the idea when you said you wished they would bring smoking back. I've been asthmatic my whole life, and I've always wanted to smoke. People like doing things with their mouths."

I tell her I can't disagree with that.

"That was the whole point of actual cigarettes," Li Ann says.

"But there was the small matter of cancer."

"Exactly! But they were cool. I mean, everyone agrees they were cool, right?"

Li Ann is passing around a small metal case. When I open it, I see thin oblongs in various metallic shades. Like very expensive lipstick. I pick one up. It is satisfyingly heavy. "This is vaping, right?"

"No," she says. She takes it from me and presses on the end, and when I inhale, the scent of rosemary fills my nostrils. It's like my mouth is getting an expensive spa treatment. "Vitamin smoke," she says. "And it comes with a microdose of pure oxygen—great for asthmatics. There are going to be way more asthmatics in the afterworld."

Destiny nods. "True."

"It's got all the good stuff—vitamins C and D, a bit of collagen, some vaporized A, antioxidants—you can customize it. It's called Breathe Life."

"Breathe Life?"

She does a toothpaste-commercial smile and says, "Do something great with your mouth!"

Li Ann sounds crazy, but in a year we're probably all going to have those things sticking out of our mouths.

"Rory's doing all the testing in the lab, and we're sourcing some great ingredients, you know, oils from the best organic farms."

"Great!" Destiny cheers, putting her thumbs up. We polish off our faux fish and make our way upstairs.

"Well, I've officially forgiven her for being way hotter than me," I say.

"Some people have it all. Every time she has a new idea, she gets to do the prototyping for free. Imagine knowing you could build anything you wanted."

"I would put a hipster café on every street east of Bayside," I say.

"Suburbs getting you down?"

"I had to get on my bike this morning and stand outside Starbucks till it opened. Starbucks in a strip mall. That's what turns you on in Merrick."

▶

We have no leads either, despite Jules exhausting his admittedly not very long list of contacts from his Sellyourshit.com days. I have taken to borrowing money from my parents, which makes me feel like I'm permanently wearing an itchy sweater. And we haven't been able to hire anyone, not even the person who is going to design the platform.

Then Jules walks into Utopia one day with the chinless investor. He brings him over to our desks, and I frantically try to hide the evidence of my four p.m. french fry habit. "Frank wanted to meet again," Jules announces.

It takes me a second or two to wipe the grease from my fingertips. "Nice to see you," I say, wondering if he can sense that I've been sticking virtual pins in him.

"I have to say, folks, I'm intrigued."

"Intrigued is good," Jules says. "We can intrigue you more."

Frank pulls up a chair. "How do you see this thing working?"

Jules gestures toward me. "Asha's the expert."

I talk him through the basics of the algorithm. He asks a few not totally idiotic questions. "This is pretty impressive," he says. "Do you have a business plan? And who's on the leadership team?"

I tell him it's just us.

"We're going to build it out, of course," Jules says. "We think a team of about twenty pre-launch, and then depending on engagement, we can grow proportionally."

I nod as if we've had many meetings about team size.

"Have you thought about roles?"

"We're all co-founders," Jules says.

"One of you has to be CEO."

"We assumed it would be Asha," Jules tells him, although, again, we have never talked about it.

"Or Jules." I shrug.

"All the technical aspects of the platform have been developed by Asha," Jules says. He shoots me this look that I think means *Stop making it sound like we don't have our shit together.*

Frank leans back in his seat and regards us, doing whatever mental calculation people like him do at times like these. Even before he starts talking, I know what he's going to say. It comes together in my mind the way things do when they're inevitable—like they've been there all along.

"Look," Frank says, "it's not up to me. But if I were you, I would make your guy—what's his name?"

"Cyrus."

"Yeah, Cyrus, the CEO. Because someone has to represent the idea—it's woo-woo enough as it is, and if you're going to pull in seed money, the person at the heart of this whole thing should represent you."

"What do you mean by woo-woo?" I ask, even though I can't say I disagree.

"He means it's going to be difficult to raise money," Jules says. "But we already knew that."

"I thought that's why you were here."

"Frank is just here to give advice," Jules says.

"Not necessarily," Frank says. "I've been doing little investments here and there. You know Countify?"

"No."

"It's a SaaS company, they do cloud-based storage for cloud-based services. IPO'ed last year, and I got in early, so I've got some funds for seed stage investments."

I have no idea what *SaaS* means. I'm assuming it is not, in fact, *sass*. "Is Cyrus being the CEO a deal breaker for you?" I ask.

"I'm just telling you what I would do if I were you."

Why do people say "if I were you" when there is no way they could ever be you? We thank Frank and he trots away, and Jules and I are left wondering what to do about Cyrus.

On the last Friday of every month, Li Ann holds auditions for the new crop of Utopians. In early December, eight months after we've moved in, it's my turn to sit on the selection committee.

Li Ann hands around the list of hopefuls. Saint or Sinner is the name of the first company. It produces wearables that turn red or green depending on your climate behavior that day. Did you take a taxi? Ride the bus? Buy a plastic bottle of water? Was it Fiji? The ring or bracelet or necklace tracks everything. At the end of the day, when you're sitting in front of your dinner, you get a personal audit of all your shitty behavior that day. And then you wake up and try again.

The two men making the pitch hand around a few bits of jewelry. Li Ann and I each get to try on a ring. Marco gets a cuff link.

"In ten years, wearables will be the only accessories around," one of them says.

"Why wear something that's purely ornamental when it can work for you?" the other one echoes.

"How do I know if I'm a saint or a sinner?" I ask.

"It's going to change color."

"But how will it know what I'm doing? Is it going to take photos?"

"We're still prototyping that," the first one explains. "We'll probably use sensors and bar codes."

"Or cameras," the other one says. They tell us more about the cameras, then give us a slightly glitchy demo.

Li Ann stands up, smiling extra-sweetly because she's about to turn them down. "We'll be in touch." She hands back the ring.

"Oh, no, you can keep that, we got a great deal on the prototypes. Excellent supply chain if we can get it up and running."

Li Ann glances at the list she's printed out. "The next one is called No Touch."

Two people in identical black suits stand facing each other. They start to move, their hands gliding up toward each other. One of them starts to speak. "In the future," she says, "the spread of antibiotic-resistant bacteria and new viruses will change the way we interact with each other. Touching will become rare." They step back from each other, then turn to face us, identical twins with matching cropped hair. "Developed by a team of social anthropologists, behavioral psychologists, and dancers, No Touch is introducing new ways to uphold social norms while maintaining safety."

They project a series of images on the screen. "We will use nudge theory and mass social marketing to promote safer greetings, such as"—and now they are folding at the waist— "bowing"—holding their palms together—"namaste"—bending at the knees—"curtseying.

"We will target the fourteen-to-twenty-five age group and introduce the new behaviors as innovations. We expect that within a generation, handshakes, hugs, and casual kissing on the cheek will completely disappear."

They paint a picture of a world where touching a stranger is akin to licking a subway seat. There are invisible threats everywhere. Their behavioral shifts come with swag: brightly painted face masks, rubber gloves, antibacterial pocket liners. Li Ann and Rory are rapt, nodding enthusiastically, trying on the gloves. Rory says the investment in public health is below par in 74 percent of all health services. The twins geek out on all the statistics, and soon it's like the annual meeting of the Pandemic Preppers Society. No Touch gets an instant yes and they move in the following week. The week after that, you can't pass through reception without pausing to sanitize your hands.

Jules and I are at the diner across the street, talking about money. It's snowing, a kind of friendly, fluffy snow falling lightly on the sidewalk. The taste of regular crap coffee is oddly reassuring. We are broke— my credit cards are maxed out and Jules is paying for our server with what's left of his allowance. "What's the game plan?" he asks.

I tell him I'm close. "But I need a front-end developer."

"And we need someone to run the community side of things. And marketing. How will anyone know about us?"

"Facebook?"

"Facebook isn't free—we'd have to pay them a shitload of money to get anywhere. Dammit, I've never spent so much time thinking about money."

"You? Moneybags you?"

"Oh, we never talk about money where I come from. My dad goes to sleep, and all the dollars just multiply."

"Do your folks even know you moved to New York?"

"They said, 'That's nice, dear,' as if I finally agreed to wear white pants to their Memorial Day party."

I reach over and squeeze his hand. "I'm sorry," I say, thinking of my own mother sending me off every morning with an egg sandwich. "Maybe we should bail," I say. "We could just go back to Cambridge."

Jules shakes his head. "Not possible. We've had a taste—even the smallest taste changes you."

I had been thinking this very thing. "Is that what happened to you last time?"

"My business succeeded for about five minutes, and I spent the next seven years trying to chase that high again. Probably why I fell on my face so many times. Cyrus was the one who finally helped me get over it, because none of this stuff matters to him."

I know exactly what Jules means. Cyrus really doesn't care. He isn't worried that we are on the verge of bankruptcy, or that there is the tantalizing possibility of something bigger. He is obsessively focused on both the present and on the esoteric distance. The middle ground, the place most of us inhabit—what we are going to eat for lunch, how we are going to pay our bills, how we are going to fulfill our petty human ambitions—those things do not occur to him. He doesn't care, because they are not on his mind.

"We're running on empty," Jules says.

"There's only one thing to do." I wait for Jules to say it.

"We have to make Cyrus the boss."

I nod. "He can make the pitch, get us our funding. You know how he is in front of an audience."

Jules looks up something on his phone. "There's another speed-dating thing in two days."

"Look me in the eyes," I say to Jules, "and tell me you're sure."

We both know that if we can get Cyrus to agree, there's no turning back. Jules doesn't hesitate. He stares right back at me and says yes. Like me, he has no idea what's going to happen if Cyrus takes charge, but that's what I love about Jules—he always wants to plow forward into the unknown. We argue briefly about who should be the one to convince Cyrus, and after I lose three straight rounds of rock/paper/scissors, the task falls to me.

Against the wisdom of the No Touch twins, we shake hands.

At home, Cyrus is reading the Talmud, a leather-bound copy that lies open on his lap. "Whatcha doing?"

"I've been thinking about Auntie Lavinia's neighbor," he says. "A person who has left his community, tried to adopt another."

"He's between worlds?"

"Being in between is one of the best things about being alive," he says. "It makes us yearn. It makes us uncomfortable, and that is the most human thing possible. But death—death requires certainty."

"Purgatory?"

"I did consider Dante, but the whole point of laying someone to rest is that he goes somewhere, even if we don't know exactly where that is. That's the only knowable thing about it." He closes the book, reaches for me. I feel that lurch in my stomach every time I'm near him. It's been over a year, and I sometimes wonder when this particular feeling will fade—it has to, I've read too many novels to imagine it won't—but right now I'm still in the swell of it, strange noises escaping my lips as he pulls at my sweater, all the time wondering what I would do if this feeling were ever taken away from me, if he stopped wanting me, if I stopped wanting him, if we turned into ordinary people who got tired of each other or simply decided to love each other in ordinary ways.

Later, we are lying on the floor among the books Cyrus has checked out from the library. I get up to fill my water bottle and decide this is the moment. "Jules and I were wondering if you would come to Utopia tomorrow. There's something we need to ask you."

"I think I know what it is," Cyrus says. His cheeks are flushed and his forehead is shiny with sweat. It's always warm in here; even when my parents are hot, they're worried they'll get cold, so the thermostat is set permanently to 85 degrees. Also: the carpets are too thick. It's like walking on a trampoline. My irritation at being here, in my childhood home with its overly plush carpets and tropical air, is mounting by the day.

"You need to lead the party, Cy."

A beat. "I thought we agreed I was only going to be the Researcher."

"We thought that might work. But it doesn't. You need to run things."

"It's just—it's not what I imagined for myself."

He leans against the bedframe and his hair flops over his forehead. His eyes are guarded.

"I know you don't want to do it. But Jules and I think you'd be great. Even the weird VC guy could tell it should be you, just from looking across the room."

"It was the martini, wasn't it?"

I laugh. "It was you. You and WAI just belong together."

He sighs. "I don't know."

"What did you think you were going to grow up to be, Cyrus?" I've never asked him that. I guess my life has been so straightforward—there was no question I was going to make something of myself. It's the brown person's code: achieve something; make it matter that your parents left their home and everything they loved on your account. I had never imagined it any other way. But Cyrus and I were from different worlds.

Did I regret Cyrus's whiteness? Truth be told, sometimes I did. If Cyrus was Bengali, I wouldn't have to explain why chewing on the end of a drumstick was perhaps the best part of a meal, or why there were outside clothes and inside clothes and in-between clothes that you wore when you got home but weren't ready for bed. I wouldn't have to explain all the complicated rules about where you can and can't put your feet, and that he could maybe kiss me in front of my parents but not on the mouth and certainly never with tongue.

But what I found infinitely worse was trying to gauge whether a man had just the right amount of brown in him. He had to know about drumsticks and shoes and not hate himself, but he also couldn't be too in love with his mother or imagine that I would change more diapers than him or ever, ever be charmed by the thought of me in a hijab. He had to be three parts Tagore, one part Drake, one part e e cummings, and that's not even getting into whether I got a rise from smelling his face. So no, I didn't want to ponder Cyrus's whiteness, I just wanted to enjoy his scent and his perfectly sized dick and the fact that, of all the people I had ever met in my whole life, he felt the most like home.

Except he isn't feeling so much like home now. "My mom and I talked about starting a school where we just read to the students all day."

I sit down between Cyrus and a copy of *Don Quixote* and curl my fist around a tuft of powder-blue carpet. My irritation shifts to Cyrus's mother. Why didn't she teach her son the basic life lesson of having dreams that were life-size instead of random and impossible?

"Um-hm. Tell me more," I say. He talks for a few minutes about the things they would read at this school. Proust. The Bhagavad Gita. *Ulysses*. Toni Morrison. Maybe, as he tells it, the story—his own fantasy about what he might someday do—sounds as remote to him as it does to me. We sit for a moment in silence; as he weighs the image he's held on to with the future I am proposing. After a long time he starts leafing through *Don Quixote*, and then he reads, "'Having thus lost his understanding, he unluckily tumbled upon the oddest fantasy that ever entered into a madman's brain; for now he thought it convenient and necessary, as well as for the increase of his own honor, as the service of the public, to turn knight errant.'"

Convenient and necessary. I'll take that.

"Don't worry, Cyrus," I say. "You'll still be you. Just with a new title."

The next day, as I'm getting ready, I see Cyrus out in the driveway, shoveling snow in a purposeful, steady rhythm, and I know he's going to take his place at the head of the table. I'm excited—thrilled, really—and at the same time, I have a small inkling of what's to come—I can almost see him flexing his muscles through the thick lining of his jacket, the way his mouth is firmly set—and despite what I said to him last night, I know that everything is about to change.

Cyrus takes the train with me and wanders around Utopia as if he's meeting everyone for the first time. He spends an hour in Rory's lab, picking apart the vegetables and getting a lecture on various forms of seaweed. He tests Li Ann's oxygen sticks and gets lessons from Destiny on how to draw an anatomically correct vulva. He is delighted by all the new things, learning everyone's first names, making little inside jokes with them about their pets or their weird eating habits. "So you're allergic to anything that grows underground except carrots. But you just hate the taste of carrots?" Once he's been suitably entertained, Jules and I run through the details of the pitch. Cyrus nods and nods. "Okay," he says finally, "I got it. I'm ready."

"The speed-dating thing is tomorrow. Should we do a run-through together?"

Cyrus is holding open a large notebook. He starts to draw with a Sharpie. "Nope," he says.

"You don't want to practice?"

"It'll be better if it's fresh," he says. He draws a series of concentric circles. The Sharpie makes a squeaking sound on the paper. I look at Jules. Jules shrugs.

"Here's what's going to happen," Cyrus says, not looking up from his notebook. "I'm going to go in there alone, and you two can wait at the bar across the street. And when I come back, we are going to have an investor."

I can't decide if that would delight me or annoy the shit out of me. "Jules and I have been working twenty-four/seven, and it's really not that easy."

He stops drawing and looks at both of us. "I'm sorry, you're right. I don't mean to make light of all the things you've already tried. That's why I'm so confident—the pitch is amazing, the platform is great, I just have to sell it. I was hesitant at first, but then I realized I just have to talk about it in a slightly different way."

"You're the golden goose," I say.

"The champion prizefighter," Jules nods.

"The leprechaun."

"What do you think?" Cyrus asks. He holds up his notebook, and on it is our logo, three small capital letters inside three concentric circles. WAI.

Six

GROWN-UPS

I wish Gaby, our new CFO, would stop wearing designer suits to Utopia. He doesn't even do it ironically, he just gets up every morning, puts on many layers of expensive clothing, and rocks up to the office.

"That's what CFOs are like," Jules tells me. "They're uptight. Don't suit-shame him."

"That's a thing?"

"I'm making it a thing."

Until Gaby arrived, I was tabulating our expenses on a spreadsheet, and I'd programmed it to beep loudly if anything went over five hundred dollars. But now that we have eleven people on payroll and we're starting to upload the platform onto our servers, the money is dribbling out like drool from an overly bred pug, and Gaby is in charge of all the numbers.

Gaby is a grown-up. His sideburns are dusted with gray, and he has a square jaw and one of those long wallets that men like to slide in and out of their coat pockets. He was the CFO of a hardware startup that went public last year and made him very rich, and now he is here to do the same with WAI. There's nothing mean about him. He has kind, crinkly eyes and he is always super nice to me, but even so I find myself a little embarrassed whenever he's around, like I just got caught picking my teeth.

Gaby is here to make sure we don't squander the two million dollars in our bank account. This seems like a stupidly large sum. The money was given to us by Rupert, a person I've met twice: first when we visited the offices of Sloane Management and Cyrus presented on the two-hundred-inch screen in the conference room, and then again when the money landed in the bank and he took us all out for drinks at Soho House. Rupert is tall, skinny, Indian, and likes to hook his thumbs around his belt loops. I hated him on sight, mostly because he started talking to me in elaborate sports metaphors and also because my parents have always told me to be skeptical of brown people who change their names to sound like white people, but he loves the platform, loves Cyrus, and treats me with an acceptable amount of respect for being the brains behind the operation. Plus, he was one of only two people willing to write a check for WAI, a fact he reminds us of repeatedly, telling us that he knows our chances of succeeding are zero, that it's not even a moon shot, more like one-putting into a black hole the size of a penny.

Rupert and Cyrus meet every week for mentoring sessions. Rupert appears high whenever he is near Cyrus. I overhear them talking about the Assyrian Empire, about Sikhism and astrology and arcane subplots from *The Lord of the Rings*. I know Rupert without asking him a single question—growing up in Jersey in a two-story house not unlike my parents' in Merrick, playing Dungeons & Dragons in the basement, and turning the volume down on his Wu Tang Clan lest his mother call down, "Rupinder, you're finishing your maths home-work or what, beta?"

Rupert has divided us into teams. There is a leadership team, an executive team, a product team, and a marketing team. We are a board of directors—Cyrus, Jules, me, and Rupert. And titles. Cyrus is CEO. Jules is COO. And I am Chief Technology Officer. I'm going to write all the code, and Cyrus is going to lend me his brain while keep-ing Rupert happy, and Jules is going to take care of everything else: the team we're going to hire, the way we're going to run those teams, the deadlines and the deliverables and the mess of running a company.

Jules is in a perpetual state of nervous excitement. He uses a standing desk so he can type things into his computer while bouncing on his heels. Instead of using Slack, he likes to shout across the room whenever he wants to tell us something. He kicks off every day with an all-hands meeting in which he leads us in singing "WAI is the word" to the tune of *Grease*. Everyone on the team adores him.

Cyrus, on the other hand, is disciplined and reserved. He takes the 7:13 train in every morning; I have to shower the night before and skip breakfast to keep up with him. He wears his signature white linen shirts and ankle-length trousers and barricades himself behind a desk and works intently, hardly ever looking up from his screen or the piles of books open in front of him. Whereas Jules is every-one's best friend, Cyrus inspires more of a hushed reverence from the team, starting with Rupert and Gaby right down to the intern who is going to run our socials, a woman called Gina whose college thesis was titled *A New Media of the Social: Networks of Power in the Era of Post-truth*.

We did not meet Rupert at the speed-dating event. Instead, Cyrus joined something called Venture Shorts, where people post two-minute Instagram stories of themselves and their ideas, then get anonymous invitations from VCs to come and pitch. Cyrus's video was one long iPhone shot of him looking deep into the camera and telling the story of how he came to believe that ritual was the central act of human life, and how, thus far, all of our technological innovations had ignored this fact. "We imagined," he said, "that we could supplant the role of meaning with other things—with advancement, with speed, with pixels and processors. But we cannot deny our essential humanity, our souls, if you want to call them that, which yearn not just for the superficial connection of social media, the followers and the followed, the influencers and the influenced, the likes and the dislikes, but for the deeper connections, enabling us to ask the questions we have pondered for millennia. Why are we here? What is our purpose? And how can we come together in our inquiry as communities of belief, human-made groups of people who commit ancient and modern acts that frame the pivotal moments of our brief time on earth, our births, our marriages, our deaths? We at WAI believe that community is about shared beliefs, whatever those may be, and that technology can help us to strengthen those ties, rather than leaving us atomized by the pull of technological progress."

Cyrus's pitch received two bids: one from a small family office run by the errant son of a Texan oil magnate, and another from Rupert. No question where we chose to get our money from, even though the magnate, Ed Junior Jr., promised us more money on better terms. No, we chose Rupert, who, after a bit of negotiation with our new lawyer, agreed to 25 percent equity and wired the money to our bank account exactly six weeks after Cyrus posted his video.

Jules now talks about time in terms of runway, "runway" being the amount of time we have until our money runs out. "We have twelve months of runway," he keeps repeating. That's six months to launch the product and six months to make it financially viable. He wants me to hurry up and hire someone to help me design the platform, but I haven't found the right person yet. The people who roll up are too young and look like they haven't left their parents' basement for the duration of their short lives. I complain endlessly to Destiny and Li Ann, but I'm feeling the pressure now, because even I'm not fast enough to get the code written in time for our launch, not without help.

One day, after four brain-numbing interviews, a man in a Mohawk shows up and introduces himself as Ren. His English is imperfect but his portfolio is stunning, and soon we are talking about the beta launch, about attach rates and UX and UI. "When can you start?" I ask, and he says, "After lunch?" I stick out my hand and take deep satisfaction in saying "You're hired!"

"You can't do that," Jules tells me later. "Did you log the interview on HireMonkey?"

"What's HireMonkey?"

"Our API. Where have you been? I did a whole workshop on it last week."

"I've given Ren all the passwords and set him up next to me." I point to my new best friend, who has headphones on and is already deep in the system.

Jules sighs. "Rupert likes process, you know that."

"I like process too. And if you want the platform to come out on time, you're going to stop sending me toddlers with laptops. If I smell another adolescent whose idea of showering is waving his pits around between wanks, I'm going to tell Rupert he can have his platform in six years, not six months."

"You're such a drama queen."

"That's a very gendered insult, Jules. You can do better than that."

"Just hire whoever the fuck you want, and finish the product." He stalks away, and I immediately get to work. Now that Ren is here, I have no excuse. Six months is only six months away.

It bothers me that Jules is such a stickler for procedure—I blame Gaby, who seems to be having an undue influence—but we are all starting to feel the high, even Cyrus. I love taking the train to work with him, love seeing him across the room. Sometimes he'll walk past my desk and brush the back of my neck lightly with his knuckle, and I swear I can feel the blood rushing to the very middle of my body where all the tingle lives. Sometimes we text. Sometimes we sext.

The other high is real estate. Cyrus and I have just signed the lease on a one-bedroom apartment in Gowanus. We are each paid sixty-five thousand dollars a year, which, after taxes, is more money than I have ever had in my bank account at one time. Between coding sprints, I'm Googling sofas on Craigslist and creating spreadsheets for our household expenses. Actually, I'm just repurposing the one I made for WAI before Rupert gave us all that money. New York is expensive and I don't want to ever be broke again.

Two weeks later, we move. It is a Sunday in the middle of April. My parents and Mira stand in the driveway as the last snow of the season melts under a glorious midafternoon sun. My mother dabs the end of her sari against the corner of her eye. She has packed two coolers full of meals, each in a blue-lidded Tupperware with a note attached: *Chicken Curry (microwave 3 minutes), Lamb Bhuna (microwave 4 minutes), Fish Curry (eat first do not freeze).* She has even packed rice because she knows otherwise we'll just eat it all on toast.

"We're just a train ride away," I say. Ammoo sniffs. My father pulls me toward him and slips a fifty-dollar bill into my hand. Suddenly, I am reluctant to leave. It would be so much easier to stay here, where there is always something to eat and some random chore to do like type up invitations for Auntie Lavinia's New Year's Eve party or pick the stones out of the dal someone has brought from my mother's village. Cyrus thanks my parents in elegant long sentences that they appreciate but are also a little bored by. Finally, we get into our U-Haul and pull out of the driveway, our van full of food and little bits of furniture left over from my childhood, the lamp I read by when I was a kid, a small table that we will put our feet on when we sit on the sofa we're about to pick up from a couple in Flushing who are redecorating, and a totally clichéd poster of Einstein that I can't bring myself to abandon.

The apartment is tiny, and the bedroom window looks out onto an airshaft, but after my parents' basement, it feels like a mansion. We heave our things up four flights of stairs and put the boxes in the vague places the boxes should be—kitchen, living room, bedroom, bathroom. We do some excellent kissing on the sofa and then we fall asleep, and in the middle of the night Cyrus gets up and rummages around and pulls out a blanket, and that's how we spend our first night. After that we don't really unpack, we just take out the things we need and shove them into whatever corners they seem to belong to. And without my parents imposing some sort of order on us, home and work start to blur. Breakfast is a microwaved frozen burrito, lunch is at our desks, and dinner is also at our desks or at the diner across the street if it's a special occasion. Jules and Gaby are almost always there. Our lives are played out in the presence of these people, but because of the moments when Cyrus leans over my desk and I can smell the inside of his shirt, I don't care that we are almost never alone and certainly never talking about anything but WAI.

I decide to take Jules at his word. Hire whoever the fuck you want, he says. So I do. After hiring Ren, which is the best thing I've done since coming up with the idea in the first place, I decide to approach Destiny. I know she's only got a few weeks of money—runway—left, and although she's putting on a brave face, the sting has gone out of her comments in the cafeteria. She's alone at her desk these days, she's lost Maisie, and even the blow-up doll is looking a little sad. On impulse, I take her to the diner and order a stack of silver-dollar pancakes and tell her we've been looking for a head of marketing for ages, and I still haven't been able to find anyone I don't hate.

"Everyone is twelve years old," I whine.

"I know," she says, "it's like they went straight from diapers to grad school."

"And smug. I hate it when they're smug."

The food arrives. I nudge the pancakes toward Destiny and she holds the maple syrup over the plate and pours for what feels like an entire minute.

"How's it going?" I ask.

Immediately, she spears a pancake, shoves it into her mouth, and begins to cry. "Disaster," she says. She looks so sad I can almost feel the tears running down her cheeks.

"Look," I tell her. "Don't make me hire one of those people on the shortlist Jules made for me." I pull out my phone. "Instagram influencer since the age of eight. Two hundred thousand followers." I turn the phone toward her. "I mean, look at this girl's fingernails."

"I think fake nails are the modern equivalent of foot binding. That and Botox."

"At least with Botox you can still wipe your ass."

"Yeah, but can you smile?" I'm relieved to see her cracking a smile herself.

"We sound like we're a hundred years old."

"This thing is aging me faster than a nicotine habit."

"So will you do it?"

"I don't want to be a pity hire."

I swirl my coffee and down the last few drops. I can't lie to her. "I'm having a hard time watching you struggle to get funding for what we both know is a killer idea."

"Is it, though?"

"Of course it is. Who doesn't want safer sex?"

"Apparently, everybody." I see her eyes start to water again.

"Just do it for a few months. You can still put out some feelers for Consentify, and if you get funded, you can abandon me to my toddler brigade, okay?"

She straightens up, wiping her face. "Okay," she says, nodding, and we stand up and hug over the mini pancakes floating in their sticky amber lake.

Gaby has implemented an executive team meeting every afternoon, which means that at three p.m., Cyrus, Jules, Gaby, and I go down to the café and talk about what we're doing that day. We have four months till launch.

It's my turn to start. "I've got the wireframes." I show them my screen. Cyrus leans down and scans the page. The logo he'd drawn all those months ago is blue, and the circles are interconnected. The home page has three panels: one where you can scroll through the rituals created for others, another that invites you to create your own after answering eight questions (we did the user testing, Ren has told me, and ten is too many, and five is too few; plus, Cyrus says, eight is a lucky number in China), and the third, where you can post messages to your community—the people who asked for the same rituals— sort of like a bulletin board in your favorite café. Or church, for that matter.

Cyrus isn't sure about the logo.

"But it's the one you sketched," I tell him.

"Yeah, but the colors."

Jules glances at the screen. "I think it's fine."

"Can you ask Ren to send me a few options?"

"Okay. But what do you think of the layout?"

Cyrus gets a notebook out and starts to sketch. "What if we put the messaging at the bottom, sort of like a ticker tape?"

"Sure." I sigh. "We can try that."

"Sorry to break up the party, but we need to talk about finances," Gaby says. "We've had some unforeseen expenditures, which means we now have six months of runway, not eight."

"I thought we had ten," Cyrus says.

"Yeah," I say, "that's what I thought."

"You guys don't read a single thing I send you, do you?" Gaby says.

I pretend not to hear him.

"Our overheads are higher than we forecasted," Jules explains.

"And we have to spend on customer acquisition right off the bat—ads are getting more expensive."

Cyrus turns to me. "How long till you can get a beta out, Asha?"

I do some calculations in my head. "I could squeeze something out in three months."

We look through the glass at the twelve people all plugged into their headphones. "I'll do my best," I say. "Oh, and by the way, Destiny is our new head of marketing." I say a number. "Gaby, you have to pay her. She can't make her rent this month."

After that, Ren and I work around the clock. We hire two other designers and a front-end developer. Ren drives them all hard, using little other than his own example and the occasional sidelong glance. We're mainlining the ginseng-doused cold brew that Rory has cooked up in his lab, and I'm up so many hours that I don't even notice the jitters. I crawl into bed (a mattress on the floor which is lucky if it sees a pillowcase), spooning myself around a sleeping Cyrus, waking up around noon, and rolling up to the office with a Ziploc of Cheerios and a single-serve pack of peanut butter.

The summer passes in a blaze of sweaty nights, dawn breaking over the Hudson and sun slanting into my eyeline; Frappuccinos, slushies, soft serve, bubble tea, the weeks bending and crashing into each other. Cyrus never asks to spend time with me, never says the word "weekend." He curates a blood baptism using Jell-O mix for a vampire couple, goes back to Cambridge for a yoga funeral, and for three weeks in July is away on a Vipassana retreat, and when he comes back, I swear his voice has dropped an octave and he is at least three times sexier.

On our two-year anniversary, we return to the Book Mill.

We stay at Sam and Sam's again, in the room with the sloping ceiling. I am more in love with him than ever. We seem to have accidentally fallen into a happy rhythm, imposing almost nothing on each other, yet maintaining a deep kind of intimacy, a secret place full of longing, scraps of tenderness we nurture and feed, a little bonsai of love. *I'm going to write a marriage guide*, I think. I'll call it *The Startup Wife: How to Succeed in Business and Marriage at the Same Time*. I'll tell everyone how great it is to mix everything together—work, love, ambition, sex. Anyone who says business and pleasure don't mix is an idiot. I can see it in Barnes & Noble, propped up on a table between *How to Stay Married* and *Startups for Dummies*.

Jules's parents, the Cabots, like to flit around the world—London, Savannah, Hong Kong—but they always spend the last few weeks of the summer in the Hamptons. Jules insists we go for a weekend in August. "You can't send me into that shark tank by myself," he tells Cyrus. "You owe me." We rent a car and drive out late on Friday after the traffic has thinned, Jules driving, Cyrus beside him, and me sprawled in the backseat. They're playing their favorite car game, where they make up stories about the people in other cars. "Divorcing," Jules says about the couple in front of us. We can vaguely make them out ahead, a woman behind the wheel with a mass of curly hair, a man in the passenger seat with wide shoulders and a thick neck. "Married for six years and they're cooked."

"I don't know," Cyrus counters. "I'm thinking brother and sister."

I sit up, peer between the seats. "They're having an affair."

"The brother and sister?"

"No, you sicko, just a regular affair. Her actual husband is nerdy and into Pokémon Go. Either way she doesn't have kids."

"How do you know that?" Jules asks.

"On the highway at midnight on a Friday? Where would she leave them?"

"That's what I said, just plain old divorce, which is what my parents should've done twenty years ago."

It takes three hours to get to Sagaponack, where the Cabots have a family home they call the Farmhouse. We go up a long driveway. Even in the dark, I can tell the house extends in all directions and that there is nothing farmlike about it. Jules hands his car keys to a man who takes our bags and gives us directions to our room. Two flights up a wood-paneled staircase, down a hallway with tiny brass lamps illuminating our way, we find a sparsely furnished room wallpapered in tiny pink flowers. There is a bookshelf crammed with paperbacks, and a window seat overlooking the garden, which leads directly to the beach. Crickets and the circular hum of the sea are audible in the background.

I flop onto the bed. "Air-conditioning!"

There's a soft knock on the door, and Jules comes in with a tray, puts it down on the window seat, and silently shuts the door behind him. Under a white napkin there are oatmeal raisin cookies and two glasses of pink lemonade. I take a sip of lemonade, thinking this is a place where Jules might have been happy, where he might have spent summers in shorts, learning to swim, catching the eye of a cute guy in the house next door. I sense the possibility of happiness, and I feel sad for Jules that this possibility has never materialized.

▼

In the morning, we sit down at a long rectangular table and eat breakfast with Jules, his parents, his brother and sister, and their husbands and wives and kids. They are all beautiful in a leggy pink kind of way. I try to remember to chew with my mouth closed, and after every bite I run my tongue carefully over my teeth to make sure I don't have a wedge of brioche stuck somewhere. I make polite conversation with Jules's sister, Brittany, whose twin daughters, Paige and Peggy, are in matching jumpsuits and pigtails, silently spooning oatmeal into their mouths.

Jules's father leans forward in his seat and calls down to us from the head of the table: "How's business, son?"

"Great, Dad," Jules replies, nudging his scrambled eggs.

"Jules is keeping the ship afloat," Cyrus volunteers.

"That's weird, because he couldn't even keep his pants up in high school," his brother, a total asshole, barks.

"He got us our funding," Cyrus says. "We're launching in three months because of him."

"That's wonderful, dear," his mother murmurs.

"What is it again?" his brother asks. "Facebook for people who want to go to church?"

"Yeah, Don, something like that," Jules says, pushing his chair back.

"Mommy says you spend your allowance on hanging on," one of the twins says. Her mother shushes her.

"Hangers-on," the other twin says. "Peggy always gets it wrong."

All the blood rushes to my face. It occurs to me that for most of my life, I have shared this island with the Cabots. Merrick is only an hour away, yet it never would have occurred to my parents to drive over to East Hampton, park their car, and unload their Bengali picnic on the beach. The summers of my childhood were spent in the homes of friends in Hunters Point or Astoria; someone might stray into the backyard for a chicken kebab barbecue, but mostly they stayed inside and sang Tagore songs, recited poetry, and talked about how terrible yet still wonderful things were back home. Summers were not for sunbathing, they were for singing and homework and waitressing at the nearest IHOP.

I'm ashamed of taking money from Jules, which is, in fact, money from his dad. There's a detailed internal monologue in my head about how I'm just another immigrant leech, another drain on the system, the system in this case being the Cabot family trust fund.

"Do you want to leave, Jules?" Cyrus says, whispering but loud enough for everyone to hear.

I lean across the table. "Come on, Jules." I am ready for us to storm out of there in a blaze of fuck-yous.

"Oh, don't *go*," Jules's sister says with a light laugh. "They're just kids, they don't know what they're saying."

Jules looks back and forth between Cyrus and his father. He puts his fork down. He mouths something to Cyrus. Cyrus nods to me. I retreat and stuff the last of the French toast into my mouth.

"Pass the butter," Jules's mother says brightly.

"Well," his father bellows, "whatever makes you happy, son. As long as you're not taking drugs or getting the HIV, right?" He looks around the table, and a few other people laugh.

We spend the day between the pool and the beach. At the pool we are given towels and more pink lemonade. Someone has taken the trouble of inflating the various plastic items that we drift around on. At the beach there are deck chairs and umbrellas, a wide stretch of sand leading to a cloudy, very cold sea. At four p.m. there are martinis. At five p.m. there are finger sandwiches. Jules tells us there is no dinner, just these sandwiches, and that we are barred from entering the kitchen and foraging for ourselves. I stuff a few extra sandwiches into the pocket of my sweatpants. The children occasionally allow themselves to shriek in delight at, say, the appearance of a hermit crab on the beach, but otherwise the silence is uninterrupted and nearly deafening, and there is the sense that the same routine has gone on in this house since the day it was built, that the rituals were enshrined even before that, brought into being by a tribe of people who say little and eat even less.

Cyrus and I barricade ourselves around Jules and try to distract him with stories of our own unhappy childhoods. I tell Jules that my parents made me eat a disgusting dried-fish dish called shutki every Friday afternoon when I came home from school, that the carpets and the sofas and even my hair took on the stench of the shutki and to this day, if someone even says the word "anchovy," I want to gag. And Cyrus said his mother had invented a kind of boiled lettuce slurry she called Green Magic, which tasted like pond moss and gave him the shits. But both of these stories revolved around mothers, and it was obvious that Jules's mother had made no attempt to shove smelly/nutritious/culturally appropriate foods down his throat, that instead, mealtimes had been wordless and cold. Perhaps she had never cooked a meal for him herself in all the summers they had spent in this house. Soon we three lapse into silence, lost in our thoughts. After we finish our sandwiches, Cyrus and Jules decide to go for a swim, and I call my mother.

"I miss you, Ma."

I haven't seen my parents since we moved out, although I call them every Sunday. We talk about ordinary things and they always ask me what I'm eating, but I have avoided getting on the train to go out and see them, even though Mira sends me threatening text messages on a regular basis. I feel like if I slow down, even for a day, everything will fall apart around me. I'm feeling it now, here on the beach, my first non-workday in months. The hours stretch out behind me, and I can't measure them by lines of code or meetings or bug fixes. The fact that it is impossible to relax in this house really helps, because even though we are taking the weekend off, no one is having a good time. If I were in Merrick right now, my mother would cook my favorite things and insist I join my father in watching reruns of *Jeopardy!*; they would remind me of a time when there wasn't a million dollars in a bank account, dwindling to nothing. So I don't go home.

"Your father is worried." My mother likes to animate my father with her own opinions.

"Tell Abboo we are fine. Really, just busy with work. I'm sorry we haven't had time to come out and see you."

"Don't worry about that. Just get your proper sleep. At least seven hours a night, that's what they say. Otherwise your life will be shorter."

"You think Jules is okay?" I whisper to Cyrus that night. We've opened the windows and there's a sorbet breeze coming in.

"It's always like this when he's with his family."

"He doesn't even sing when he's here."

"Let's enjoy the silence for a few days." Cyrus laughs. He pulls me closer, kisses me lightly on the forehead.

"Are we hangers-on?" Peggy's slip has been bothering me all day.

"If you count the free rent and meals Jules has given me over the last four years, yes, you could definitely classify me as a hanger-on. But not you."

"What if WAI crashes and burns?"

"We've both read the data. We know that's more likely than not."

"I've been instructed by my parents to act against type. Succeed where others would fail—it's the immigrant mantra."

He turns to me and tucks a stray lock of hair behind my ear. "I love this," he says.

I'm surprised. "Really?"

"Yeah. This is the most fun I've had since . . . since all those projects with my mom before she died."

It occurs to me that Cyrus is having the best time of all. Jules and Gaby are worrying about things like runway, and I'm building the platform brick by brick, but Cyrus is just being Cyrus—feted by Rupert, making decisions about the color of the banner on our website, interviewing people who will then go on to beg us to hire them. I'm trying to enjoy the fact that Cyrus is having a grand time, that I've been able to give him something he might have been looking for without knowing it, but a part of me is also a tiny bit envious, wondering how I've managed to set up a situation where I'm doing all the work and he's having all the fun. *Never mind*, I tell myself, *I'm having fun too.* I must have been a Spartan in my previous life, because nothing pleases me more than work.

Seven

THE LAUNCH

In the first twenty-four hours of launch, WAI clocks up 270,322 users. In the days ahead, we're going to talk endlessly about how this happened: what alchemical mix allowed us to hyper-trend, how our spend multiplied, how the video of Cyrus went viral, how our logo was posted and tweeted and 'grammed to millions, but right now, at the moment when it is happening, we don't have time to do any of that, because right now we are trying to keep the site from crashing as the users come flooding in like shoppers on Black Friday.

Cyrus doesn't want a big launch event, so we decide to do a kombucha and gin party at Utopia. It's four hours before the site goes live, and I'm hunched over my keyboard feeling decidedly unfestive. Ren is beside me, and our fingers are tapping as the voices rise around us. It smells like feet, which is what authentic kombucha is supposed to smell like while it's brewing. At least that's what Rory says, and because he wears a lab coat almost all the time, everyone believes him.

Cyrus strolls in with a glass of something pink and frothy. "You gonna come join us?"

"I found a possible bug," I reply, not looking up from my screen. "A giant pothole in the middle of the road."

He offers me a sip of his drink, and it's every bit as rank as I'd imagined. "Is it going to affect the launch?"

Ren gives Cyrus a look that only I can decipher. I explain, "If too many people log the same interest at the same time—say, two thousand people watch an episode of *Peaky Blinders* and decide they want to get married running through the streets of Birmingham dressed like Ada and Freddie—the system crashes. It's not made for high volumes of people wanting to do the same thing, it's optimized for individual algorithmic outcomes."

"We didn't factor in the group mentality," Ren says.

"The herd will kill us if I don't fix this."

Cyrus crouches down beside me. He has started shaving more regularly, and now I can see the lower half of his face darkening with stubble. He puts his hands on my knees, and I have to stop what I'm doing and pay attention to him. "Let's take a moment," he says. Cyrus always wants to take a moment.

"I don't have time," I complain. "The platform has to be stable, otherwise we're finished."

He closes his eyes. "It's going to be fine."

"No, it's not. I mean, it might be, but then again it might not, and I'm the only thing between possible disaster and definite disaster."

Cyrus rises. "Okay my dear," he says, planting a kiss on my forehead and retreating. I barely have time to register his disappointment before I get back in, trying to chase down the lines of code that might sink us.

I sit out most of the party, although Jules and Destiny interrupt me every few minutes to tell me what I'm missing. "Rory's lecturing everyone on plastic use. Says he's trying to get Li Ann to ban products that have any form of plastic in them."

I nod, making it obvious that I don't care.

"He's projecting enormous photos of the whale that was caught with garbage for guts."

"Li Ann's giving out free Breathe Life vapes and the room's getting cloudy."

"It smells like Whole Foods in there."

"I've always wanted to smell like Whole Foods. She should bottle that shit."

"Cyrus is making a toast and he asked if you wanted to join."

"Sure," I say. I wonder why lately I've had this small urge to roll my eyes every time Cyrus opens his mouth. I tell myself I need to stop, plaster on my most encouraging smile, and waltz into the room with it.

Cyrus is holding the same pink kombucha cocktail, and I'm able to catch most of the speech. He spends some time thanking everyone by name, making Jules, and Li Ann, and Rory all blush, making the rest of the team, Gaby, the devs, Destiny, cheer and clap for him and for the promise of WAI, and then finally, he thanks me, an elaborate, giving-me-all-the-credit kind of thank you that has everyone in the room turning toward me, glasses full of funk raised in the air, thinking, *God, that girl is lucky.*

The party breaks up at 11:23 p.m. I know this because I'm back at my desk, and so is the rest of the team, and we're about to press the go button for launch. Ridiculous to launch something at midnight, I've told Cyrus. No one will be paying attention. But he's looked up all sorts of arcane books and star charts and decided nope, midnight it's got to be.

At midnight, we go live. At this point we're just a bunch of slightly drunk people hovering around a computer. At 12:04, the algorithm gets its first request, a bar mitzvah for a person who is not Jewish yet is interested in marking a moment in her child's life. She's a single mother. She once traveled extensively throughout Australia. She makes hats for a living. She likes Daft Punk.

The platform welcomes this woman—she calls herself Alanna, but we know that's not her real name—and then asks her a series of questions. After only 2.3 seconds (which is as fast as I could make the algorithm run), it presents her with a possible ritual she might enact to mark this moment in her son's life. Then it connects her with two other people—by now, seven minutes in, we have passed the hundred-user mark—who also love Daft Punk and Australia. It's up to her whether she wants to form a micro-community with these two strangers. Six minutes later, we have our reply: she does. Twelve minutes after that, the others have accepted her request.

At 12:26 we have 2,893 users. At 12:58 we have 6,147 users. We are all transfixed by the rising numbers; only Ren appears impervious. I take this as a signal that I'm allowed to remain calm, knowing he'll raise the alarm if anything goes wrong. Destiny makes coffee. When dawn breaks over the Hudson, we're into the tens of thousands. Jules and Gaby are in a corner, whispering to each other. I think Jules is panicking and Gaby is trying to get him to calm down, or maybe it's the other way around. Cyrus dozes in a chair.

We debate whether to go home and sleep for a few hours, but then Cyrus's phone buzzes and it's Rupert and he wants to come over right away and take us out to breakfast to celebrate. Gaby makes his excuses and heads home while the rest of us take a taxi uptown. At the upscale twenty-four-hour restaurant perched on the top floor of a skinny sky-scraper in Chelsea, we order champagne and Rupert insists we all get the duck waffles, even though the thought of food is making my stom-ach do somersaults. Everyone seems to be talking at the same time, Rupert the loudest, but I can't concentrate because Destiny is sending me updates by the minute. The numbers are rising and so is my panic.

My conclusion is that it must be a fluke. "It happens sometimes. The crowd gathers around some shiny new object, but before you can blink, they've moved on to the next thing. People are gnats. This isn't even a mathematically relevant sample."

"You could be right," Rupert says, "but we scored a goal from midfield, and I'm not going to let you tell me I was offside the whole time."

Maybe it's the sleep deprivation, but I can't help being the Bad News Fairy. "I'm the only person who's just a tiny bit worried about this? About what it means?"

Jules laughs. "You and Cyrus are perfect for each other, have I ever told you that?"

"Wait," Rupert interjects, "are these two playing doubles?"

"Cyrus here is always thinking about what everything means, and apparently, so is his wife."

"You guys are married?"

I'm so annoyed at Rupert that I ignore the next three messages from Destiny. "We are," I tell him. "We told you ages ago."

"I must have forgotten. Too much going on." Rupert smiles, and I notice how white his teeth are. He definitely has them whitened at the dentist, none of that at-home bleaching with a creepy plastic tray. Rupert calls to the waiter, who pours us each another glass of champagne. "To you," he says, raising his glass, "best Quidditch team ever."

Before I can ask, Cyrus explains: "Because there are three players on a Quidditch team."

"Gaby is an integral part of the team too," Jules adds.

"The Three Musketeers!" Rupert says.

"There were four," I snap. "Four Musketeers." I finally look down at my phone. *Motherfucker*, Destiny has written. *We've just hit 100,000.* "We have to go," I say. "I don't think the system can handle this kind of volume."

"This growth is going to require more funding," Jules says to Rupert.

"I'm your linebacker," Rupert says, waving his arms. "Go score your touchdowns."

Three days later, after the sign-ups have plateaued at around 500,000, Cyrus and I go home, order poke bowls, and watch multiple episodes of *Black Mirror*. When I wake up, I have my hands in the vicinity of his crotch, which tells me we had intended to have sex and one of us fell asleep and the other was probably too tired to notice. He's still sleeping, his hair all Rapunzeled behind his head, his nostrils flaring a little as he exhales. My eyes must have been boring into his skull, because he wakes up with a start and then, seeing me, gives me the most glorious of smiles. Then I remember why I'm annoyed at him.

"Why didn't Rupert remember we were married?"

Cyrus blinks, rubs his eyes. "I didn't want to make a big deal about it. I wanted him to respect you on your own terms. Not just as my wife."

"What if he saw you just as my husband?"

"I wish the world worked that way, but it doesn't."

"I thought we were going to remake the world."

"We are," Cyrus says. "Thanks to you."

"Can you believe it?" I ask him. "The launch—it's really happening."

"Nothing has happened," he says, which is both deflating and reassuring.

He's right, of course. I turn to look at the time on my phone. "If we rush, we can make it to free sprouted buckwheat waffles at Utopia," I say. We leap out of bed, both knowing that it isn't the waffles, it's WAI that wakes us up, drags us out of bed, and keeps us cheerful and loved up, even when small doubts begin to take hold.

Every morning, Destiny greets me with the latest numbers. I've also tasked her with the job of finding the quirkiest stories from among the many rituals the algorithm has been asked to produce. "Turtle wedding in LA," she says. "Ouija-slash-resurrection ritual by a Catholic group who loves the book *Possession*, which features a séance."

"People are weird."

"But they want a piece of you." Destiny folds her hands on her lap. We're at the diner, sharing our second plate of pancakes. "It's happened, Asha. You made it."

I've decided to adopt Cyrus's line on the launch. Yes, we made a big splash. Thousands of people are signing up every day, and WAI is taking on a life of its own. But I'm too nervous to celebrate. Or maybe I'm just superstitious, like if I say it out loud, it will disappear. "We have a long way to go."

"Try to enjoy it," Destiny says. "Women never get to enjoy anything."

This feels like the right moment to ask Destiny why she's so angry with the world. "Did something happen to you?" I ask gently.

She laughs, a dry, bitter laugh. "Isn't it obvious? Daddy issues, abandonment—my mother was desperate for male attention, my father was absent when he was present, and then one day he was actually gone—the usual cocktail of clichés."

We sit in silence for a moment.

"I used to be a stripper," she says. "That's how I got my name."

I can't help it—a small frown crosses my face, and before I can shake it off, Destiny has seen it. "You're judging me."

"No, of course not. I was just—I'm surprised."

"It was when I first moved to New York, and it was only a few months. I'd run out of money, I didn't know anyone." She hangs her head. "I saw some shit, did some shit. Some shit was done to me."

She looks out the window onto Tenth Avenue, and there is an old woman on a mobility scooter and a young woman on an electric scooter, and they glance at each other and smile at the exact same time. "I love New York," Destiny says. "Every single person in this city is in love with this city. They might hate it, but they're also a little bit in love. You walk down the street, and you can just tell people are self-high-fiving themselves all the time, just for being here."

"True," I say. "It's one of a kind." I don't remember loving the city as a kid—at least not this part of it. This part was remote and inaccessible to people like me, those few stops on the train like falling through the looking glass into a world of skyscrapers and people in taxis. And now here I am, totally at ease; even, in moments, feeling like I too possess a tiny piece of it.

"I'm so sorry," I say. "I can't imagine what it must've been like."

While she's telling me the story—of those eleven months of dancing, the back rooms, the way the dollar bills chafed against her skin, and how she did it because she had nowhere in the world she could go—I can't help but think of all the ways this could never have been me. My mother had told me there were always uncles and cousins around when she was growing up, and it wasn't unusual to be touched or pinched in a way that felt wrong but was always covered up with a laugh. "I will never let anything like that happen to you and your sister," she had said, preemptively angry at the thought of it. And when I was in college and grad school, and on all the holidays in between, weekends and Thanksgivings and spring breaks, my parents always knew where I was, they were always begging me to come home; I had never walked the streets of any place because I had nowhere to go. Destiny was telling me what an extraordinary privilege that was. She was also telling me something else, and if I listened carefully, I might have heard a little warning. But I was too busy believing we had nothing in common except that she was my friend and I wanted to make things right for her. As for me, I was protected, cocooned against such violences. No, it would never, could never, be me.

"I like to look on the bright side," she says, brandishing her fork. "My stripper name is my superhero name now."

Eight

THE RAISE

Cyrus won't do any interviews. He won't speak to the press, the networks, the bloggers, the influencers. He will only talk to the WAIs. Yes, that is what they are called. It's pronounced "wise," of course. We didn't call them that, they decided to name themselves. They have uploaded photos and Medium posts and TikToks about their rituals, and some of those posts have gone moderately viral. They have printed T-shirts and hats. They have authored Instagram stories and videos and clickbait.

The press is hungry. They want to know the story behind the story—how we built the platform, how the three of us met. Mostly they want to interview Cyrus, but Cyrus refuses, so Jules does it instead. Jules is made for prime time—he's funny, self-deprecating, yet brimming with confidence as he talks about how we're going to turn social media on its head. The tech news loves him.

Cyrus won't talk to the media, but he will talk to his people. So every morning, at exactly seven a.m. Eastern Standard Time, he posts a five-minute video he calls the WAICast. He is always in the same place, in front of a fixed camera that's set up against an exposed brick wall at Utopia. He dresses in the same clothes, and his hair is pulled into a ponytail behind his head. He talks about a range of things, about the state of the world, myths, stories from archives that have been covered over with dust and ignored by history. He sometimes talks about himself. One morning he tells the story of his mother's death, how she slipped away from him over the course of that terrible year. He is responsible for a lot of tears that day.

After starting the WAICast, the following goes from passionate to obsessive. It isn't just that the videos rack up thousands of views or that there are letters—actual letters—in the mail every day. It is the language. Life-changing, life-altering, transformative. Saved my life. It's as if people can't limit their experience of him to a single moment or even a period; the experience has to encompass their entire time on the planet. This troubles me more than a little, and Cyrus, to my surprise, not at all.

Gaby and Jules are busy preparing PowerPoint presentations listing the details of the business. They call them decks. These decks make frequent use of the word "engagement." Apparently, our engagement is off the charts, and this is the thing that indicates WAI may not be just another flash-in-the-pan business that's going to crash as quickly as it rose. The decks include graphs and charts showing the number of hours people spend on the platform, how many times a week, a month, they return. The things people say about us. The number of times they use the word "love." We love you, Cyrus! We love being WAIs!

Ren and I start to add features to the platform. First we create a way for people to group-message one another. They start to have conversations among themselves about the rituals we have given them. They talk about wedding dresses and baptisms and rituals to mark the day they start new jobs or fall in love for the first time. They offer suggestions—*I tried walking around the fire eight times but we got a little dizzy so I would cap it at four.* They riff on what we send them, make their own meaning, change the order in which the ancients did things. They iterate. They create. *We are infinite*, they say, *our possibilities are infinite.*

And they talk about Cyrus. Is Cyrus a shaman or a priest? Philosopher or prophet? Friend? Charlatan? Cult leader? Visionary?

And while, on the surface, not much has changed—we spend as little time in our apartment as we did before; our diets are just as questionable; our ability to keep plants alive as poor—in some parallel world, it seems, we are rich.

Jules is the first to break this news. "I'm crunching the numbers with Rupert, and it looks like we're at about ten mil."

Jules, Cyrus, and I are at a restaurant where everything is pickled. It's called Pikld. The drinks are called vinegar and taste like soda. The vegetables are called kraut and taste like vinegar. "Our company is worth ten million dollars?" I ask.

Jules leans over to me and whispers, "Ten million each, Asha. You, me, Cyrus, and Rupert. Rupert figures WAI is worth about forty given our engagement."

There was that word again. I wonder, not for the first time that day, if Cyrus and I should've gotten engaged before we got married. It's not that anything is wrong, really. I still feel a little seasick whenever I see him, and as we get deeper into this thing, he continually surprises me, like the other day when I saw him add a thread to the algorithm. "Do you know," he said, "about the Morrigan?"

"No."

"She was a tripartite goddess of the Celts. She was a goddess and also three goddesses at the same time: a goddess of war, a goddess of the land, and a goddess of fate."

I knew where this was going. "What are you telling me?"

"That you are the warrior of WAI. And you are the protector of our little tribe. And you are the holder of my fate."

In anyone else's mouth, those words would have come out like synthetically flavored syrup. But in his, they sounded sincere. Because Cyrus believed every single thing he said.

"What the fuck do you mean, ten million each?"

Jules raises a glass of vodka spiked with vinegar. "We are rich."

Cyrus spears a piece of kimchi with his fork and shoves it into his mouth. This is his way of telling us how much he doesn't want to be rich. Still, I find myself raising my glass and clinking it against Jules's. I don't mind being rich. In fact, I find I'm quite enjoying the idea of it, even though the money is imaginary and I'm still working to pay off my credit card debt.

The main courses arrive. I'm having cured sardines and Cyrus is having cured and torched sardines and Jules is having a steak that has been hung for several years and is probably more fossil than animal. "Mmm," Jules says. "This tastes like burp."

The vinegar starts to climb up my nose. "I can just feel my liver detoxifying."

Cyrus is not participating in the pickle jokes. "Don't worry, bro," Jules says. "We won't actually enjoy any of it. Like this food, see— we can afford it, but it tastes like shit."

"Yeah, cheer up, Cy," I soothe. "It's just money."

"You're right," Cyrus says. "We're not actually rich. And we said we were going to make sure that didn't happen."

This makes him feel better, and we all agree, since we are not actually rich, we can put off figuring out what to do if that ever happens.

Cyrus is mollified. He makes a speech. He tells us how much he loves what we're building together. He admits to being wrong before, when he was skeptical, when he was half in, half out. He is so lucky to be here, with me and with Jules, expanding our family in the best possible way.

It is a typical Cyrus moment. At first he shies away from something, and then he drives himself deep into it and it's hard to imagine he was ever doing anything else.

And yet. And yet. I feel the thing is running away from us. I don't want to complain to Cyrus, because I'm worried he's going to think I'm jealous. A woman sent us a photo the other day with I LOVE CYRUS JONES written across her breasts. Cyrus glanced at it, said, "Let's hope that's not permanent ink," and moved on to something else. But I stared and stared. Her breasts were not just slightly better than mine, they were better in every possible way. First of all, they were bigger, which meant they were inherently better. But they also seemed perkier on top of being bigger, which made it all so much worse, and her nipples seemed ludicrously well proportioned, like a perfect dinner setting for two. She smiled at the camera, her hands holding up her T-shirt, with the sort of smile only a woman with those breasts could possibly possess: light, smug, 100 percent confident that the person who was looking at her would have major trouble ever erasing the image of her tits from their mind.

And there is more. Although Cyrus is impervious to the boob flasher, I can tell he's enjoying the rest of it. The fan mail in various digital and analog forms, the numbers going up every day, the way the people who apply for jobs talk about the privilege of working for him, just being in a room with him. Even Rupert takes a different tone now, the tone of a person talking to another person who has real power in the world.

None of us has ever had real power. Jules has been smacked down by his family for as long as he can remember; Cyrus hasn't even had a family. As for me, even though I've never thought of myself as a symbol, I can't help but feel like every little success is a small fuck-you to all the people who glanced ugly at my mother in her sari in Walmart, or mispronounced my name even though it was only four letters long, or said something casually racist and then said, "But I don't mean you." I feel like I'm coming for all those people, and that fills me with a kind of satisfaction I didn't even know I needed. I understand my sister a little more now, how she always insists that everything means something bigger than it seems. But instead of getting angry, I'm doing something about it. I'm knocking the air right out of the argument, me and my algorithmic genius.

Jules, Cyrus, and I try talking about other things, but our conversation always circles back to WAI. "Remember," Jules says, "when you wanted to call it the Infinite Wisdom?"

Cyrus denies it. "I never wanted to call it that."

"I wanted to call it Why the Fuck Not?" I say.

"Well, why the fuck didn't you say anything?"

I've had two gin-egars, so I decide to tell the truth. "Because somewhere inside my little immigrant heart, I'm not interested in telling the truth. I just aim to please."

Jules shuffles over to me and squeezes all the air out of my lungs. "You're safe here," he says. And I believe him.

It doesn't take long after that—just enough time for our fermented rhubarb chia puddings to arrive, and for Jules to start humming Money money money, *must be funny, in a rich man's world*—for me to banish my doubts and feel like we've returned to old times, old times being last year when Jules and I were standing in front of Li Ann trying to explain why on earth we belonged in her little oasis of magic.

▸

These days Jules is looking like he goes to the dry cleaner instead of swishing things around in the laundry basket and pulling out whatever smells the least bad. He shows up in blazers and ties, and when he sits down, his socks announce themselves in flashes of color and bright patterns. And he sings all the time, not just in front of Cyrus and me but in the hallways and before we start meetings and in line for Rory's latest vegan shake. *Is he in love?* I wonder, but then I would've known, and anyway, when would he have had time to fall in love? He's always here, locked away in a corner with Cyrus or Gaby. He hasn't said so, but I can tell he's feeling a little tortured about the Cyrus worship, too. And while Cyrus is crafting handwritten notes to his fans, Jules and Gaby and I have to keep things moving. Thousands of people sign up on the platform every day, and we're busy hiring, troubleshooting, debugging, and monitoring the community. So far it's buzzing along like a raucous Asian wedding, but I have this feeling of dread that something terrible will happen and everyone will start hating each other—not unlike a wedding, late at night when the guests have gone home and the mother of the bride discovers the caterers have made off with the leftover biryani.

Even though we have decided not to become rich, and even though—and possibly because—WAI seems to have gotten off to the best possible start, it is a hungry beast that requires constant feeding.

"We have seven weeks of runway," Jules says at the next board meeting.

Rupert tells us not to worry about the runway. "As long as you're willing to take on more investment."

Cyrus has booked Utopia's boardroom, a soaring space on the top floor with a table the size of a small cruise ship.

"Rupert, you've made yourself clear, and for the record, let me restate my position: I will only take additional VC dollars if we are approached by someone who shares my vision of the company and its future."

"Our vision," Jules says.

"Clearly, the vision is a three-pointer. Unquestionable."

"I've heard too many stories of founders raising too much money because they get undue pressure from their board," Cyrus says.

No one has asked my opinion, but annoyingly, I have one. "It's going to depend on how we plan to monetize."

Rupert turns to me like I've just been teleported onto my seat. "Of course it does," he says. "That's the number one question everyone is going to ask."

"Great," I say, applauding the sound of my own idea. "So, how are we going to answer that?"

"We're not going to monetize," Cyrus says. "We are not doing this for profit—that was the whole point."

"Then we have to shut down in a few weeks," Jules says. He pulls out his laptop, takes a few seconds to connect to the monitor on the far side of the room, and projects a spreadsheet onto the screen.

"If we're not spending anything on customer acquisition or marketing, why is our burn so high?" Cyrus asks.

"Burn is better than churn," Rupert says.

Churn, I am told, is just not the latest fad in cultured butter but the number of people who sign up, then abandon, the platform. In our case, once they've asked the platform to give them a ritual, they're hooked, perpetually asking it more questions, coming back daily and sometimes multiple times a day to see what their friends are doing, posting photos, commenting on other people's rituals, and in general just hanging around like they have nothing better to do than to sit around not worshipping God.

"It's the team, the servers, the constant updates. And we need customer support."

Rupert stops scribbling. "Customer support? The WAIs need customer support?"

Jules and I have been talking about this. "All the social media platforms—Google, Facebook, Instagram—they spend a lot of money policing their users. Making sure we don't get exposed to the dark side of humanity."

"I don't see why we need to police our own community," Cyrus says.

"So we don't let them do something colossally fucked up," Jules snaps.

"We're mitigating risk," I explain. "Plus, we need a way to take care of the community. People are getting emotionally involved, and these are some of their most intimate moments, their fears, their desires, all coming out, and we have to find a way for them to talk about it, or we risk them getting hurt."

"Can't they talk to each other?" Rupert asks.

"They do," Jules replies, "but we need to give them something more."

"I understand," Cyrus says. "That's why I've been doing the WAI-Cast."

"They need more than five minutes a day."

"What's the damage?" Rupert asks.

"Maybe I should make the videos longer," Cyrus muses.

"If we open a help line, we need to staff it. At least ten full-time staff, maybe more."

"Can we outsource?"

Jules says we can't outsource. "This isn't like returning your dishwasher because it won't fit under the counter."

"I like the idea of providing the community with more resources," Cyrus says.

"Then you have to agree to fundraise," Rupert tells him. "And before that, we have to agree on how to monetize. I have some ideas." He shares his screen. We all turn our chairs. "Number one. Advertisements." He shows a slide of the platform, only with ads for yoga pants that can be worn to the office and office pants that feel as comfortable as yoga pants.

In glorious chorus, Cyrus and I shout, "NO."

Rupert sighs and leans back in his chair so I can see the shiny quarter-size circle of bald at the top of his head, a sight that makes me hate him a tiny bit less.

"It's important to remain calm," Jules says. "Rupert makes an interesting point, but we would have to significantly change our idea of what we are doing and why we are here to go down that road."

"Number two. Selling data—not the personal stuff, just a few limited things, all aboveboard."

We repeat our opinion, louder this time.

His third idea is this: "We get people to pay ninety-nine cents for each ritual."

This is met with cheesecake-thick silence.

He closes his laptop and groans. "I knew it wasn't a content play, but you guys really need to get a handle on optics. How's this thing going to look like anything more than a social experiment? A very expensive experiment that I put money into."

"Rupert, it was my impression that you'd come on board because you believed in the vision," Cyrus says.

Rupert throws his hands up. "Of course I believe in the vision. I just expect the vision to deliver on revenue. I didn't do it to make a bunch of hippies feel better about the state of the world." He puts two fingers between his neck and his shirt collar. "This is a business, not a charity."

Jules puts on his most soothing Caboty voice and says, "We understand. Of course you want to see a return."

"I have investors too," Rupert whines.

"Totally get it. And we will come up with a solution. We will."

Cyrus is trying to appear to look busy by arranging a piece of paper in front of him. I reach over and put my hand on his elbow. "It would be so much better if we didn't have to think about revenue, I get that." I let my words sink in and soften him. "But there are realities here that we have to contend with."

Cyrus meets my gaze, nods.

"In the first place, let's just raise a bit more money. That'll give us time to consider our options."

"Look, I'll go in for a little more. But then you'll have to find someone with a heart as big as mine," Rupert says.

"There's no one like you," Jules soothes. "We really appreciate it, Rupert."

Rupert settles back in his seat. "Fine. I'm agreed. Here are some people who might be interested." He brandishes a list. "Most of your premier-league funds aren't going to get into social media. The market is mature, and there's no guarantee anyone will make a significant dent. But there are a few who have cropped up. The first is a new fund called Woke VC."

I'm trying to keep a straight face. "Are they . . ."

"Yes," Rupert says, grave. "They are targeting diversity."

"What does that mean?"

"Five percent of their funding goes to companies founded by minority women."

"Five percent?"

"That's the target. Right now it's about one point five."

"Sounds cutting-edge."

He rolls through a list of funds: GreyGrey, Founders Friend, Telepathic, Bolton Steinberger, Crush, Firework. He lists the pros and cons of each, the probability of landing one of them. He tells Jules and Cyrus they have to go to the Valley to make their pitches. "Get your gloves on," he says. "We're going into the ring."

Nine

KILLING EVERYONE

Jules and Cyrus go on a road show. They take their decks, their projections, Gaby's financial models, and they fly back and forth from the West Coast and return with stories about all the boardrooms they pitched at, Prets they ate at, rooms they shared at Holiday Inns. Now that Cyrus has signed off on our plans for WAI, he's as ready to pitch it as the rest of us. That doesn't mean he sticks to the script—part of the Cyrus/Jules routine is that Cyrus goes off book and behaves and speaks as if he has wandered off a mountaintop and into a boardroom. There's the time he leads the partners of Steiner Jenkins in a group meditation in which they sit facing the wall of their boardroom and chant "om" in three-part harmony. There's the other time, when someone asks him while scrolling through a phone, why on earth anyone would rather talk to people about how we die rather than to their friends about how to make homemade yogurt, and Cyrus reaches across the table, puts his hands on the man's shoulders, and looks so deep into his eyes that the guy starts crying right there in front of his boss.

On neither of these occasions are they invited back for a second meeting.

Then there is the usual party trick, of which Cyrus appears to never tire, when someone volunteers their three deepest commitments—a partner from Van Dreeson Janowicz said his father was a lapsed Mennonite and that he was obsessed with *The Sopranos* and that he was starting classical guitar lessons and that he thought he was really, really good. What would Cyrus recommend for his fourth marriage, which was actually his second marriage to his first wife?

The way this used to work was that Cyrus would close his eyes or walk around the room for a few minutes, but now he just asks the platform and WAI gives up its answer. Sometimes the partners ask Cyrus if he agrees with what the algorithm produces, and Cyrus always says yes, of course, he wouldn't change a thing, but I wonder if he occasionally thinks he'd do better if left to his own devices, or if it annoys him that I've burrowed so deep into his thoughts that I've actually transplanted his brain to a code that is now replicating him to thousands of people around the world.

Despite Cyrus's winning eccentricities, Rupert's assurances, and the sheer success of the platform, three months before we are about to run out of money, we get interest from only two firms: Accelerate Capital and Play Ventures. Cyrus says we have to go back in and give presentations and that this time I have to come too.

Destiny has hired a small army of very young, very cheerful people to continue to spread the word about WAI and its many virtues. Whenever I'm online, I get chased around with ads telling me I need to bring meaning back to my online experience, that ritual, community, and contemplation—the pillars of WAI—will bring joy and sustenance to my otherwise empty shell of an existence.

Whatever they're doing, it's working. People are piling on like it's the last express train to Bushwick, and Ren and I are working around the clock to keep it all running smoothly and with the speed that users now expect of every other device in their lives.

Destiny seems to have been born for this. She barks sweetly at her charges, waking them up in the morning with pallets of lattes, showering them with praise, posting their numbers on a giant billboard, taking them to late showings of Hollywood classics and then dragging them back to the office for one last push/sprint/stab.

She spends marketing dollars we don't have on T-shirts for the whole team. WAISER, they say, with the three-circle logo underneath. I wear mine till it nearly dies. Destiny is magnificent; just looking across the room at her gives me a thrill. We stick to our eleven a.m. donut habit and high-five each other all day long.

One day she asks Li Ann and me to meet her in the cafeteria. Rory is there, having a meeting with his team, a group of somber scientists staring into their laptops. His vegan superfoods grace the menu at the cafeteria, and occasionally, Li Ann will talk about how Rory is going to disrupt the way we consume everything, but I've hardly spoken with him since we moved in—I can't shake the feeling that he knows something I don't, something dark and groundbreaking that makes whatever I'm doing totally irrelevant.

Destiny tells us she wants to take the sisterhood to the next level. "I want to start a thing for female founders."

"There are already things like that," Li Ann says. "I'm in the 24/7

Club, the Women@work collective, the Google Women working group. You can join if you want." She scrolls on her phone.

I'm not sure the title applies to me. "I don't know if I want to call myself a female founder."

"Which part are you not sure of, the female or the founder?"

Li Ann takes something out of her bag. It's about the size of a small tablet or a large phone. She opens it, and inside, there are five long metal cylinders that look like cigars except they are bright blue, purple, and orange.

"What's that?"

"A hundred percent pure oxygen," she says. "Little miniature oxygen tanks. You get high from the purity." She passes them around and I take a blue one. "Tap twice to turn it on," she says. I do and then inhale, and a cold hit of—well, air—flows into my mouth.

"I liked the other one better," I say. "This one doesn't have any flavor."

"Yeah, but it's better for you. And if the apocalypse hits super-suddenly, you can have twenty minutes of oxygen to get to your panic room."

Destiny pulls hard on hers. "It's like a blow job without some guy's hand on your head."

"Or the warm spunk."

"That too."

"Get this," Li Ann says. "Smoking is out. Breathing is in. Breathe Life."

"I'm in," Destiny says. "So will you join Fucking Female Founders?"

"What?"

"Yeah, the 3Fs club."

"It sounds like you're pimping female founders."

"Female Founders Say Fuck You? Fuck You We Are Female Founders?"

"How about just Female Founders Club?"

"That doesn't have a fuck-you in it."

"Does the rage have to be in the acronym itself? Can it come later, like in the press release?"

Destiny rolls her eyes. "We need to bring this shit down, all of it."

"First we have to raise funds for WAI, and then I will join your revolution," I say.

"How's it going?" Li Ann asks.

"Cyrus and Jules are on the road. Every few weeks Gaby joins them and they send me selfies from VC parking lots."

"You don't go with them?"

"I gotta keep my head down and make the magic."

"Asha's good at following orders," Destiny says. She waits for about three seconds, and then she's all over me apologizing. "I'm sorry, that was shitty."

I find myself getting a little tingly around the eyes. "It really was."

"I guess I just don't want you to get overshadowed by the boys."

"It's Cyrus, for God's sake. He couldn't screw me over if he tried."

"But he's a man."

"It's real between you two, isn't it?" Li Ann says.

"I've been in love with him for as long as I can remember."

"Then you just have to keep it all going, the marriage, the business, it's all one messy thing."

"I see it more as a happy symbiosis. Imagine if I had to go home and explain what I was doing all day."

"Now that would be fucked up," Destiny says. "Oh, I know! How about Female Founders Society?"

"FFS. I like it."

Li Ann, Destiny, and I tap our oxygen cigars together. "Here's to us. May we take over the world."

▼

Cyrus picks me up at the San Jose airport on a Sunday night in September. It's cool out and he's wearing a long-sleeved T-shirt and a baseball cap. His skin has a reddish tint that makes him look like he's been out surfing all week. I don't realize how much I've missed him until we're walking toward the parking lot and he stops to kiss me.

"I don't want you to go anywhere ever again," I say.

"That's uncharacteristic of you, Ms. Ray."

I turned thirty while he was away, celebrating at the office with Destiny, Ren, and a bottle of grapefruit gin. "I'm getting sentimental in my old age," I say. "And that's Mrs. Jones to you."

He starts to sing the song.

"You know that song is actually about Mrs. Jones straying à la Mrs. Robinson, right?"

"I know. But since we're disrupting everything, let's disrupt that too, okay?"

"Pioneers."

"Revolutionaries."

The hotel room looks like a bomb exploded in it. Cyrus's clothes are all over the floor; there are two laptops stacked on top of each other and several empty cartons of hotel cashews on the bed. I'm about to say something, but Cyrus peels my T-shirt down over my shoulder and kisses me right where my pulse is strong and hot, and so we just push everything off the bed and do our thing.

Cyrus dozes off while I text with Ren about a few fixes we're planning to launch next week. I don't know how Cyrus manages to sleep so much, or maybe it's that I've got so much accumulated caffeine in me that I can't sleep more than a few hours at a time. When I look up from my screen, it's dinnertime, and I nudge him and we drive to a diner nearby and order omelets.

"So what should I say tomorrow?" I ask.

"Just be yourself," Cyrus says. "You'll do great."

"What do they want to know?"

"They want to ask you how you did it. They asked me and I was, like, damned if I know, ask my wife."

I still get a thrill every time he says the word "wife." It's not a fantasy, not anymore, but it doesn't feel like marriage—the shitty parts of marriage, I mean, like actual responsibilities and getting tired of sex and one person feeling like they're less beautiful than the other. It's all the good things about being in love with all the good things about watching movies on the sofa with an old friend. It's sexy and tender and sweet. For the thousandth time, I feel grateful for that day in city hall, the small woman behind the podium, the way we just went ahead and did it without asking anyone's permission. Even now I feel myself unfurling into something light and airborne whenever I think about it.

I'm taken aback by the amount of space around everything in California. On either side of the road there's grass, and after the grass there's more road, and before you get anywhere you go through a long, entirely unnecessary length of driveway. Oh, and the parking lots. So many parking lots. I have never been this far west, and west, it seems, has a very high parking-lot-to-people ratio.

The offices of Accelerate Capital are on the grounds of a "think park," a little cluster of buildings with similar ambitions. We pull up to a four-story building with a curved glass facade. The doors slide open, and stepping into the air-conditioning is like diving into a very large glass of cold milk. They're expecting us; our name tags are already printed out. I try to find somewhere to clip mine on the dress I've bought specifically to be here.

In the elevator I redistribute my lipstick while Jules and Cyrus do things to their hair. When the doors open, we are greeted by a tall woman in a yellow jumpsuit who asks us what we'd like to drink, and when I say, "Oh, anything," she takes a bottle out of the cooler and hands me an activated-charcoal lemonade.

The boardroom is empty, so Jules and Cyrus get on the network and plug in their laptops. I follow suit. On one side are two extremely large screens built in to a recessed wall. The table is made of white marble and looks like a very wide kitchen island. I'm about to say this out loud when the double doors open and three men in identical navy polo shirts and khaki slacks shake our hands.

"Hi," they say.

"I'm Larry."

"I'm Gerard."

"I'm Hans." Their hands are soft, their handshakes firm.

Larry, Gerard, and Hans sit at one side of the table, and Jules, Cyrus, and I sit on the other.

Larry, dark hair, long face, speaks first. "We met last time, and I was impressed with what I saw, so I thought I'd bring my partners in so we could dig a little deeper."

"Dig away!" I say. Nobody laughs, and I realize too late that this is one of those speak-when-you're-spoken-to moments.

Jules clears his throat. "This is our CTO, Asha Ray."

"I don't get out much." I laugh.

"Why don't I go through the deck again, for Gerard and Hans, and if you have any questions, please feel free to interrupt."

They nod. Cyrus begins. An image of our logo appears on one of the giant screens. "We created WAI to introduce a new kind of interaction with social media. Instead of being built around what people like, it's built around the things that mean something to them."

I see an image of the platform—my platform.

"Instead of user-generated content, the platform features rituals created by Asha's algorithm based on a short questionnaire."

Our questions pop up on the screen.

What are you looking for? Ritual? Daily practice? Just exploring?

List three things that you care about most in the world.

List your three most powerful memories.

Do you subscribe to any form of organized religion?

"The algorithm produces a ritual or a set of rituals for the user. It then asks the user if they'd like to match with others who share similar interests or have similar meaningful events coming up in their lives—weddings, funerals, the birth of children." Cyrus projects an image of the community message boards.

I'm suddenly overcome with feeling. I glance up at the ceiling to distract myself, but the tears are still gathering. I reach up and dab the corner of my eye in the most top secret way I can muster.

"What we've found is that, using the rituals as a starting point, people build small and meaningful communities. They share ideas, photos, messages. They return to the platform—even after the service is delivered—because they have now connected with a group of people with whom they shared a meaningful experience."

"It's beyond friendship," I find myself saying. "It's like discovering a new family." At this point, my nose begins to tingle, so I excuse myself. The woman in the yellow jumpsuit, who seems to be positioned just outside the doors, points to the bathroom.

I close the stall and cry hard. "Why?" I ask myself. This makes me cry harder and also makes me laugh. "Why? WAI!" I announce. I'm so busy cracking myself up, I don't notice there's a person in the stall next to mine. She's got some kind of machine in there with her, something that wheezes and sighs.

"Are you okay?" I ask.

"Are you?" she replies between wheezes.

"I'm fine. I was just crying on account of my own awesomeness. Is that a nebulizer? Do you have asthma?"

"No, I'm pumping."

She comes out of her stall and I come out of mine. She looks like a half human, half cyborg, with her dress pulled down around her waist and two cups attached to her breasts. The cups are each half full of milk.

"My kid is two years old, but she refuses to drink any other kind of milk."

I nod, fascinated by the engineering of her bra, which appears to be holding the entire contraption upright.

"We've tried cow, goat, almond, oat, soy, and hemp. Everything except rice. You're not allowed to give them rice."

"Because of the arsenic?"

"Do you have kids?"

"No, I'm just a nerd."

"I used to be a nerd," she says. "Now I'm producing the milk of human guilt."

"And there's nowhere else in this fancy office where you can do it?"

"It's all open plan," she says. "It's more democratic that way."

"I'm Asha Ray," I say.

"Amanda Wakefield," she replies, shaking my hand. "So what were you crying about?"

"I built this thing, and I was suddenly realizing how amazing it is, and it made me cry," I say.

"That's great," she says. "I'm really happy for you." She looks like she's about to impart some wisdom, but instead she throws her hands up. "I'd better go, my cups runneth over."

I stumble back into the boardroom, where Larry is grilling Jules on the MAU-WAU-DAU of the platform.

"Ah, Asha," Jules says. "Gerard was just asking how you set up the framework for the community side."

I run through the technical points with Gerard, who is at pains to inform me that he started his career as a programmer. "I was employee number eighteen at DeepMind," he says.

I talk about how Ren and I have instrumented the platform so that you can see exactly what people are doing, how long they're spending with us, how many posts and photos they're sharing. "Our minutes per session are going up every month."

"How do you deal with people who break the rules?" Hans asks.

It's a good question. "The algorithm will not provide a ritual that goes against the values of the platform," I say. "It's programmed to send a red flag, and then we reach out to the user and let them know we are suspending their account." It was one of the things Cyrus, Jules, and I had agreed to from the start— we wouldn't tolerate any bullshit, we would just turn peoples' accounts off if they behaved badly. There would be no bullying, no trolling, no lying, no conspiracy theories, no anti-vaxxers, no neo-Nazis or All Lives Matter activists.

"We've only had to do it a handful of times," Jules says. "The community is pretty self-selecting."

Gerard, Hans, and Larry put their heads together on the other side of the table. Cyrus, Jules, and I pretend we are busy doing other things, fiddling with our laptops, unplugging, rearranging the printed-out presentations in front of us.

Finally, Larry speaks. "We like it," he says. "We like the growth, we like the ambition. No one's really come up with an alternative social media platform in a decade, and we see this as a contender." I'm waiting for the but, and then it arrives: "But we see some major risk factors here."

"It's about the burn," Gerard says. "Five years ago, if you told me you needed a million a month just to police these people and make sure you head off a shitstorm, I would've said sure, as long as you have that kind of engagement, it's worth it."

"But you're going to have to front all that without knowing where the monetization of the platform is really headed, and digital ad spend has already peaked," Hans adds.

"And," Larry says, "We're concerned it's too . . . political."

"Political?" I ask.

Larry glances at the other two. "Yeah. Like only for certain kinds of people. A liberal echo chamber. Don't get me wrong, we're all on the same page here. But it might be off-putting to some."

"We don't ask people to declare their political affiliations," Jules says.

"But you said so yourself, it's a self-selecting group, isn't it?" Gerard asks.

"Happy to take a deep dive into the numbers and give you a solid answer, but just to be transparent, those are our concerns," Larry concludes.

They stand up. We stand up.

As I'm leaving the room, I figure I have nothing to lose, so I turn to Jules and say, "I think there's a law, isn't there, about women having the right to express breast milk in a private room?"

Jules looks at me like I just belched in front of everyone. "Um, I don't know, I guess."

Cyrus has gone ahead, but we are still inside with the other three. Yellow jumpsuit is holding the door open for us.

"We had to read all the workplace laws, remember, when we started hiring."

"No one is even pregnant yet, Asha."

"It's just important to make sure we mitigate all forms of risk," I say. And then the boardroom doors close behind us and I glimpse the last of the beige decor. "Bye, Larry!" I call out.

In the elevator Jules pounces. "Jesus, Asha, what the fuck was that?"

I tell him the story about the woman in the bathroom. "She was like a cow. In a cow stall."

"You mean a barn."

"Whatever. They're not going to invest in us, anyway."

"I thought it went well," Cyrus says. "A liberal echo chamber. Now why didn't I think of that?"

We step into the lobby. My knees are extremely cold.

"What makes you think it went well?" Jules asks Cyrus.

"They were really impressed with what we've built. I think we might get there."

A second ago Jules was ready to throttle me, but Cyrus has a way of bringing us together. "Were we at the same meeting? They just broke up with us."

"You heard them. They said they hate the status quo as much as we do."

Cyrus is heading to the parking lot. "He drinks his own Kool-Aid," I say to Jules, stating the totally obvious, which is that Cyrus is the smartest person in the world—except when it comes to getting rejected.

On the drive back, Cyrus tells Jules to run the financials again. "Just model it with a lower burn."

"It's too risky. If anything goes wrong, we'll never be able to bounce back."

Jules and I have run through all the scenarios. What if someone does something awful with one of the rituals from the platform. Uploads photographs of unspeakable things. Forms communities around racist bullshit. Ren promised me, swore there was nothing that happened without his knowledge, that he had built eyes into every corner of the platform, but we had all been taken aback by the speed of growth. There was something out of control about it already—that's what Larry was alluding to. And if we didn't spend a truckload of money assuring ourselves that everyone was behaving, sooner or later people would start to do bad things and it would be our fault.

Cyrus doesn't see it this way. The platform is built around him—and the community, by extension, is also a part of him. Believing that the people who join WAI are inherently good is important to Cyrus—or, rather, imagining that people might do terrible things to each other in his name is admitting a personal defeat. He can't do it. Now Jules has to recalculate all the numbers and claim we can monitor the site with half the staff and half as much money devoted to customer support.

"Did you know," Jules tells us, "that there are entire warehouses full of people in the Philippines who are hired just to sift through the human trash that's put out on Facebook? I mean, all day long people have to look at photos of the kinds of dark shit you and I don't even have the words to describe, and they have to scrub all of it from the pretty blue-and-white-bannered site so that we can believe we live in a world of unicorns and cupcakes."

"That's never going to be us," Cyrus says. "Asha would never let that happen, would you, Asha?"

I'm touched that he thinks I can solve the problem of human degradation with an equation. "Sorry, love," I say, "my genius has its limits. Or rather, people are so fucked up that even I can't build a code to fix them."

Jules glances at me in the rearview mirror. "It's not that we think anything terrible is going to happen. It's that when it does, we need to be prepared."

When we arrive at the offices of Play Ventures, at the top of a hill overlooking the San Fernando Valley, we are given electronic bracelets and asked to surrender our shoes, then led through a corridor, beyond which is a trampoline the entire width and breadth of a high-ceilinged room.

A small man hands us each a pair of socks with little plastic buttons on their soles. We understand that we are meant to jump up and down on the trampoline in order to cross over to the other side of the room, beyond which is our meeting. We step onto the trampoline with our bags. The small man, whose name is Craig, leads the way. He is clearly practiced. He leaps, flips, lands on his feet, and leaps again. He apparently feels no need to explain. I attempt a medium-size jump. Craig does a somersault in the air with his hands clasped under his knees. Cyrus dumps our stuff on one corner of the trampoline and starts to jump quite high. Jules just stands there, wobbling with the ripples of other peoples' jumps. Our bags wobble too. Cyrus attempts a flip and lands on his butt. He laughs, gets back up. I've found a comfortable rhythm with my medium-size jumping and try not to think about how much longer this will continue. Cyrus keeps attempting the flip until he gets it right, then he does it again and again.

Finally, it ends. Craig crosses over to the other side of the trampoline and takes us through another hallway, this one with green lights running along at floor level. He turns and opens the door and we are in a boardroom, which, by contrast, is rather normal, a corner of the building with panoramic views, a large oval table, and the requisite pair of screens at one end.

I'm surprised to see Craig taking a seat at the table. I thought he was a kind of acrobatic house butler, but it appears he's the investor. We make our pitch. Cyrus talks, Jules reads out the numbers, I follow up with the technical details. Craig is on his phone. He occasionally looks up, smiles, gives us a thumbs-up, and then continues to do stuff on his phone. It's obviously nothing important; I can tell he's just scrolling his Instagram.

When we are finished, Craig stands up and applauds. "That was great, guys," he says. "Really great."

Jules asks Craig if he has any questions.

Craig rubs his chin. I wonder if he thinks this gesture makes him look older. "Yeah," he says. "I think it's great, I mean, I think it's fantastic. But the question is: are you going to kill everyone?"

Cyrus, Jules, and I glance at each other. Is it the liberal thing again? Is he worried we're a bunch of socialist murderers?

"I mean, are you going to kill everyone?" Craig asks again.

"We're not sure—" Cyrus begins.

"You gotta be sure. You gotta be one hundred percent abso-fucking-lutely sure you are going to totally crush-kill everyone out there."

"We really don't have any competitors in the marketplace," Jules says.

"You have to crush the church, and you have to kill Facebook. You're like a church/Facebook mash-up. You gotta kill both of those guys."

"I think, realistically, we would get a decent amount of growth even if we didn't try to compete with Jesus or Zuckerberg."

Craig springs toward Cyrus and eyeballs him. "I always check for the killer in everyone. The assassin. Are you an assassin?"

I see Jules give Cyrus an imperceptible nod. "I most certainly am, sir," Cyrus pledges.

"Fuck yeah!"

"I will kill everyone and anyone." Cyrus's tone is like the EKG of a dead person. "I will assassinate all my enemies, and I'll even kill a few friends while I'm at it."

"I knew it!" Craig says. "You look like a hippie, but you're a fucking ninja."

He leads us out, back through the green hallway, across the trampoline, and to reception, where we surrender our bracelets and retrieve our shoes.

"Thank you for your time," I hear Cyrus and Jules say, and then I shake little Craig's hand and we're back in the parking lot, falling over ourselves.

For weeks, we pretend to be Craig. "What do you want for dinner, Cyrus?"

"I want to kill everyone and eat their eyeballs."

"Should we hire the very serious woman from Vassar to do our accounts?"

"I don't know. Is she an assassin?"

"Can we please talk about runway?"

"Nope. I'm too busy killing everyone. Every fucking one."

The joke never gets old.

Ten

BRINGING UP BABY

Finally, Cyrus agrees to an interview for an online magazine. He asks me to come with him. They've said something about a photo shoot in a disused church. On the way, we consider all the angles the story might take. "What if they secretly hate me?" he says. "What if they don't put it in the tech section or the business section but in the sexy-minister section?"

"They could call it Missionary Style."

"Hey, maybe they'll let us borrow one of the outfits and we can go home and play nuns and priests," he says.

"Totally. But only if I can be the priest."

"That would be super sexy."

"I guess your suit won't fit me," I say. Suddenly, I'm annoyed at having to accompany him. "Why isn't Jules here?"

"He said he wasn't going to stand around and watch me tell everyone how important we are."

"Guess that makes me the sucker."

The taxi swerves and he slides toward me. "Let's ask them if we can do the interview together," he says. "I would love that."

Now I feel ridiculous. "No, don't be silly. They want you."

"It'll be even better," he insists. "I'll call them right now."

"Why didn't you ask in the first place?" I say.

The taxi swerves again and this time it's me sliding over to his side.

"I guess it didn't occur to me. That's shitty, I'm sorry."

By the time we roll up to the address, I'm in a foul mood. "I'm going to get a coffee," I say, and disappear for an hour. When I get back, he's in full Cyrus mode, talking Rubik's cubes around the poor interviewer. The guy can't get a word in edgewise, but instead of being offended, he is rapt, listening to Cyrus riffing on everything from climate change to online privacy. Lately, I've realized that because of the popularity of the platform, and because of what it is—a replacement for religion—people are looking to Cyrus for answers to the questions they ask themselves all the time. And the most we can hope for is that Cyrus will tell them he doesn't have the answers, only his own opinions, which they should take as the thoughts of one man with a limited understanding of what is beyond the horizon.

We all think a little press will help us get our funding back on track—unsurprisingly, neither the khaki triplets nor the trampoline assassin came through. Rupert is getting nervous, calling Gaby every week and demanding to know how much money we have in the bank. He's suggested we make cuts, maybe take a few of the devs off the team, but Cyrus has refused to fire anyone. "Asha and I will hold our salaries," he volunteers. "Jules too."

Jules, Cyrus, and I meet every morning to figure a way out. We call it Bad News, Good News.

Jules begins by writing the bad news on the whiteboard. A list of investors who have said no.

"Rupert sent me a new list for outreach," Jules says. "I've drafted all the emails—Cyrus, you just have to review and press send."

Cyrus reads through the list. "How evil are these people?"

"Just your average evil funds."

"Rupert says these guys are all tier three."

"What happened to tier two?" I ask.

"They rejected us. I've made a word cloud of the reasons." Jules turns his computer to me. The word VERTICAL is the biggest, followed by UNUSUAL and then RISK.

"They didn't give us money because we were too vertical?"

"Our business didn't fit into any of their verticals."

"What were their verticals?"

Jules runs down the list. "Fintech, agritech, real estate, cloud, and gaming."

"I have some good news," I announce. I always have the good news. The good news is that the community continues to grow. Every day there are new people joining the platform. They chat, share photographs, form little groups, call one another family. Recently, there was a cat funeral, and the cat's mother, someone by the name of Rose, live-streamed it to two hundred thousand other cat lovers. "In fact," I said, "the Cat Lovers are the biggest group."

Cyrus rolls his eyes. "No surprise there."

"Also on the good-news front," Jules says, tapping a pen against the side of the table, "I'm seeing someone, and I need you not to judge."

Cyrus and I both sit up and say, "YOU'RE SEEING SOME-ONE?" at the same time.

Jules clears his throat. "It's Gaby," he says.

"Gaby?" I ask. "But we've been making fun of him for months."

"You've been making fun. I've been secretly dating. And now we're moving in together."

"You're moving in together?"

"Stop repeating everything," Jules laughs.

"Let's go out and celebrate," I say. Then I wonder aloud, "But does Gaby have to come?"

"Seriously, you guys cannot be assholes about this. That's why I didn't tell you."

Cyrus walks over to Jules and hugs him. "This is really great, my friend. Don't mind us. We're just—you know, Three Musketeers and all that."

"First of all, we never called ourselves that. And second, as you constantly remind us, Asha, there were four musketeers."

"Why do they always call them the Three Musketeers, then?" Cyrus asks.

"Because D'Artagnan was the narrator, and he joined last."

We think about finding a restaurant, but by the time we clock out for the night, it's late and we end up at the diner. Gaby and Jules sit together on one side of the booth and Cyrus and I sit on the other side. I go between feelings of tender warmth toward Gaby, the way he pours water into Jules's glass and asks if he wants to share the Cobb salad, to something I guess must be jealousy, because Cyrus is right, even if we didn't call ourselves the Musketeers, we were a gang, and it's possible the gang will never be the same. I'm a terrible person for thinking this, not least because I was the one who got between Jules and Cyrus in the first place. How annoying that must have been for Jules. And I can't believe we didn't see it, Cyrus and I, our best friend falling in love right before our eyes. Anyway, I tell myself, Jules deserves someone of his own, someone who will go to every Hamptons weekend with him and tell his brother to go fuck himself. Cyrus has his hand on my knee, and from the way he's going around in circles, I can tell he's thinking all the same things I am.

Gaby is perfectly lovely. He has a soft voice and he smells like limes. "Here's to you both," I say, and we clink plastic cups. "I thought I knew everything that went on around here."

"We're very happy for you," Cyrus says.

"How did you two meet?" Gaby asks Cyrus and me. I realize we've never really sat down and talked to Gaby. I'd just put him in the Rupert category—someone to count our money and tell us what to do.

"We've been in love the whole time," Cyrus says.

"It's true," Jules tells him, "they have. They met in high school and that was it."

"Well, not really. I was into Cyrus, but his head was in the clouds."

Gaby smiles. "That sounds about right."

"It took me ages to ask Gaby out," Jules says.

"Yeah, because you hired me."

"I was sitting there in the interview wondering if it would be better if you worked here or not, but then the thought of seeing you every day was too tempting."

"Wow, I had no idea," Cyrus says. Jules must have been lonely, and we've been so caught up in each other that we never noticed. Cyrus puts his arm around me and I nudge closer, and I realize it's been weeks since we've had a moment together. We're always too tired when we get home from work, or we get home and spend the last bits of our energy talking about WAI. I haven't minded until now, but seeing Jules and Gaby holding hands, I feel a twinge of longing. Cyrus and Gaby are talking about someone on the team, and I just want to wrap up and go home. I yawn. "Shall we get going?"

"Why don't you come over?" Cyrus says. "We have—what do we have, Asha?"

"Nothing. But you're totally welcome," I add, thinking of the trail of dirty dishes I ignored on my way out the door this morning.

In the end we decide to go to Jules's. He instructs us to take off our shoes at the door, and I'm about to make a joke about Crazy Craig, but I stop myself. I've been here dozens of times, but it's different now: Gaby takes our coats and asks if we want anything to drink, and then he glides easily around the kitchen, opening drawers and taking out glasses. "We should invite people over more," I say to Cyrus.

"I love you," Cyrus replies.

We sit by the window with all the New York lights before us. Jules lives by the High Line now, just a few blocks south of Utopia, with bouquet after bouquet of buildings on either side. Gaby hands me a glass, and the wine goes down slow and warm. Again I feel a surge of desire for Cyrus; I study his face to see if he's with me, but he's looking at something on the other side of the room.

"I have some ideas about the funding situation," Gaby says. "I was going to bring it up tomorrow, at our exec meeting, but we could talk about it tonight if you're up for it."

"You're in the family now," Cyrus says.

"Well, Jules and I have been brainstorming." Gaby finds his laptop, turns the screen toward us. "I've modeled it. With our current runway, we hit a wall in three months."

We all know this—Jules has said it a hundred times. I even have an hourglass programmed into my screen at work.

"But we could stretch the runway, if we make a few cuts, and launch subscriptions in December."

Cyrus leans forward and examines the screen. "Subscriptions?"

"We ask the community to pay a small amount every month."

Cyrus turns to look at Jules and me. "You've heard about this plan?"

I shake my head. "Not me."

"It's just an idea," Jules says. "Hear him out."

"It can be ten dollars a month or even less—seven or five. Less than your Netflix subscription. Certainly less than all the other things people pay for—gym, phone plan, Amazon Prime."

Cyrus pulls out his wallet and takes a folded piece of paper from inside it, and I realize he's been carrying our manifesto around with him. "It says it right here," he says. His voice is cutting in and out like an analog radio. "We said we weren't going to sell anyone anything. We said it would always be free."

Jules leans forward on his chair. "That was naive of us, Cyrus—I should've told you that right off the bat, but I was too eager to get you to say yes."

Gaby points to his screen. "It would mean controlling our own destiny. We would only need twenty-five percent adoption."

"You agree with this, Asha?"

It hasn't occurred to me before, asking the cat lady and the couple who wanted to get married beside Karl Marx's grave to give us money. It doesn't sound quite right, and I know that if I'm having trouble wrapping my head around it, so will Cyrus. But I can't deny it's a good idea. "It costs money to run the platform. We either raise venture funds or we get money from the people who use it."

"It's the principle," Cyrus says.

"Could a part of it remain free?"

"We don't think there should be two tiers," Gaby says. "But we could offer three months free to new subscribers."

Cyrus starts pacing up and down the room, his hands in his pockets, his face turned toward the window.

"I think we should consider it," I say.

"So do I," Jules says.

Cyrus pauses and tosses his head the way he sometimes does when he's agitated. "I can't believe what I'm hearing," he says. "You're asking me to change the vision and, most important, my boundaries, which I made perfectly clear before we ever embarked on this thing."

Before any of us can speak, he's stormed into the hallway and slammed the front door behind him.

"Shit," Jules groans.

I take out my phone and start texting. **Did you just walk out without me?**

"What happened?" Gaby asks.

"We pushed too hard," Jules says. "I knew this was going to be a touchy subject. We probably should have waited."

He's not texting me back. "Wait till when?" I ask. "Till we run out of money?"

"He was ambushed," Jules says. "Hard to get him to come around if he feels we ganged up on him."

"It was news to me too," I say. I don't say: *And yet he just fucked off and left me here.* I text: **Did you just fuck off and leave me here?**

"You should go find him," Jules says.

I don't want to run after him. "Are you guys serious about the subscriptions? We won't need to raise funds?"

"That's what it looks like," Gaby says. "Look, I don't want to get in between you all."

"I guess that makes you D'Artagnan," I say. Then I turn off my phone so I'm not waiting like a horny teenager for it to buzz, and fly out of there myself and take the biggest steps I can manage all the way to Utopia.

Ren and Destiny are dancing. We bought a record player a few weeks ago, and there are exactly six records, and one of them—the original Amy Winehouse album—has been playing on repeat. I hug Destiny and we slow-dance for a minute or so, and by the time the song ends, I'm feeling human again. I tell Ren about the subscriptions, and we start working out the back end. We make a sprint schedule, debate the various payment platforms, Shopify, PayPal, Google Pay, Apple Pay, and then we get right into building it, and by the time I look up from my screen, it's morning and I have never been happier to see daybreak. But then I turn on my phone and there are no messages from Cyrus, and I'm right back into my lather, with that weird feeling in the pit of my stomach like I have a guilty secret even though I know I haven't done anything wrong. Did we gang up on Cyrus? Did we stab his vision in the eye?

On the R train home, I veer between different emotions, all equally pathetic. I'm angry at Cyrus for storming off and not even looking over his shoulder once and asking me to join his rebellion, and I'm racking my brain to see if I've done anything wrong (*No. No. Maybe. Maybe?*), and then I'm worried about him, what if he accidentally hurt himself, like if he stood on the edge of the Brooklyn Bridge and then just tripped? Or stepped out on the road, half-hoping something would crash into him, and it's a sixteen-wheeler delivering cabbage to Fairway?

When I open the door, it's quiet and I think maybe he isn't home, but there's a bump in the comforter, and when I lift it up, there he is, wide-awake, his face like a piece of wood.

"Did you get any of my messages?"

"Yes."

"Why didn't you call me back? Or text?"

"I thought we could talk once you got home." He sits up and rolls his shoulders back, and suddenly, he's eight feet tall even though I'm the one standing up.

"Let's talk, then."

He takes a deep breath. I would have to do yoga for seven or eight years to get that much air into my lungs. "I'm hurt by what happened last night."

"What exactly happened?"

"You and Jules know what WAI is about—it's not about making money. It's about giving people a safe place, a community. We promised them that. For you to renege on that promise is unacceptable to me. And hurtful."

"No one is asking you to give up your principles."

"I refuse to be treated like a commodity."

"No one is treating you like a commodity."

We go on like this for what feels like a hundred years. Cyrus levels accusations at me, I deny them. He defends his vision, his beliefs. I ask why he's the only one allowed to have visions and beliefs. He denies this. He tells me I've lost the plot. I tell him he's lost the plot. This is all going to go away, I say, if we don't find a way to raise money. And anyway, why was he willing to take money from Crazy Craig and not find a way to not take money from Crazy Craig?

Halfway through this sentence, I realize I am so hungry I'm starting to sweat. I make myself a peanut butter sandwich with the one remaining knife in the drawer. Then we are back to whatever it is we were doing, which has no name, except maybe "fucked if you do, fucked if you don't."

Finally, I apologize. "I'm sorry I hurt your feelings, Cyrus, I didn't mean to." I don't know if I am sorry, I just know that I'm so tired my teeth hurt.

Immediately, Cyrus leans over to my side of the bed and puts his head in my lap. I can feel him crying, so I stroke his hair, the back of his neck. Eventually, we both fall asleep, and at some point in the middle of the day, I wake up with peanut butter on my tongue, and when I get up to brush my teeth, he cradles me and whispers he's sorry too, for not calling me all night, and when he kisses me, I relax, absolved, and fall asleep again.

The next few weeks pass in a blur. Ren and I work around the clock to get the subscriptions going, and Jules and Gaby try to stretch the last of our money as far as it'll go. Cyrus and I don't get paid, so I'm back to asking my father for a loan, which means I have to go out to Merrick and suffer the humiliation of him silently handing over a check without asking me a single question.

Cyrus hasn't said yes and he hasn't said no. We've all just gone on as if nothing happened that night, and everyone is acting normal except Gaby, who avoids making eye contact with any of us when we're at the office. Then, four weeks later, Cyrus calls us into the meeting room. "Thank you for all your hard work," he says to Jules and me, as if we just walked in yesterday and started putting up shelves in the empty alcove. "I really appreciate it. Although I was disturbed by the manner in which you brought up the issue, I don't dispute that we have to find a solution to our financial situation."

I glance over at Jules, wondering where this is going.

"I've decided to accept your proposal about the subscriptions. But I have two conditions." He pauses while we get out our laptops and take notes. "The first is that the contributions will be voluntary. In that people will contribute what they can every month and there will be no upper or lower limit. If someone wants to give us a penny, they can do that, and we will give them the same service we would if they gave us a hundred dollars a month."

I wait for this news to land with Jules, who is shaking his head.

"They have to give something," Cyrus continues. "But it can be a tiny amount."

"How are we supposed to model that?" Jules says.

"Let me finish, and then you can state your objections," Cyrus says. "Second, we don't give people a set amount of free time on the platform, we give them one free ritual." He shows us something on his screen. "As you can see, our attach rates are through the roof. So presumably, a person who has received a free ritual will want more."

He leans back, takes a sip of his coffee. He has started drinking seven or eight cups a day, just black, no sugar, in an old-fashioned thermos he found in my parents' garage.

"Thanks, Cyrus," Gaby says. "I'll go and crunch the numbers."

"But what do you think?"

"I think it's great!" I say before Jules can speak. "I love it."

Jules nods. "It's a really great way to solve the problem," he says finally. Gaby agrees.

Cyrus is pleased with himself. "Isn't it? We get the revenue, but we also get to keep the spirit of the whole thing, which is that it's essentially a community."

"Like passing your hat around at church," Jules says.

"Exactly. You don't get less church if you pay less." Cyrus was getting more comfortable with the religious metaphors. "Asha, could you get Ren to mock up a few designs of how we might introduce this? And Destiny should come up with a marketing message. You'll know what to do around the back end."

Ren and I had already come up with a way to take payments and track subscriptions. But we would have to find a way to allow people to pay whatever they wanted instead of a set amount.

"Let's call it membership," I say. "That way we can use things like GoFundMe to let people donate whatever they want."

"It's not a donation. But yes, we could call it membership."

We've reached a truce. In five weeks, we'll see what it yields.

When I come out of the meeting room, I find my sister sitting at my desk, her hands wrapped around a mug. "This place is unbelievable," she says when she sees me.

"I've been asking you to come visit."

"What, and get seduced by your capitalist wet dream?"

"Toba Toba," I say, mimicking the way our mother slapped her own cheeks whenever we used the f-word at home. "Do you want a tour? We have a chocolate fountain."

"No, thanks. I came to tell you I'm pregnant."

Everything else melts away. I try not to knock her over. "You did it!"

"It's horrible timing. I won't have time to finish my manuscript, so I won't have a book when my tenure review comes up, and then they'll hire someone else and make me an adjunct."

"Never mind about that. How are you feeling?"

"Like shit, but apparently, that's a good thing. It means I'm more pregnant."

"What does Ahmed say?"

"He's already starting talking to my stomach."

"I'm really happy," I say, hugging her again and again. "I'm going to be such an awesome aunt."

▼

Mira is pregnant for thirty-five weeks after I hear this news, and in those thirty-five weeks, WAI becomes, in the words of Rupert and his endless sports metaphors, the Patriots in 2002. In other words, we hit the big time.

The subscriptions are a success. People begin to donate to the platform in huge numbers. We draw graphs and bell curves and pie charts, but they all tell us the same thing, which is that, far from giving people the impression that they can get away with contributing as little as possible, the voluntary donation has made the WAIs reach deep into their pockets. They send us twenty, thirty dollars a month, sometimes more. They pay us when they don't have to, in the middle of the month, two weeks before their money is due. They ask if they can donate for others, if they can give the gift of WAIsdom to their friends. Yes, WAIsdom is a thing. It's the opposite of wisdom in that it makes no fucking sense at all.

So as my sister goes nervously to her twelve-week scan, her jeans starting to get a little pinchy around the waist, we turn our first ever profit. And by the time she's had all her blood tests and knows she's having a girl and that the girl has a near perfect set of genes, WAI is generating $3 million a month in subscriptions, a subscription rate of 47 percent with an average rate of $14, which is 44 percent higher and $7 more than we'd projected. In other words, while the baby is perfectly average, as one wants a baby to be at that stage in its life, WAI is breaking all of our average-size predictions and doubling its growth every month. And by the time little Gitanjali comes into the world, twenty-two hours of pushing accompanied by much cursing, and her father whispers the opening lines of the Quran into her left ear and my mother whispers into her other ear, "And though she be but little, she is fierce," we are spinning with the strangeness of it all. And Gitanjali, suffering from colic or from an abundance of fierceness, cries for the next three months, keeping her parents up at night and harassing the neighbors, and at the end of those three months, we are all transformed, our entire tribe, not only Mira and Ahmed and my parents and Ahmed's father, who sits up and cradles the baby all night long as she wails into the heavens, but Cyrus and me and Jules and all the people who work at WAI, all two hundred of them, crowding into the top two floors of Utopia, and the rest in the Valley, and London, and Hong Kong.

Eleven

FFS

When Li Ann gets an invite to the Girls Who Boss networking night, Destiny and I tag along. It's at a bar called Composite, and when we walk down the stairs to the basement and enter the windowless room, it is already full of women in skinny jeans and blazers. Destiny and I hover around the edges while Li Ann gets us drinks. "What are we supposed to do here?" I ask.

"I don't know. Be awesome, I guess."

"Are we supposed to go around and introduce ourselves?"

"Yes, you talk to other people. It's called mingling."

"My inner geek is my outer geek," I say.

Li Ann returns with our drinks. "We could talk about sex," she says, handing us each a flute of something orange and bubbly. "I would really like to have sex with Rory."

"Vegan Rory?"

Destiny takes a sip of the orange bubbly. "What the fuck is this?"

"Skin-contact champagne," Li Ann says. "We almost did it, but then I told him about Breathe Life and he was not supportive, and I never sleep with a man who doesn't fulfill my need to be affirmed."

"I would never get laid if that was my rule," Destiny says.

"Yeah," I agree. "High bar."

Li Ann takes out yet another sample of Breathe Life. These look more like the first ones. I switch one on, take a deep breath. "This tastes like marijuana," I say.

"It is marijuana," she says, nodding. "Best thing for your lungs. All-natural, wild-grown, foraged, and dried on sustainably sourced sheepskin mats."

"What was Rory's objection?" I ask.

"The inside of the hardware contains plastic," she explains. "He's against plastic in all forms."

"I guess there's going to be a lot of leftover plastic in the afterworld," Destiny says.

"Rory lives in a plastic-free commune in Bushwick, and they make their own toilet paper."

"Out of what?"

"Out of other pieces of paper."

"His poor butt," I say. "You should definitely have sex with him. For the sake of his raw behind."

"What? I'm not going anywhere near that thing."

"I just meant in general—never mind. Let's go talk to other people." Just then the host takes to the stage, and the room goes quiet. "I'd like to introduce our panel for the evening," she says. "Ladies, welcome to Mary McGreen, Manishala Brown, and Selina Lewis."

We clap. Three impeccably dressed women take seats onstage. The woman in the middle, Manishala Brown, has long braids falling down over her shoulders and enormous boots on her feet. I love her immediately. She is flanked by two white women, both sporting the kind of calm confidence and grooming that comes from being older, wiser, and richer than everyone else in the room. "Each of our panelists has had enormous success in crashing through the glass ceiling. They've started companies, taken companies public, sat on boards, and seen the whole funding cycle through from seed to IPO. What would you tell your younger selves about the challenges and opportunities of being a female founder?"

The woman on the left, Mary McGreen, speaks first. "I would tell her to relax and have more fun," she says, and the audience titters. "No, but seriously. Ask yourself if you're enjoying the ride. Because with all the pressures heaped on us, it's easy to forget that we need to find joy too." I nod, feeling joyful, or maybe just high from Li Ann's pot.

"I would tell her to take less bullshit," Manishala Brown says.

"Amen!" someone from the audience shouts.

"The number of times I brushed off some sexist or racist comment, thinking, well, that guy's a product of his generation, he didn't mean it—each of those times, I knew I was giving a free pass to someone who did not deserve it, but I didn't have the confidence to call him out."

More cheers. I find myself doing a "Woo-hoo!" and thinking of Crazy Craig and those guys in suits and even Rupert, who almost never looks at me, even if he's asking a direct question about the algorithm I invented.

Selina Lewis clears her throat. "If I may," she says in a clipped British accent, "I must disagree. Let's be realistic. If we don't sometimes give men a free pass, as you say, we are going to sabotage ourselves. You may think, from reading the newspaper or social media, that the world has fundamentally changed, but it hasn't. It's still the same people in power, and if you want to get into the club, you have to first play by the rules. Then, perhaps, you might have the fortune to change it from the inside."

"Selina, with all due respect, I just don't buy that," Manishala says.

Selina does an exaggerated shrug. "You can buy it or not—it's reality."

"So you're saying we should all be on board with a little light workplace harassment?"

"Harassment, absolutely not. But giving a man the benefit of the doubt, not pouncing on everything he says, so that he takes you into his confidence, yes."

Manishala leans back, rolls her eyes. I sense that the audience of women like me, founders and wannabe founders, are on the fence. They want to agree with Manishala. They want to say "fuck you" every time some guy uses a woman's body as a way of describing something—*We're already pregnant, let's just push this thing out* or: *Should we open the full kimono?*—but they know they're going to walk into that office or that pitch meeting, and they're going to feel like they have to bro it up with all the other guys, because who wants to be the uptight girl who makes everyone shush the minute she walks into the room? We want to be on the inside, we want to hang. We want to be cool. And we want to win.

Manishala is talking about how she started A Friend in Need, a fintech company focused on lending money to women. She tells us no one would fund her until a female VC stepped up and saw the opportunity. "We have to back each other," she says. "Not because we're being nice or because of the sisterhood. We have to back each other because we see things—financial opportunities—that men don't. My company is worth two hundred million dollars, and I have made money for the woman who bet on me. No one gets to tell her she did me a favor, she just valued the investment on different terms."

The crowd cheers. We see ourselves on that stage, each one of us, hoping we're going to defy the odds. And for the first time, I feel a little pang of regret. Why didn't I front the WAI? Why did I wed my idea to a man and push him to take center stage when I was the one who stayed up nights making it a reality? It wasn't Cyrus's fault—at least not initially—that I couldn't have imagined putting myself out there and saying, *This thing is real. Back me.* Now it's too late—the cult of Cyrus has begun, and although I have a seat at the table, it isn't my table, it's his. His and Rupert's and all the other men who are going to fund the business.

Destiny shoulder-bumps me. I look over and I see that her eyes are shining because Manishala has put the same fire into her as she has into me, and she's thinking about Consentify.

After it's all over, I grab Destiny's hand and push us to the edge of the stage. The speakers are gathering their things, taking off their mikes. "Ms. Brown?" I say. She looks up, smiles. "You can call me Manishala," she says, though I can tell she liked that I didn't presume to use her first name.

"This is my friend Destiny. She had an idea, but like you, she hasn't found funding."

"I'm sorry to hear that." She fumbles with her handbag. She's heard a thousand sob stories.

"It's technically sound," I say. "But the narrative didn't sit well with most investors. I can vouch for it—I programmed the algorithm that powers WAI."

"You built WAI? You're Asha Ray?"

It has only just started happening to me, that thing where people I have never met have an opinion of me based on things they've read or heard. Six months ago I never would've approached Manishala, and she never would have given me that look she's giving me now, like I'm a person to notice and be reckoned with. I earned that. I give myself a silent high five.

"So what's this thing?" she asks.

Destiny explains. "It's called Consentify. It allows partners to pre-agree to their sexual activity."

Manishala laughs. "You're kidding, right?"

"Nope."

Destiny hands over her phone. Manishala swipes, scrolls, presses a few buttons. "Interesting." She clicks open her bag, takes out a business card. "I'm not making any promises," she says. "But send me your deck and I will take a look."

Cyrus, Ren, and Destiny are crowded around a screen. Cyrus is pointing and gesturing. I haven't been called in, but I can see through the glass that there are moments of conversation and then long periods when no one is saying anything. Cyrus has his own office now, a glassed-in section on the fourth floor. We've talked about moving— Utopia is an incubator, and WAI's incubation is definitely over. But Cyrus wants to stay, and he convinces Li Ann to let us. We take the top two floors, raise the ceilings, create an internal staircase, and re-build the roof garden. It looks like the old Utopia, but there is more steel than exposed brick, and everywhere you look, there are people on their laptops and hunched over desks, all in the same pose of self-satisfaction, because they are doing their dream jobs at a place that in-spires envy. And there are other benefits besides the bragging rights: excellent health care and paid maternity leave, karaoke Tuesdays (led by Jules), the I Think Therefore I Am Club (led by Cyrus), and the "How to Make Your Robot Joke Authentically Club" (led by me).

Jules has tried to get me to take my own office—he and Gaby have side-by-side ones downstairs—but I want to be with my team, so I just perch wherever suits me. Right now I'm trying to focus on what I'm doing, but I keep looking over and wondering what Cyrus is up to. I have a bad feeling. Finally, I decide I can't wait.

"Sorry to disturb," I say, knocking on the glass door. "May I borrow you for just a minute?"

"Sure, we're done here." Cyrus turns to Ren. "So send me those mock-ups by lunchtime."

Ren nods, drifts away. I see a large drawing pad on Cyrus's desk. He's attending to it with a thick pencil. "What's that?" I ask.

"The redesign of the platform," he says.

"Which platform?"

He looks up from his drawing. He is not smiling.

"It's cluttered," he says, turning his screen toward me. "I don't like the copy at the top. The messaging part is buried below the line. And the colors don't work."

It takes me a moment to realize what is happening, and once it dawns on me that Cyrus wants to redesign the entire platform I built, I have to try very hard not to throw a chair against the glass wall of his office. I take a deep breath. "Maybe you could've run this by me?"

He pauses. "Right, yes. I'm sorry. But I want it to happen before the raise, and there's not a lot of time."

As it turns out, even though we have real people sending us real money every month, if we want to keep growing, we have to raise funds. This time Cyrus isn't opposed; in fact, he's the one driving things. Gaby and Jules have drawn charts, and all the arrows are pointing up—more users in more countries doing more things with

WAI—but we can go further, reach more parts of the world, if we pour money into the platform. And Cyrus wants to get to everyone.

Now that we have a steady source of revenue, investors want a piece of WAI. Woke VC is only one of the funds that come calling, except they don't call, they send texts, emails, emissaries, and sometimes flowers. One offered to set up a meeting with the pope. Would Cyrus be interested in meeting His Holiness? The only His Holiness Cyrus is interested in is the Dalai Lama, and they will be appearing onstage together in two months, at a conference in Aspen. We have been offered money at sky-high valuations, and when people cotton on to the fact that Cyrus is not swayed by money, they start bigging up their other forms of cred. We are now up to 2 percent, Woke VC tells us proudly. A full 2 percent of their funds go to minority women. They donate to Black Lives Matter. They're all Democrats. Some of them are even socialists. Would Cyrus like to meet AOC?

Cyrus is still busy doing Cyrusy things. He attends the Mami Wata Society the first Friday of the month. The Athena Club every alternate Saturday. He has become friendly with a group of Shinto priests. Comic-Con is a big commitment, because so many people on the platform ask for superhero rituals. Cyrus has a personal assistant now, a bloodless woman named Eve whom I have come to dislike intensely because she is the guardian of his schedule, and if I want to get a dinner date, there are three competing Google calendars to wrestle with, and Eve's placid face telling me that two Fridays from now might work for a ninety-minute reservation no more than four blocks away.

Cyrus and I are fine—mostly we just laugh about the ridiculous attention he's getting, the army of people who suddenly work for us, the millions who crowd our platform. We do this thing where we look at each other and say "Am I me?" And the other one will say "You're still you, baby." But once in a while, like right now, Cyrus is frustratingly incomprehensible. It doesn't seem like there's time for a single new thing in our lives, but apparently, on top of everything else, he's redesigning the platform.

"You went ahead and gave Ren directions on the design?"

"It's just a mock-up. You can come to the meeting this afternoon."

"I was not invited to the meeting."

He smiles. "That was an oversight. Please come. I would love to have you there—you have a great sense of design."

"It's fine, you do it. Ren can catch me up later."

"I love you, Asha," he says. "You know I like to improvise. Let's try it and see what happens?"

"Sure." When he raises his fist for a bump, I bump him back.

And that's me getting Cyrused, where I roll up, fully dressed, to my own irrelevance.

To get my mind off of whatever Cyrus is doing to the platform, I take a walk around Utopia. The rest of the building is unchanged, except for the new companies whose logos adorn the walls. The latest one is Freud, a matchmaking service that asks people real questions about who they are instead of random ones about what books they like and whether they prefer skydiving or streaming. Freud's questionnaire is like this:

> Would you call your mother a) loving and largely present, b) loving but largely absent, c) unloving but largely present, or d) unloving and largely absent?

They have a small following (who wants to look at the painful stuff?) and a shocking success rate.

In the stairwell, I run into Rory. He's holding a tiny metal box with great care. "Is that an engagement ring?" I ask.

"It's much better than that."

"Yeah, diamonds are not a girl's best friend." I follow him downstairs while monologing about the absolute terribleness of diamonds.

We're at the entrance to his lab, and to my surprise, he touches his finger to the pad and invites me in.

Rows of long benches frame a large open area. Although we are in the basement, there are solar tubes bringing light from aboveground, and bright LEDs directed at the plants. One breathtaking wall is a spectrum of green, from pale moss to dense, bluey emerald. "This is our Popeye Project," Rory says. "Lots of companies are trying to wean the world from its dependence on meat. We support all of those because, really, whatever it takes. What differentiates LoneStar is that we're trying to increase the nutrient density of the entire food chain."

He brings me over to another area, where there are three raised soil beds. One contains cabbage, another a tangle of tomato vines, and the third, he tells me, has potatoes growing underneath the soil.

"We can gene-edit the most eaten plants in the world and increase the protein content of those vegetables by fifty to a hundred percent without altering the taste."

"Superfoods."

"Yes, but that term has been hijacked by the upmarket food industry. With LoneStar foods, people can subsist entirely on a plant-based diet without purchasing expensive meat substitutes."

"Wow. So I can eat a whole plate of french fries and it'll be like I just inhaled a bowl of raw kale?"

He tilts his head and I realize he doesn't know I'm joking. "Not exactly," he says. "All foods will never be equal. But we can substantially increase the nutritional qualities of a vast majority of vegetables."

I am reminded of his plastic-free commune and feel a surge of tenderness toward him. He's a geek, just like me. "So what's in the little box?"

"If I tell you," he says, "when they come to arrest me, you can't claim you didn't know."

I awkwardly laugh. But again, he's not smiling. Is it because he doesn't know how to smile or because he's actually serious? Then I think, *It's very possible this man is part human, part machine*, and that train of thought makes me sad all over again because if I had just gone ahead and built my Empathy Module, then all the robots would be able to smile realistically.

"I'm not afraid," I say.

He opens the box. At first it looks like it might be empty, but in the corner, I see a tiny insect that looks like half an ant.

"This is the LoneStar tick," Rory says. "If it bites you, you can never eat meat again."

I pause. Is this a biological weapon? "Wait, did you engineer this thing?"

"No, it already existed. We are just making them more effective and less lethal."

"Less lethal?"

"It gives you an allergy to meat-based products. We genetically modified it so that you also become unable to eat dairy, honey, or eggs. But whereas some people react to an allergen by going into anaphylactic shock, the bite from this tick just makes it so that meat makes you very, very sick."

"Sick as in cancer?"

"As in diarrhea."

I'm not sure what to think. On the one hand, Rory is insane. On the other, his version of changing the world is way more radical than my version of changing the world. I'm having changing-the-world envy. Rory is looking right at my mouth instead of generally in the direction of my face, and I wonder if maybe he's leaning in to kiss me, so I jerk my head back because God that would be weird, and thankfully, before either of us tries to register what's going on, I get a text from Jules. **Come to the meeting room now pls.** I bolt up the stairs, but by the time I get there, the design review is over. Destiny, Gaby, and Jules are huddled together around the conference table looking wilted and gray.

"It's okay," Jules is saying. "We'll figure it out." I peer over his shoulder and see a drawing of the site that is unrecognizable.

"What's that?" I ask, even though I already know.

"It's the new design," Destiny says.

"But people like it the way it is."

"Cyrus does not like it the way it is, so we're going to change it," Jules says.

"On the basis of what?"

"On the basis of he's the CEO," Gaby says.

I want to say, *Oh, fuck that*, but I know Destiny and Jules have already gone through the arguments with him and that he's won. "Look," Destiny says, "why don't we mock it up, do some A/B testing, see what people say."

Jules agrees. "Good idea. The data will speak for itself." He looks at me. "Everyone happy with that?"

I'm far from happy, but I don't see that I have a choice. Gaby winks conspiratorially at me and I feel a little better.

I don't go home for several days. I stay up all night and take naps in the sleep pods at Utopia. Ren and Destiny and I take turns playing DJ, and then the turntable breaks. We order the same thing from the diner every day, going old-school and picking it up ourselves.

"Are you okay?" Cyrus asks, and I nod, tell him I'm just tired because the deadline is so tight, and he accepts that, doesn't dig any further. I'm actually not tired, I feel rather refreshed. The sleep pods are quieter than the apartment, and I don't have the feeling every time I go home that I should be there more often, like normal people, and keep food in my fridge. Last time I checked, there was half a bottle of sparkling water and half a lemon and half an avocado that had gone brown the week before. Cyrus and I live like wolves, but when we are at the office, it doesn't matter; in fact, Cyrus's desk is always spotless, and my code, I know, is uncluttered and elegant. Nothing like my bedside table, which is not a bedside table at all but a crate I once picked up on the sidewalk and on which I precariously balance a number of items, including a stash of cookies, an alarm clock, a bottle of water, birth control pills, and when it's not under my pillow, my phone.

All this is about to change. Cyrus and I are closing on an apartment on the Lower East Side. It too contains an abundance of glass and steel and, underneath, the bones of an old building. There are two floors, multiple bathrooms, and a six-burner stove. We are going to cook meals, make our beds, and take our coffee cups to the sink. We are going to purchase furniture and flower vases. We are going to return the mugs we stole from the diner. I have visions of dinner parties, people laughing, their delighted faces reflected in our excellent choice of cutlery. And through it all, I see us, Cyrus and me, our lives entwined ever more, shrugging off the last two years and returning to the time when we had acres of things to talk about, things that weren't related to fundraising and redesigning a website to which I have grown attached.

I can hear Mira in the baby's room, cursing. "Oh, for the love of God, how is it possible for you to shit so much."

She comes back, slides onto the sofa, pulls her top aside, and silences the baby. "She poops, I change her diaper, and then ten seconds later she poops again, and while I'm changing that, her pee comes out in a little arc and hits me right in the face."

"We don't put diapers on babies in Bangladesh," our mother says.

Mira groans. Ammoo has been staying at her house every weekend for the last two months, making food and generally driving everyone crazy.

"Here," Mira says, handing me the baby. "You burp her."

I stand up and stroke Gitanjali's back while doing a bouncy dance that just came to me the first time I held her. Her head smells so good. "I'm thinking we have heroin pods in our vaginas," I say. "When the baby comes out, a little heroin gets sprinkled on top of their heads, and then all you want to do is sniff them instead of counting the number of times you have to wipe their butts."

"Heroin-laced vagina! If only. My vagina feels like the Hulk stepped on it."

"Yeah, but a baby came out of your vagina. Your vagina is magic."

"Can you two please stop saying vagina?"

"Don't mind me, Ma. I'm just mourning the loss of my previously perfect vagina, which is now the size of a Big Gulp."

"I'm getting you a night nanny," I announce.

"What's that?"

"It's a person who comes to your house and stays up all night so you don't have to."

"What kind of person?"

"Whatever kind of person you want. You get to pick them."

Mira gives me the side-eye. "How much does it cost?"

"Don't worry about that, it's on me and Cyrus."

"Like the crib, the Bugaboo, the car seat, and the baby monitor that tells you everything except when you're going to die?"

"'Death is not extinguishing the light; it is only putting out the lamp because the dawn has come.'"

"Ammoo, please. Seriously, Asha, you have to stop paying for everything."

"Why? Why do I have to stop paying for everything?"

"Because you're making everyone uncomfortable."

Gitanjali has fallen asleep in my arms. I gaze at the little face poking up out of her swaddle. She has Ahmed's wide forehead and Mira's and my mouth, something I am extremely proud of. Right now there is a circular rough patch on her upper lip, a milk blister that gives her a small pout. Mira has banned us from the following things: commenting on Gitanjali's beauty, the color pink, calling her a princess, informing her there's a thing out there called Disney, or forecasting professions that require fewer than two graduate degrees.

"Well, I'm sorry if I've overdone it."

"I don't mean to be horrible," Mira says. "It's just that Ahmed's parents wanted to get her a high chair, but I overheard them saying you would probably come over and say it was toxic or ugly."

"Why would I say that?"

She shrugs. I can see she's fighting tears, so I walk over and hand Gitanjali back to her, and she relaxes while the baby rustles and pecks at her shoulder, a current of needs passing back and forth between them like Morse code.

The testing on Cyrus's redesign comes back, and the results are clear. People like the old version better than the proposed new version. I turn all this data into a presentation with slides, graphics, and pie charts. Then we go back into the meeting room and deliver the results. "In our opinion," Destiny says, "while some of the color changes are an improvement"—I told her to say that, to give something so that Cyrus could feel like he'd made it better—"the rearranging of the primary features of the site have not been considered a value add by the people we surveyed."

"How many people?" Cyrus asks. I've hardly seen him this week, but now, instead of congratulating me on all my work, he's peering at the screen like he's left his reading glasses at home.

Destiny checks something on her computer. "Three thousand and thirty-seven," she says.

"That's not a good sample size," Cyrus says.

"I guess not," Destiny agrees. "It's less than point one percent of our user base."

"It's all we could do on short notice," I say. "They represent the demographics of the broader community."

"Can I see the raw data?"

I was prepared for this. I take out a thick folder and hand it to him.

"These replies are not decisive," he says, flipping through the material. "They say they prefer the old one, but they don't say why."

I text Jules. **Do something.**

"Cyrus," Jules says, "we've already told the community there are going to be new features. The redesign is going to add three weeks to the timeline, and that's if Asha and Ren and the team work around the clock."

I wait to see how Cyrus will respond. "Couldn't you use the same codebase? You're doing the wireframes again anyway, right?"

"It's not the same part of the site," I start.

"But you are, right?"

"I guess so."

"Then it's probably fine." He flips through the questionnaire again. "Yeah, I don't buy this. See, this woman says she doesn't like it, but she also says she doesn't actively dislike it. I don't even know if we asked the right questions here." He shows Destiny.

"Right," she says. "I mean, it's not completely clear. I guess we were just reading between the lines."

"I think we need to be precise in our assumptions," Cyrus announces. He catches my eye. "Look," he says, reverting to negotiation, "why don't we do a little more research. Let's create a few options, and once we've got a new investor, we can get the green light from the board?"

"So you want us to create entirely new designs when the old one is working fine."

"Yes."

"But why?"

"Because one of them might be better."

He is right. One of them might, indeed, be better. We won't know unless we try. Cyrus wants to try everything. In the same way that he wants to meet the three people on the planet who have written PhD theses on the Japanese goddess Ame-no-Uzume, and then he wants to go to Japan and have the original texts recited to him while someone simultaneously translates them into his ear, and then he wants to learn a few characters so he can check his own interpretation against the translations, Cyrus wants to know absolutely everything. The more he knows, the more he believes he can know. He is constantly entering new data into the algorithm and teaching it new ways to think, new connections between seemingly disparate threads. This is how he approaches everything these days, with a maniacal need to try every available option before making a single decision. And that leaves the rest of us—well, it leaves the rest of us in what we have started to call the Cyrus wake, the dizzying, turbulent, stirred-up waters that follow wherever he goes.

Twelve

THE CUDDLE PUDDLE

Cyrus and I go to Sicily. We eat a lot of ice cream and we have a lot of sex without a care in the world because I had an IUD put in after spending one terrible night with Gitanjali. We rent a car and visit a necropolis, graves carved into limestone hills, where Cyrus tells me about the Mycenaeans, and at a Greek amphitheater on the edge of the sea we reenact the final scene in *Antigone*. Cyrus plays Antigone and I play her brother's corpse. By the pool at our hotel, we hold hands and doze side by side. Away from the office, the loud static of New York, in sweet, unhurried moments, Cyrus is warm, familiar, and mine again. We have long, unfocused conversations about important and totally not important things, and we play multiple rounds of Old Before My Time.

"I don't understand Keanu Reeves," Cyrus confesses.

I gasp. "That's not being old before your time, that's not having a heart."

"I'm being honest. Don't judge."

"I suppose there are people who don't understand you."

"Me?" he says with a shudder. "No way. That is impossible."

"Only really terrible people who do terrible things."

"True. There are some really awful people out there."

"I don't understand dick pics."

"Hm, yes."

"I mean, at any given moment in time, there must be hundreds of thousands of dick pics flying around the world, and why? It seems to me the demand is not really that high. A penis out of context is not a beautiful thing."

"You really think there are people who don't get me?"

Cyrus receives equal amounts of fan mail and hate mail. Some months the fan mail outweighs the hate mail, but other months, like this one, the hate is especially thick. Last Monday, he received a letter from a man whose daughter had decided to read a passage from *The Handmaid's Tale* at her bat mitzvah, and on Tuesday a woman had written to say she had singed her eyebrows while attempting to cremate her novel-in-progress with the hope that it might be reborn into something she could actually get published.

Jules and I almost never share these letters with Cyrus; once, after receiving a message from a lapsed Catholic who was now trying to rewind two decades of atheism, the last year of which was on account of WAI, Cyrus spent several days corresponding with his friend Father Douglas so that he could find a scripturally appropriate response to the lapsed Catholic, and then he invited this man to meet Father Douglas, who agreed to rebaptize him and formally absolve him for twenty years of denying the existence of God.

Since we don't share the hate mail, Cyrus has reason to believe there isn't a person in the world who doesn't think he's totally amazing.

We also have a new game called Should I Go to This?

Cyrus reads an email from Eve listing out his invitations. "Founders First Forum?"

"Where is it?"

"Vegas."

"Are you serious? No."

"You're right. How about a month at Bellagio to work on my memoir?"

"You're writing a memoir?"

"Started it last week."

"I'd miss you."

"You're right. No. How about Davos, should I go to Davos?"

"Sure," I say. "Rub shoulders with your people."

He texts Eve with the results of our survey, and the holiday ends with twenty minutes of hot Mediterranean making out, a late checkout, and one last, perfect scoop of lemon gelato.

When we return to New York, Eve has moved us into the new apartment. Our sad little clothes, which are dry-cleaned and hanging in the walk-in closet, have come with us. But our furniture, our dishes, our pots with scratched bottoms, our disgusting excuse for a rug, our dead plants, all have been discarded. In their place, there are things in sets. A dining set, which is an oval table framed by six very upright chairs. A sofa set, which is an L-shaped sofa with a matching armchair. There are clusters of things that look good together, like bookshelves and curtains and potted plants. Color schemes. Ideas. Everything is easy on the eye, and when it isn't, like the jagged, angry abstract painting in the hallway, it is meant to be there, like a sprinkle of salt on a slab of chocolate. Cyrus and I bounce on the bed, sprawl out on the sofa, press buttons on the remote control and find that it opens and closes the blinds and not the television, hunt around for the television remote and find that it responds to voice requests, and then, about an hour later, after pressing buttons on the coffeemaker and the ice maker and the lighting and the sound system, we unpack our suitcases, shower, and head to the office.

At Utopia, the first thing I have to do is congratulate Destiny on her funding from Manishala and graciously accept her resignation.

"I'll be right downstairs," she says. "Like literally two floors away."

"Do you still have the inflatable doll?"

"Von? Hell, yeah. I just need a bike pump to bring that baby back to life."

"What's your plan?"

"Hire two engineers, beta-launch in November. See what happens. Why, you need a job?"

"Would you hire me?"

"In a heartbeat. In the meantime, don't worry, I'll be sure to find a replacement before I go."

Li Ann bounds up to us. "I have something for you," she whispers, taking what appears to be a pillbox out of her handbag.

I tell her I can't do drugs. "It would interfere with my genius."

"Shut up, no one does drugs anymore." She opens the box, and inside there is a tiny pink hair clip. "Meet Flitter," she says.

"It's a vibrator, isn't it," Destiny says.

"We are going to need a lot of orgasms in the afterworld." Li Ann lifts it out of the box and holds it up for us to see. "You just clip it to your clitoris." She presses on the sides and it opens its tiny mouth.

I tell her it looks painful.

"It's a hundred percent not painful."

"I can't believe you made a sex toy," Destiny says.

"It's not a toy. It's a handbag essential."

"You're going to carry it around in your handbag?"

"As far as I can see, there are three distinct use cases for this product. Number one, you have sex with your partner, and he comes and you don't. What are you going to do? Run an entire bath just so you can hump your showerhead? No, you just clip Flitter on and lie there, and boom. You can rest peacefully beside him instead of tossing and turning because his tongue got tired."

"I hate men," Destiny says.

"Use case number two. You have a stressful meeting at work. Your colleagues are repeatedly ignoring you and backslapping each other. 'Excuse me,' you say, and you run to the bathroom, get your Flitter out, and while they're congratulating each other on the size of their dicks, you can have a totally silent orgasm."

"You want me to come in the office bathroom?"

"It *is* called Utopia." Destiny laughs.

"You don't think the guys are jerking off constantly at work?" Li Ann says.

I really don't want to think about that. "Gross."

"Men have orgasms all the time. That's why they walk around looking like they own everything."

"They do own everything."

"What's the third use case?"

"Thanksgiving."

I'm starting to feel queasy. "That is just wrong."

"If your family is anything like mine, you need a little something to get through the holidays."

"So you're telling me you would just have an orgasm in front of everyone."

"If you can keep a straight face, yes. Because Flitter is totally noiseless. It doesn't even really vibrate. It uses centrifugal force to tug on your—"

"Okay, that's it," Destiny says. She plucks the box from Li Ann's hand and strides toward the Disabled toilet. Li Ann and I talk about other things, trying not to look at our watches to see how long it will take for Destiny to return. After approximately seven minutes, she reappears. "I'll be keeping this," she says, putting the little case in her pocket.

Li Ann squeals. "I told you! I told you!"

And with that, one of our many problems is solved.

"We won't need to replace Destiny," Cyrus says. "I'm going to run marketing." He turns to Eve. "Eve will help. She'll schedule everything and I'll make the decisions."

Everyone agrees Cyrus has an excellent eye for marketing. Those changes he made to the platform—the redesign—have proved successful. Our user base is going up, and our surveys have come back positive. Cyrus starts drawing and writing copy and booking digital ad campaigns. People start to wonder if there's anything he can't do.

There are two hundred and forty-four employees on our payroll. We have hired programmers and designers and creators of apps, and also, historians and anthropologists and graduates from seminaries and madrassas and astronomers and psychologists and futurists. Jules knows everyone by name—he prides himself on walking past the rows of desks and calling out individualized hellos to Lydia, James, Sachin, Brian, Murtaza, Sophie, Selina, Richard—and he has promised not to stop until we get to three hundred. He takes everyone out to baseball games and throws parties on boats floating in the Hudson and keeps employees feeling like they work more for the sheer fun of it than for the paycheck. Cyrus still does his WAICast, but the production values have gone up significantly, and instead of standing against a bare brick wall, he has a purpose-built VR studio so that people with headsets can be right there in the room with him. The whole thing lasts about an hour, so Cyrus has to get to the office by six a.m.

I enjoy being alone in the apartment in the mornings. Sometimes I take a long bath, and other times I just pad around and allow myself to be surprised by the very white walls or the very tall windows. I marvel at the kitchen, how effectively it gleams. Boiling water out of a tap. Ice cubes on demand. Cyrus has his own study/meditation room, which is immaculate and smells like patchouli. I think of that room as the Old Cyrus room, the tatami mats, the calligraphy on the walls, framed photographs of his mother. I have a room to myself too, an office that looks like a meth lab. We talk a lot about inviting people over, but we never do; we are always working.

My mother told me a story once about the first time her parents had an indoor bathroom installed in their house. Before that they used an outhouse built against the back boundary wall outside, and before that they lived in one third of her grandparents' ancestral home and shared a toilet with her cousin's family, and before that, before my mother was born, people like her grew up in villages where the women walked out into the fields early in the morning and didn't piss again until after sundown.

For this reason, my mother hates camping. Not because of the tents or the inconvenience of cooking outdoors but because of having to pee in the woods. Plumbing is one of her life's great pleasures, and therefore, because we inherit these things, it is also one of mine. I take that bath every morning and listen to the splashy sounds of my limbs arranging themselves in the warm, soapy water, and I try to enjoy it while also reminding myself of the vast distance between the me I might have been and the me I have become. *Am I me?* I ask myself. *Yes, you're still you.*

In the midst of it all, Cyrus conducts a funeral for Auntie Lavinia's neighbor Jed, the lapsed Jew who wanted to convert to Hinduism. His long battle with cancer finally lost, Jed's final wish was to find a way to honor his split faith, as he liked to call it.

The service takes place at the cremation chapel in West Babylon. Jed has no surviving relations; his wife died ten years before, and they'd never had children. It is just me, Cyrus, Auntie Lavinia, and a handful of Jed's former colleagues and students from the Rabbinical College of Long Island.

Cyrus stands up against the cheap plywood paneling. "Jed often told me his right side was Jewish and his left side was Hindu, but his whole self was a Nets fan—on that matter he had no ambivalence at all."

We laugh softly.

"What does it mean," he says, "to devote one's entire life to a faith only to discover, at the end, that this faith does not sit solidly in the body, that it has shifted like the sands on a seashore?

"Those of you who remember him from his student days know that when Jed was in rabbinical college, he was fascinated by the Urtext—the uniform text that some believe preceded all the known versions of the Hebrew Bible. Although the text is now thought not to exist, Jed carried the idea of this mythical first testament with him. Perhaps this is why he was drawn to the earliest Hindu scriptures, the Vedas. These texts, recited over centuries, written down three thousand years ago, are so unlikely they seem almost fabled. It was through the lens of the Urtext that Jed interpreted the earliest Hindu scriptures, almost as if what the biblical scholars were looking for was right there all along, if they only knew to look beyond their own traditions. I read to you now from Jed's favorite passage in the Rigveda:

> *'Who then knows whence it has arisen?*
> *Whether God's will created it, or whether He was mute;*
> *Only He who is its overseer in highest heaven knows,*
> *He only knows, or perhaps He does not know.'"*

Cyrus speaks in his lowest, softest voice, a voice that seems to contain everything that can be known and so many of the things that cannot, until we are all dabbing at the corners of our eyes.

"Did you know Jed?" I ask him later.

"He sometimes texted me in the middle of the night. He had trouble sleeping because of the chemo."

I had no idea. I still can't quite get my head around the sheer number of people Cyrus cares about. Cyrus is a circuit board, lines of connection stretching far beyond what I can see. There are the people he knows or has met in real life, like Jed or Mrs. Butterfield, and then there are the others, the millions who are having relationships with Cyrus through the platform, asking him questions about how they should live their lives, receiving small coded versions of him on their phones every day. I have done this. I have expanded Cyrus's reach to encompass everyone, and people everywhere are now getting a little piece of him, and he is expanding, like a cloud, covering the whole world. In the meantime, he is also my husband. And he is also my boss. How have I managed to make it all so complicated, and how have I managed to put myself on the margins of this story? There is no way to answer that, at least not without questioning the very bones of our life, and so I don't, I just let Cyrus's presence wash through me, and that, as ever, is enough.

In the spring, Cyrus, Jules, and I return to the Valley. This time it's more of a victory lap. I measure it by the number of drinks people offer us when we arrive at their offices. "Can I get you anything at all? Coffee? Coconut water? Birch water? Rosemary water? Pink coconut water?"

There are no vacant faces this time, no people dipping their heads and reading text messages under the table. And no one cares about our politics. They just pay full attention to Cyrus, who tells story after story of the platform, the Viking death rituals, the Wonder Woman prayer circle in Madras, the Bhagavad Gita recital group in Dallas, the little cluster of communities that have formed around the worship of living people, Greta Thunberg, Margaret Atwood, Malala Yousafzai. What would Greta/Margaret/Malala do? These are the things the WAIs ask themselves. They do not want to try the latest skin-firming cream, they are not interested in celebrity gossip. They do not bow to influencers because we don't give them any. They are the curious, the wondering and wandering, hungering for connection, searching for meaning. They are the best of us. And we give them a place to be those people.

The next few days are a catwalk. Woke VC shows off a diverse portfolio. Another firm claims to donate most of its profits to charity. Another has a founder who personally put millions into George Soros's fund. They all pretend to be the good guy.

Cyrus makes everyone beg to be on our board. They would do pretty much anything. It's beyond social media. We are creating a new category. The growth curve is only going up. There are more people on the platform, more people spending more time and recommending us to their friends and using us as their way of interacting with their screens. We are creeping onto their home pages and staying there. We are commanding their interest. We are educating and ennobling them.

"You're a visionary," the investors say to Cyrus. "You're a dreamer. You're a hero. You're just what the world needs."

In our hotel suite, we consider our options. "I would like another woman on the board," I say. "I'm tired of being the only one."

"Absolutely." Cyrus nods. "Let's solve for that." We put all the names of possible female board members on a table. "We could also get some non-investor directors to join. In fact, we probably should."

Cyrus and Jules bandy a few names back and forth.

"I want to add one more person to the mix," Cyrus says. "Craig Boize."

"Crazy Craig? Craig of the trampoline?" I ask.

"Craig of the call to mass murder?" Jules echoes.

"They're all the same," Cyrus says. "Craig is just more honest about it than the rest of them."

We argue about Craig for a few minutes. Jules and I tell Cyrus he can't possibly be serious. Cyrus tells us that Craig has the biggest fund, and that he shares his vision for the future of WAI.

"Which is what, exactly?" I ask.

"We want WAI to reach every single household in the world."

I roll my eyes. "That's preposterous."

"I'm with her," Jules says. "What are you smoking, Cy?"

"My feedback to you two"—he looks at each of us in turn, and we shrivel up a little inside—"is that we lack ambition. If we're really going to change the world, we need to reach the world in the first place."

"Did you borrow that line from Crazy Craig?" I say.

"Please stop calling him that. You might end up saying it out loud."

"I just said it out loud. Crazy Craig."

"I mean in front of him."

Jules puts a hand on my arm, and I know it's time to stop.

"You've made up your mind, haven't you?" I say.

Cyrus nods. "I believe this is in the best interest of the company."

"So you were just pretending to ask our opinion?" Jules says, a notch of hurt in his voice.

Cyrus has made up his mind. I don't know why I'm surprised—I should've seen it coming. Cyrus has always believed that tech companies are evil, that the whole system is rotten. But with WAI, he's changing things from the inside, giving people a reason to be better. The only way to truly make it worthwhile is if it takes over all the badness, if it overwhelms the greed and the inequality with the sheer force of its popularity. He needs it to grow, and if he's going to make it grow all the way to the stars, he needs Craig. He has found someone whose hunger matches his own. We of the small appetites have no choice but to step aside.

We take Craig up on his offer to meet before we sign the documents. The trampoline has been replaced by a swimming pool. "No way," I say to Cyrus, so he leads us down a side entrance, and about twelve turns down a polished concrete corridor later, we're in the boardroom, where Craig is waiting, looking blissfully normal in a polo shirt and shorts.

With a flourish, he offers Cyrus the head of the table, which Cyrus accepts. A young woman arrives with a tray and places steaming mugs in front of us. "Ginger turmeric toddy," Craig says. "Always makes me feel invincible." He looks meaningfully at me, which I take to mean he knows that my people invented turmeric and his knowing that makes him super enlightened.

I take a sip. It's as if someone took my mother's biryani, removed the salt, and added boiling water. "Mmm," I say, dribbling some of it back into the mug.

"I want to hear stories," Craig announces. "Make me feel good, Cyrus."

Cyrus is prepared for this request, and he knows how to play to his audience. "Well, we created rituals for seven hundred funerals yesterday," he says. "Thousands of weddings, birthdays, initiations, baptisms, commitment ceremonies, graduations. Every part of the human life cycle is touched by WAI."

"Sayonara, church," Craig says, waving his hand and bidding farewell to millennia of organized religion.

I look over at Jules, whose face is unreadable. I tell myself I'm the Miss Manhattan statue at the Brooklyn Museum so I don't give away a single one of my thoughts.

"I think you'll like this one in particular, Craig: the CEO of Einstein X, the driverless car company that's about to IPO—"

"Jeremy Rubenfeld-Castro?"

"He's a WAIser, has been from the start, and he says that next week, when they debut at the stock market, they're not going to ring the bell. They're going to perform a Jupiterian ritual instead." Cyrus puts his hands together but slightly apart, as if he's holding a ball, and he moves it around and says something about prosperity, kabbalah, and planetary alignment.

Craig stands up. "Goddammit, Jones," he says, clapping. "Right there on the floor of the NASDAQ! That is going to be all over the news. Motherfucker."

"It's all due to Asha's incredible algorithm," Cyrus says.

I really, really don't want to take credit for the Jupiterian ritual of Make Me a Lot of Fucking Money. "No, no," I say. "It was a team effort."

"Asha's been working around the clock to deliver the subscriptions platform, and that's what brought you to the table."

Jules tells Craig the good news. Subscription revenue is holding steady. New users join the platform every day, and they are as loyal as ever. "Sticky" is what we call it, as if the thing we should be most proud of is having the pulling power of flypaper.

"But it's not all roses, is it, Jules?" I signal to Jules, and Jules gives Craig the bad news. "The way we designed the subscriptions was a PR coup," he says. "People are talking about Cyrus as the people's CEO, the guy who makes money while also maintaining his integrity. But giving people the choice to pay what they want creates some uncertainty going forward. It's difficult for Gaby to build a financial model off of that. And there's a downward trend." Jules pulls up a spreadsheet showing that the average contribution from each member of the platform is going down.

"You need to find an alternative revenue stream," Craig says.

Cyrus shifts in his seat at the head of the table. "I don't see why we need to take any immediate action."

"If the trend continues," Jules says, "we'll be down year on year."

"We can't have that," Craig says. He sits up and puts his elbows on the table. "We need to acquire a company that gives us strategic leverage while providing us with potential revenue we can use in case your WAIs old men decide they need to put money aside for their funeral plots instead of their eulogies."

He says that whole sentence without taking a breath. Maybe he does have some kind of superpower, I think for a minute. Maybe Cyrus saw something that Jules and I missed. Then his assistant comes in with bowls of what she calls beet polpetti, and when I take a bite, they are indeed little balls made of beets that taste exactly like beets.

"Look," Craig says, his teeth stained purple, "a lot of folks are going to approach you now that you're the flavor of the month. They're going to sit on your board and suck up to you and not tell you that the ship is about to sink, or that you're two mistakes away from being Keanu Reeves in *Speed 2*, you know, the one where the cruise ship is about to crash into the shore? I'm a value add because I won't bullshit you. What you see is what you get. You're gonna have to grow, open new offices, fund a global expansion, and buy up a lot of assets. And you definitely want someone on your team who's willing to go all the way with you, not just sit back and watch the dollar signs but actually jump in there and get the work done."

Jules and Cyrus are nodding. I guess Cyrus understands Keanu now.

We go through the rest of Gaby's slides, and then we wrap up. Craig tells us we should come up with a list of possible companies to acquire ("You find 'em, I'll bring 'em home," he announces, suddenly Texan), and then we call it a day, but not before Craig attempts to entice us to base-jump out of his helicopter, an invitation we politely decline.

▼

We're in our hotel suite with a tray of room service between us, and Cyrus is listing the companies he wants to buy as if he's writing a last-minute letter to Santa.

"We could buy Headzen," Cyrus says. "Or Meditate.io."

"We can't afford them."

"It's important that we think big. Craig has deep pockets."

Jules suggests the dog collar that sends a message when a pet owner has died.

"What's that? Never heard of it."

"It's called HereBoy. Did you know that over fifty percent of solo pet owners who die in their homes get eaten by their pets?"

I gasp. "What the fuck?"

"It's the dark side of domesticated animals."

"Cats or dogs?"

"Equally out for blood."

"Pets would be a little left-field," Cyrus says.

"But somewhere in the area of death might be a good place to start," Jules suggests.

"Death Tech," Cyrus says. "Has anyone coined that?"

I'm going to look back and regret what I'm about to say. But it's me who suggests it. "What about Marco's thing?"

"That AI app that kills you online?" Jules asks.

"It doesn't kill you because you're already dead. It manages your death. Turns off all your socials, informs your contacts."

"Sounds like a great idea. Is it in market?"

"I think they're a few months away."

"Still think we should buy Headzen," Cyrus repeats. It grates on him, I know, that the CEO of Headzen is not himself as into meditation as one might expect. In fact, he told Cyrus jokingly at a CEO mixer last month that he never really cared for all that mindfulness crap, but boy, did it light up people's phones.

"It's a lot of extra work," Jules reminds us. "Buying someone out, all the legals. And then you have to integrate them into your team. It can take months, and even then it's rough going."

"I don't mind," Cyrus says. "Sounds like fun."

"Just buy someone who uses React Native," I say. "Oh, and check their bathrooms to make sure they don't force their female staff to pump milk in them."

"Right," Jules says, pretending to make a list. "'Fun-loving CEO seeks small to medium company with a focus on arcane rituals to merge with his already impressive portfolio. Must speak Native and treat women with a modicum of respect. Accepting applications.'" He starts singing a tune from a musical called *Once Upon a Mattress*. "I did it in high school," he announces.

> *We have an opening for a business*
> *A beautiful bonafide business.*

He says in the original, it's princess. *A beautiful bonafide princess.* Cyrus and I throw pillows at him and order him out of our room. "I'm going for a swim. See you later fellow assassins!"

We're getting ready for bed when Cyrus's phone rings. It's Craig. Cyrus puts him on speakerphone.

"You gotta come meet me," Craig says. "I'm at this party, you'd love it."

I make a slicing gesture across my neck.

"Asha and I were just about to retire," Cyrus says.

"Retire? What're you, ninety years old?"

"Where is the party?"

"Not far. My driver will pick you up."

I'm shaking my head, but Cyrus is looking at his phone. "Maybe just for an hour? Asha, what do you think?"

"Um, I'd rather not, to be honest. Why don't you go ahead without me."

"Asha, seriously, these people are great, you're going to love them. C'mon, let me show you some Californian hospitality," Craig insists. I'm not sure I want to find out what this entails, but Cyrus has already said yes.

"My car's on the way," Craig says. "See you guys soon."

"Californian hospitality apparently means dragging your friends to the middle of nowhere in the middle of the night," I whine. We've been in Craig's car for nearly an hour. The tiny tide of energy I rode in the first moments of getting dressed is long gone, and I am regretting not putting my foot down. "Why couldn't you just go by yourself?"

"Because we roll together."

The car goes up yet another winding road, but this time it stops at a gate, where a man with a big head leans in, checks the driver's name, and waves us through.

The house is large and flat and wrapped in glass. We walk through room after room of brown, low-slung furniture, tables of food, and a row of television screens turned vertically so that they resemble paintings, except they are video installations. I watch fifteen seconds of multicolored lines moving up and down.

In the last room, like a pot of gold at the end of a rainbow, there are clusters of bodies melting into other bodies. They are mostly naked, and without needing to stare, I can tell they have all been born with perfect proportions, and whatever God neglected to give them has been provided by working out and eating whole foods. All the kissing and fondling is very quiet, so we have to whisper.

"How the fuck are we supposed to find Craig?"

We back out of the room and into a courtyard fringed by small gecko-green trees.

Craig appears at Cyrus's shoulder. "Who says all the fun happens in New York?" He smiles, waving his arm as if he's conjured it all himself just to prove an East Coast/West Coast point. "Let's get you two a drink." He disappears for a few minutes, during which I beg Cyrus to leave, and then he comes back with a pair of martini glasses. No way I'm drinking this. It's probably spiked to make me want to lasso my bra around one of the small bronzes in the hallway.

"So do you guys hand out condoms at the door?" I ask brightly, as if I've ever seen thirty people naked at the same time before.

"Oh, there's none of that," Craig says. "The cuddle puddle is a strictly non-penetrative ritual." He looks to Cyrus for approval. Cyrus, who has finished his drink, appears not to have heard him.

"Want to microdose?" Craig asks, removing a small vial from his pocket. I shake my head, but Cyrus doesn't, so Craig passes him the vial and Cyrus casually tips the contents into his mouth. Cyrus and I have never done drugs and never really talked about doing drugs, and I wonder if there was a time before he met me when things like Molly were regularly on the menu.

Within a few minutes we've lost Craig's interest, and he has disappeared into the crowd. "Let's wander," Cyrus says, taking my hand. The house is shaped in a giant U, and in the middle of the U is a swimming pool. More cuddle puddlers are in the pool, their bodies bobbing gently in the water.

Again I tell Cyrus I want to go home. Cyrus suggests we take one more round of the house and then leave. I am offered another drink; this time I accept it and down it quickly. Cyrus strikes up a conversation with a man who introduces himself as Quinn and tells us he's been a member of WAI since the first month it launched. "When my wife had a late miscarriage," Quinn says, "your site was the only thing that helped us. No one knows what to do with a tiny body." Cyrus is unruffled by the abruptly personal account; he's used to people telling him things, secrets they'd never reveal to anyone else. And I know he's taking mental notes which he will dispense later. *What are we doing to protect people who lose pregnancies? And who was it again, ah, that's right, Saint Catherine of Siena, the patron saint of fertility. Must make a note of that for later. And saints in general. Have we taken a close enough look at saints?* The two of them wander off together, Cyrus's hand on the man's back.

A woman emerges from the pool. Her body is long and entirely unaffected by the laws of gravity. I stare and stare as she towels off. She gets a drink from the pool bar and sits down beside me. She's just as improbable up close. "I'm Eleanor," she says. "You're wondering where I came from, aren't you?" She pauses, smiling. "You were thinking escort agency."

"I totally wasn't," I lie, trying not to rest my gaze on her breasts, or her ass, or any other part of her that she has neglected to cover up but probably should have. "Why, do you get that a lot?"

"I didn't mean to sound defensive—it's a bit of a fishbowl in here."

"So what are you?"

"An associate at Pemberton."

"*The* Pemberton?"

"The very one."

"God gave you brains too?"

"It's not fair, I know."

"What about all the other women?"

She looks around. Points to a couple with their arms entwined. "She's a partner at Believe Capital. That one over there is a corporate lawyer, and my friend Adrienne—in the swimming pool with the bald guy—just raised seven million in Series A funding."

"You guys do this a lot?"

"My third time. I've gone to other things, similar vibe. I find the small talk at receptions painful. At least we all know why we're here."

"Why are we here?"

"To put our shoulders to the wheel of the patriarchy."

"But seriously. Why? Did someone tell you you had to come?"

"It's not that obvious," she says. "They just invite you, and if you don't come, it's like everyone else is in on a joke and you're left out. Then the next time, you hear them whispering around the coffee bar, and maybe they give you one more shot. And see if you show up."

"That's disgusting."

"But we're disrupting everything," she says with an exaggerated laugh. "Surely we can disrupt the mono-normative sexual rules we inherited from the Victorians?"

I nod. "Totally. Tech is here to set us free from all that." Eleanor's drink is finished. She glides away, and I'm left thinking I probably imagined her.

Someone taps my shoulder. It's Cyrus. "Hey, I've been looking for you."

"Oh, hello." My voice quivers.

Cyrus kneels down beside me. "I'm really, really sorry," he says.

I start to cry. "Whatever."

"We shouldn't have come. I will talk to Craig, okay?"

"Okay."

"I was . . . I was curious."

"Curiosity killed the Cyrus," I say, sniffing.

He cups my cheek, brushes my tears away. "Look, we have three options here. We can go upstairs, find an empty room, and have sex like everyone else. Or we can keep watching to see if there's anything else on the agenda, like maybe a movie or a late-night buffet. Or we can go home."

"But the cuddle puddle is strictly non-penetrative," I say.

"There are other things we could do."

"Do you wish you had more sex before you married me?"

"No."

"How much sex have you had?" I ask, wondering why we have never had this conversation.

"I would say a medium amount."

"Me too," I offer, even though he hasn't asked. "Medium to small. Although I guess it's all relative. What do you mean by medium? Under ten or under a hundred?"

"Under ten," he says.

I'm relieved. We link arms, pick our way back through the house, passing another bar, a vinyl library, a man stirring a giant vat of paella, a circle of people chanting om, and finally, through the double doors in front. Our cab is here; we get in and fall asleep on opposite corners of the backseat in the hour it takes to return to our hotel.

Thirteen

BFFS

On the surface, Marco is a normal person. He can make eye contact and have perfectly ordinary conversations about things that other people might be interested in, say, the weather, or how lovely it is that we have our own nondairy mixologist called Mylkist at the cafeteria now. But a few sentences in—and I check this multiple times to make sure I'm not just being judgmental—Marco will always steer the conversation in such a way that he ends up telling a story about someone, or something, or all of humanity, dying. At times the transition is so subtle that you wouldn't even notice it, but occasionally, it's obvious that while he's commenting on your shoes, he's really thinking death/apocalypse/end times thoughts. Let's say the conversation starts like this in the stairwell:

"Hey, Asha, how's it going?"

"Going great, how're you?"

"I was just heading to the seminar on work-hobby balance."

"Work-hobby?"

"Yeah, you know, if you love something enough, it doesn't even feel like work, so you call it a hobby, but really, it's taking all your time and you're totally obsessed."

"I know what that's like. Anyway, see you around—"

"The thing is, we talk about people working themselves to death, but we never say 'He hobbied himself to death.' Still, there must be a lot of people who do that."

"Oh, okay."

"My uncle Gennaro had this thing for gardening, I mean, he just loved all kinds of exotic plants, and so he set up a business selling seeds online."

"And did he? Work himself to—? I'm sorry."

"No, heart attack. But everyone said he worked too hard. I think he hobbied too hard."

Or this:

"If a pandemic wiped out ten percent of the world's population, as a society, would we become inured to the loss of our loved ones? Would we just care about them less?"

Or this:

"I'm setting up a probabilities algorithm for all the ways humans are going to get wiped out, and I think climate change is definitely winning. Closely followed by antibiotic resistance."

Cyrus does not see a problem because Cyrus and Marco have become instant best friends.

They're together all the time, eating lunch at the café, hanging out on the rooftop among Rory's Popeye plants, booking out the meeting rooms so they can close the door and hatch secret plans. Gaby and Jules are tasked with getting under the hood of Obit.ly's financials.

Ren and I look at the tech. Since Marco is always around, it's difficult to get Cyrus on his own. He gives off a kind of hummingbird vibe, flapping wildly while appearing to stand perfectly still.

I try to warn Cyrus. "I think Marco is unstable."

"What's wrong with him?"

"He can't stop talking about the end of the world."

"I thought that's why you liked this place. Because we're preparing for the afterworld?" He circles his arm around to indicate the rest of Utopia and to remind me that I'm just as weird as Marco.

As far as I'm concerned, I am doing a great job of adjusting to the new situation. Craig has joined the board, and I've stopped trying to make the big decisions. Cyrus has a vision, and the WAIs are so devoted to him, they'll follow him anywhere. I'm starting to think about other things—a mentorship program I might kick off to help young women get ahead in tech. I might even ask Cyrus if I can spend some of our WAI money on building a lab for the Empathy Module. Jules is encouraging me to stay in stealth mode. "Just let him do what he does best—talk to the brethren—and the rest of us can enjoy being mortal," he says. Jules is also busy keeping the team steady; the talk of acquisition has made everyone a little jittery.

Jules's advice is all well and good, except I have to go home with Cyrus every night, and lately, the office Cyrus and home Cyrus are starting to sound like the same person. I find myself organizing more and more of his life, even though he now has two assistants. I answer the door when the dry cleaner comes to take his shirts, and I run through his calendar to make sure Eve is scheduling his meetings in the right order, and Jules and I coordinate when to give him little bits of bad news, like if someone quits or posts a Glassdoor review about how Cyrus is a controlling micromanager with a God complex.

We argue about money. Cyrus deals with having money by spending it fast, before it can accumulate. He sends checks with multiple zeros to multiple charities and monasteries and GoFundMe campaigns. He clicks on every Indiegogo film, travel pillow, and illustrated book project. He funds a school in Bangladesh. He pays a company called Green Taxi a huge amount of money to send him the same driver, a man called Daniyal, to take him anywhere beyond a five-block radius because he has developed an allergy to the subway.

The truth is, there isn't enough money that we can't burn through it. At this point, the millions are still imaginary. I want to pay off our mortgage and start a college fund for Gitanjali and buy my parents the kind of end-of-life insurance that means they will never have to worry about paying their medical bills when they get really old. Cyrus wants to send our money to Bangladesh, and I want to buy end-of-life insurance, and this of course means he's a hero and I am a Grinch.

Still, we have our moments. I see the person I married inside the person in front of me. In some ways the new confidence, the swagger, is powerful. I love what we've created together, this world of people who suddenly find themselves with a center, something they never imagined they'd have—a social network that goes beyond selfies and humblebrags. We are woven together by these strangers who appear at once distant and intimate.

In the meantime, Cyrus has set up a giant easel in his office, and right now he is holding a palette of paints and a little knife with a triangular point. A landscape is starting to come into view, a blur of blues, grays, and whites. Along with painting, Cyrus has taken up capoeira. A large man named Gil comes to our apartment every morning to yell energetic things at Cyrus.

"It's far healthier to confront death than to avoid it," Cyrus says. "Ancient civilizations were obsessed with death."

"Our civilization is obsessed with never having to think about death," I say.

"The Anthropocene is corrupt."

"I'm concerned about bringing Marco on board."

"We're developing a great working relationship," Cyrus says, scooping up a dollop of paint from his palette. "Marco respects what we're doing, and he agrees that we could bring the two companies together for everyone's benefit."

I'm not sure what he means, exactly. "Crazy Craig said to buy a company, not merge with a company."

Cyrus puts his little knife down gently. "No decisions have been made."

"You say that, but I recognize the tone in your voice, the one where you've already made up your mind and come up with a million arguments for doing something your way, and by the time you're done, the rest of us have no choice but to fall in line."

"It's a merger, Asha, not a war."

"See, you said it. Merger, not acquisition."

"Craig wants us to find new revenue streams, so that's why we are buying Obit.ly. It was your idea. Integrating the tech into our platform is just the natural extension of that. There's no grand conspiracy, darling."

"Dammit, Cy, don't call me darling."

He puts down his paint, reaches over, and kisses me.

"I don't think this is a good idea," I mumble. "Glass wall and all that."

He pulls me tighter against him, and the smell of turpentine rises from his body. "I hear you," he says. "I really do." He leans down and looks into my eyes. "You're so beautiful. Is that a new eyeliner you're wearing?"

It is, and I hate that he notices everything. I kiss him back, my lips softening. Maybe he's right, maybe Marco's idea will flourish, and maybe Marco himself will be neutralized by the force of Cyrus. God knows the rest of us have been.

Marco is presenting Obit.ly to our board. "I've bootstrapped the company myself. I'm the only shareholder, and I've built all the tech."

Craig has dialed in. "No big dev team around you, huh?" he asks. His face is enormous on the screen, and I feel like the question is directed at me, because Ren and I have fifty-two devs on our team, and Craig has been asking annoying questions about our cost base.

Marco keeps smoothing the hair on the sides of his head like he's in a high school production of *Grease*. "Just me. I'm one hundred percent committed to my mission."

"What is your mission, just so we're clear?" I ask.

"I want to bring the benefits of the digital age—transparency, efficiency, ease of use—to our online deaths." When he puts it that way, it doesn't sound so crazy.

"You're ready to launch in twelve weeks, right, Marco?" Cyrus prompts.

"That's right, Captain." Captain is Marco's new nickname for Cyrus. This does not irritate me at all.

"There are some amazing synergies between the two companies," Cyrus says. "Death rites are our most requested rituals, making up twenty-three percent of all queries on the platform."

"What's Obit.ly actually going to do?" Rupert asks.

"You give us permission to access all your social media accounts in the event of your death," Marco says. "We close things down, write to all your friends, inform everyone about your final wishes. It's like a will, except for your online presence."

"What's the market size?"

"Well, so far there's no competition—no one else is trying to do this. But dead people are going to outnumber living people on social media within ten years. You obviously don't want to give anyone access to your accounts while you're still alive, but once you're dead, there needs to be a way to put an end to your online presence."

"I don't know," Rupert says. "You're dealing with a lot of sensitive information."

Craig loves it. "This is awesome," he says. "I get so freaked out when a dead person suddenly appears in my feed."

"Have you done a risk assessment?" Rupert asks. "What's the tech behind the security?"

"Asha's in charge of that," Cyrus says. He turns to me.

"Ren and I will run all the stress tests," I say. Then I turn to Marco, "Tell us what inspired you to start Obit.ly," hoping that he'll tell some kind of creepy story about keeping his mother's corpse locked in the attic.

Marco looks down at his shoes and then up at the ceiling. "My mother passed away when I was very young. And my family—my father and my grandparents—thought it would be better not to tell me the truth until I was older. I can understand where they were coming from—it wasn't a pleasant story—she took her own life. But I've always been haunted by those years of secrecy." He clears his throat. I can't help feeling a surge of sympathy for Marco; it's impossible not to be moved by a grown man standing up in front of a roomful of strangers to talk about his mother's death.

Craig is shaking his head. "This is mind-blowing."

"And there's more," Marco says. "I think the world is going to have a different relationship to death in the next ten, twenty years."

I perk up. Here comes the crazy.

"Climate change is going to create events that wipe out large portions of the human population. Pandemics, natural disasters. Our sense of safety is going to collapse around us. Obit.ly is about confronting that inevitability, about using tech to help us prepare for what's to come."

I look around the room to see where this last statement has landed. Rupert looks a little worried, but no more than usual. Craig is practically drooling with excitement.

"Thank you, Marco," Cyrus says. "That was illuminating." He shepherds Marco out of the room, telling him, "We're going to talk and get back to you later today." After closing the door with a swoosh, he says to us, "Well, I think you can all see that Marco's product is revolutionary. He's built it all himself, the team is basically just him and a CFO and a marketing person. They've taken almost no funding to date and are ready to beta-launch in twelve weeks."

"How much does he want?" Craig's voice is faint and breathy, and the screen has gone blank.

"Craig?" Jules says. "Is your video working?"

"Yeah, but I've switched to my treadmill desk, so I'm gonna keep it to voice for now," he says, panting. "How much does the guy want?"

"He wants ten, but I can probably get him down to six or seven maybe a mix of cash and shares."

"I don't think we should pay more than five," Rupert says. "He hasn't even got off the starting block. No users, no data."

"But the tech is solid. Asha, did you want to speak to that?"

"It's good," I admit. "Relatively bug-free, although I'd want to stress-test it a little because there's so much sensitive information going through the system."

"So there are no major problems with the tech," Cyrus underlines.

"That was kind of a crazy story about his mom, wasn't it?" I say.

Craig tells everyone it's great when founders are motivated by personal events.

"In this case, personal tragedy," I add. "You don't think that's a red flag?"

"Asha's right," Gaby says. "Maybe we need to get a little more confidence around Marco, whether he can build a leadership team as the company scales."

Cyrus tells everyone he's going to recommend a full integration with WAI.

The screen blinks and Craig appears, a towel around his neck. The San Fernando Valley is a blur behind him. "I love it," he says. "It's just what we need, it's taking things to the next level."

"What do you mean by full integration?" Rupert asks.

"We leverage our customer base to get people to sign up for Obit.ly's service. It's the same sign-in, same platform, just an add-on to what we offer," Cyrus explains.

"Only for when you're dead," Craig says. "It's genius."

Cyrus tells everyone it was my idea. "It wasn't even on my radar. Being in the same space means the integration can be quicker. We'll have to build up the team, of course. I think I probably need to spend a couple million in year one. Gaby has modeled it."

"I don't know," Rupert counters. "I'm imagining all the ways this can go wrong, and there are many."

I can see Cyrus getting irritated. "Such as?"

"Well, for one thing, the system mistaking a very much alive person for a dead one. Imagine waking up to your own obituary."

Cyrus turns to me. "Asha, what are the chances of that happening?"

I want to say yes, there is a chance of that happening, not least because it's the first time Rupert has ever agreed with me. But I can't lie. "Not high," I say. "There's a verification process that's pretty watertight. I do have other concerns, though—"

"Let's move on, and we can address those in diligence," Cyrus interrupts.

"I want to hear what Asha's concerns are," Rupert says.

Cyrus sits up in his chair, tents his fingers, and gets a scary Zen face on.

"It's okay," I say. "I don't want to waste too much time if there's consensus on this."

"This is our go/no-go moment," Rupert says. "So let's put everything on the table."

I blurt it out. "I think Marco is crazy."

Craig's screen pixelates, then comes back into focus. "You're all crazy," he says, laughing. "That's why I gave you so much fucking money."

Gaby clears his throat. "I think what Asha's trying to say here is that it's been a little difficult to disambiguate Marco's passion from what can sometimes appear to be mania."

"CEOs are all the same," Craig says. "Rupert, you've met your share of loonies, haven't you?"

Rupert is on the fence, I can tell. He has the same gnawing feeling in the pit of his stomach, and he wants to back me up. But I also know that in the VC jungle, Rupert is a zebra and Craig is a lion. Even if he has reservations, he's going to defer to the big cat. "I sure have," he says. "You founders are pretty much all the same."

"If you're not an assassin, you can't do your job. So unless there's anything else, Asha, I say we put our weight behind Cyrus."

I should stop here, but I can't. I address myself to Cyrus. "We are walking into a minefield here, and I really don't think you've weighed the risks."

"I've done my homework, Asha."

"I'm sorry, Cy, but I don't think you have." I turn to the others. "None of you mind that Marco is a potential hazard?"

"No, we don't mind, Asha," Craig says, as if he's just added a lemon to his voice. "In fact, it's what I want in my CEOs. I want madness, I want ambition, I want fuck-itness. I told you when we first met—were you even listening?—that I want you guys to KILL EVERYONE." He's rubbing his palm against his forehead, and then suddenly, his video feed goes dark. "I gotta go," he says. "I need a gong bath. Let's just vote."

"All in favor of merging Obit.ly onto the WAI platform, raise your hand," Cyrus says. Cyrus, Rupert, and Jules all raise their hands.

"I'm in," Craig says.

"All against?"

Gaby and I raise our hands.

Cyrus instructs Eve to take note of the vote. "The motion passes four to two."

When the meeting ends, Cyrus is out of there in an instant. I figure he's going to go upstairs, blow off some steam, and then read me the riot act later. I find Destiny and ask her what the hell a gong bath is.

"You've never heard of one?" She laughs. "You lie down in a room and someone plays gongs for you so you can relax."

"You're kidding me."

"Not a joke. A real thing that people do. To whom do you owe the pleasure of this revelation?"

I tell her about Craig, about Obit.ly and Marco.

"Oh, honey," she soothes. "I see a bruise forming on the left side of your face. Did you get hit by a swinging dick?"

"Not funny."

"Look, I agree with you—Marco's totally insane. But he's a lot like Cyrus. Single-minded determination. You'd be smart to bring him on board."

"I'm worried he'll put something volatile into the code and we won't know until it's too late."

"I don't think he'll get past you, will he?"

She's right. I can take Marco. "Probably not." I turn to her. "But I have a bad feeling. Anyway, enough about me—you ready to hit the road?"

"Almost. I can't believe it's actually happening."

Destiny and Manishala are leaving next week to sell Consentify to school districts around the country. It was Manishala's idea to get the app approved by school boards and sex education teachers before launching to the wider public.

"Those Bible Belters are going to love me," she says. "Wait till I tell them I used to be a stripper."

I can always count on her to cheer me up. "I miss you, girl."

"With all those enormous egos around? Aren't you too busy trying to find an air pocket?"

Jules and I ignore Cyrus's vanishing act until the third day. On the third day, we start to worry. Should we call the police? What would we say? No, he hasn't been home. No, he hasn't replied to any of our calls or messages. No, he hasn't logged in to his email. He also hasn't taken any money out of our bank account, but that doesn't surprise me or Jules because we both know Cyrus can subsist on very little.

I'm surprised he hasn't been spotted by one of the WAIs, but I've kept tabs on the platform and all our socials, and no one has speculated on his absence, even though Jules had to front a video saying that Cyrus was taking a break from the WAICast but would be back soon.

Jules, Destiny, and I are at the diner. "He's totally fine," I announce. "I made him mad, and now he's licking his wounds."

Jules is more worried than I am. "I thought he would at least reply to my email."

"He's not checking his email," I tell him. "I've got access to the system."

"Doesn't he have a Gmail account?"

"I hacked it on day one. Trust me, he's not checking."

Destiny suggests we go to a movie.

"Why would we go to a movie?" Jules asks.

"Because that way, for two hours, we can't check on Cyrus."

My phone rings. It's my sister. I don't answer.

After the movie, which exits my brain immediately, we make our way to a small bar with a blue awning. AGAVERIA, it says on the door. It's four p.m. and I have a shitload of work to do, but Destiny and I decide to get drunk. It turns out Agaveria is a tequila bar. I don't think I've had tequila more than a few times, but other than the fact that it burns my throat on the way down, I don't have anything against it. Soon Destiny and I are sprawled on a sofa in the back, and Jules is plying us with water. He calls Gaby, and Gaby turns up in a taxi, and we all pile in and return to the office.

By the time I turn my phone back on, it's dark. I've had three hours in the sleep pod and a vitamin drip courtesy of Rory, and I'm feeling great. There are six missed calls from my sister, so I call her back.

"He's here," she says. She exhales loudly and creates a huge static cloud in my ear, which makes me suspect I'm still a little drunk.

Even though I've been searching for the whereabouts of only one person over the last three days, I say, "Who?"

"Your errant husband." She sighs. "Who else would turn up in tears and crawl into Ammoo's lap like a teacup pig?"

"We had a fight," I say. "Did he tell you?"

"He hasn't said a word to me. He just showed up at the house, Ammoo fed him, and he's been hiding in the basement ever since."

"He's probably meditating," I say. "Or sticking pins into an Asha doll."

"I've done that—it doesn't work."

"Why didn't you call sooner?"

"Bitch, I've been calling you all day. Ammoo wouldn't let me before."

I'm going to have to rescue my husband as if he's an alcoholic on a bender, except instead of being in a dive bar, he's with my parents, and I am the one who's drunk. "I'll be there as soon as I can."

I could take a cab, but I don't want to be trapped with someone else's sad breath, so I start walking to Penn Station.

The LIRR seats always stick to my thighs, and today is no different. Fluorescent lights, and the announcer whose accent I can only describe as Annoyed Conductor, all reminding me of the hundreds of times I've gone home before, the warmth and the feeling of slight dread and the anticipation of food, trying to shadowbox all the questions my mother will ask.

Mira's car is at the Merrick station. I climb in the back and give Gitanjali a kiss on the forehead. "How's the baby?" I ask.

"She sleeps all day and screams all night, so, the same. Oh, do you mean your baby? Well, I heard him moving around downstairs, so at least we know he's still alive."

After I've gazed at my niece's face for long enough to make me feel human again, I squeeze through and jump into the front seat. "Good. I don't want to enter a murder scene." Then I think, *Would Cyrus do it, would he off himself?* Should I have that fear somewhere in the back of my mind whenever I disagree with him? More things to worry about.

Mira is about to start the car but then pauses to look over at me. "I want to tell you something."

"You want to stop covering your beautiful head."

"No. I want to tell you that the only way I can poop right now is to stick my thumb into my vagina and push it out."

"Why, why the fuck would you tell me that?" I press a button and the window rolls down. "That is the worst thing I have ever heard."

"Not so loud, you'll set off Gitanjali."

"Then don't make it Halloween in here. Goddammit, now I'm imagining it."

"I've been awake for eight thousand hours. I smell like yogurt. I weigh two hundred pounds. And even though my tits are fabulous, I can't let Ahmed anywhere near them because if he even looks at me that way, I want to murder him."

"I'm an asshole."

"No, you're not. You're the only person who can code that thing that is taking over the world. But you're also my sister, and if I can't shit unassisted, you have to hold that in your big brain along with everything else."

Cyprus is expecting me. Sitting with his legs crossed as if he's the Buddha.

"Everything's approved, Cyrus. We're going to buy Obit.ly. Ren and I have some great designs for the integration." I show him.

He nods.

"Can we go home now?" I ask.

Cyrus isn't done. For the next forty-five minutes, he talks at length about all the ways my outburst was destructive, and I have to admit, yes, he's right, I shouldn't have questioned his judgment in front of everyone. And then I try to say that maybe he should've given me a little more airtime when I expressed my misgivings in private, and he says yes, maybe, but the important thing is that I have an anger problem and I need to address that.

My mother calls us up for dinner, and I'm hungry, so I just say yes, that's true, I was angry, and we hug, and I say sorry about a thousand more times.

"So," Auntie Lavinia asks, "when are you two going to make us grand-parents?"

"Cyrus and I already have a baby between us, a very demanding baby who keeps us up all night."

"Means you have practice," she says.

"I think Gitanjali is enough baby for now," Mira says.

Cyrus is plowing into my mother's shrimp and okra curry. "Not a lot of white people like okra," I announce, desperate to change the subject.

"It's time you stopped calling him white people," my father says. My father hasn't had an opinion in several years, so I feel I shouldn't disagree.

After dinner, my mother leads me into the kitchen, hands me a pineapple, and says I should peel it very thinly, then go around and around and dig out its eyes and cut the whole thing into triangles. This takes me about a year and gives her time to impart some wisdom.

"Your father has his head in the clouds," she says. "Cyrus reminds me of him." She's chopping some green chilies to go with the pineapple.

"Oh, great. So I married my father. That's not a cliché."

"I always knew, even when we came here and started a family, that I was going to have to leave him to his dreaming. When you take people like that and force them to carry a job, responsibilities, they don't always react well."

"I thought Abboo loved the pharmacy."

She puts her knife down. "Every day he didn't want to go, and every night when he came home, it was my fault. He wanted to be a writer, but he could never finish his novel. So he blamed me for killing his dreams."

"I had no idea."

"That was between me and him. And see, now that he's retired, things are much better." She puts the slices of chili into a bowl and squeezes some honey over them. I thought of my father as unchanging, exactly in childhood as he is today, all of his words going into his little notebook instead of coming out of his mouth. I can't imagine anger or resentment, and I guess it must have been my mother absorbing all of that, acting like a membrane between him and the rest of us, allowing only the soft, kind version of his dreaminess to permeate.

As for Cyrus and me, I'm sure my mother is about to tell me to suck it up.

"These are the things I had to do, and I don't regret them. Marriage is an epic poem."

I'm almost done with the pineapple. It's eyeless now and waiting to be sliced.

"But you are young, and smart, and God gave you some very unique gifts. So I don't think that kind of compromise should be assumed."

I was sure, about three minutes ago, that Cyrus had achieved a permanent place in Ammoo's pantheon, but maybe not. Maybe she actually loves me more than she loves him, even though, unlike Cyrus, I've never sat at her table and asked her, at length, why she prefers *Twelfth Night* over all the other comedies. Maybe she was playing the role of his mother for my sake. My head spun with the thought.

"You think I should leave him?" I ask, finally down to my pineapple triangles.

"No, I'm not saying that." She examines the platter. "I'm just saying: 'To thine own self be true.'"

Later, on the cab ride home, Cyrus says, "I wish you wouldn't call me white people either," so I gather he's still angry about the other thing, and just as I was too tired to argue with him before, I'm too tired to say sorry again, so we go for another round or two until we

get across the bridge, and by the time we pull up to the loft, I feel like
I've aged at least a dozen years.

◥

A month later, WAI purchases Obit.ly, and Cyrus, Jules, and I all
become part owners of Marco's company. I've scoured his tech and
haven't been able to find anything that would convince the others
to back out, yet I continue to feel suspicious of Marco. I can't figure
out what his motivations are. I find it scary that he's not turned on
by money—in the end, he sold his company to us for less than we
were willing to pay for it, and that's because he hardly negotiated. He
seems genuinely, passionately committed to making sure that when
people die, all their friends will come to hear about it immediately. He
speaks in terms not of the market or the opportunity but of people's
right to know. Why are we still depending on obituaries and word
of mouth? When someone dies, everyone they ever knew should be
notified straight away.

He also talks a lot about AI. How we should use AI to allow
people to continue to live indefinitely. He is obsessed with films in
which people's brains live on in robots or in the bodies of other people. Cyrus is no longer listening to me on this subject, and I do not
have the guts to bring it up again. Fuck it. This is not on me. Then at
other times I want to shake Cyrus and tell him again and again that
Marco will ruin us. I know it in my bones—but because at this point,
not only am I afraid of Cyrus, I believe in him more than I believe in
myself—I don't say anything.

Fourteen

NOBODY WANTS TO BE MARRIED TO THE MESSIAH

Sometimes being right is actually worse than being wrong. Six months after we merge with Obit.ly, Marco ruins everything and we are done.

He and Cyrus have been working on a secret project. They hold meetings to which the rest of us are not invited. Cyrus puts black paper up on his walls and a sign on his door that says, DO NOT DISTURB— NO EXCEPTIONS, which I take to mean NO EXCEPTIONS, NOT EVEN MY WIFE. Jules and Gaby invite me over for dinner on a regular basis, and in their super-clean apartment, we speculate endlessly about what Cyrus and Marco are up to. When we ask Cyrus and Marco, they giggle like a pair of kindergarteners who have just discovered poop, and finally, when they break the news, it is too late for us to do anything: they've already convinced themselves it's a brilliant idea.

Crazy Craig is jubilant. "THIS IS GOING TO KILL EVERY-ONE," he says when he shows up at Utopia. "I knew it, I knew you two were a force, a super-fucking-natural force." He waltzes around the office hugging people and passing out cannabis-laced lollipops. All this because, to everyone's horror and Craig's utter delight, for the first time in history (drumroll, please) . . .

A dead person has sent a text message.

Yes, it's true. Marco has used the WAI code—my Empathy Module—and combined it with Obit.ly's database to get people to communicate with their loved ones from beyond the grave. Cyrus has named it AfterLight. It mimics the tone, the written diction, the vocabulary, of a person based on an entire history of texts, emails, Instagram comments, likes, memes, and retweets. It takes all of that and creates new texts and sends them as if the person were still alive.

Now, if you want your family to hear from you after you're dead, and if they want to hear from you, you can all go on as if nothing has happened. "Most people only call their parents once or twice a year anyway," Marco argues. "They've got a family WhatsApp group, they exchange all their news there. So the AI just keeps going as if the person hasn't died, the family chat stays the same. And you can postpone your grief for as long as you want. Maybe forever."

There must be some kind of law against this, I figure. At the very least, it's an idea ripped off from a TV show. I consult our lawyer, and she does a little digging, and two hours later, she calls to tell me that although it's a gray area, the thing itself is so new that the law hasn't really caught up. The people who invented messaging didn't imagine they'd have to be solving for this particular situation, so we have no legal way of handling it.

I try to get Cyrus to change his mind. "Is it possible that I'm the only one here who thinks this is a ticking time bomb?"

Cyrus looks at me and I know he's secretly calling me the girl who cried Marco is insane.

Jules has doubts too, I know he does—he and Gaby and I have gone over it all again and again—but it's like he is programmed never to disagree with Cyrus out loud.

"I agree, there are risks," Cyrus says. "I've thought about them, and I have to tell you, I believe this is the culmination of everything we dreamed of when we started this company."

"What, that dead people will speak? What does that make you, the Night King?"

Cyrus lowers his voice to a near whisper. We are in his office, and there is a song playing in the background that I can't place. "When I think of the number of times I've wished I could talk to my mom just one more time, and what that would've meant to me, I feel it's my responsibility to offer this to the WAIs."

So this is what it's been about all along. How could I have been so stupid? This whole romance with Marco is about Cyrus and his dead mother and the fact that he still has things he wants to ask her. Questions that had been left unanswered by her death, and goddammit if he isn't going to raise her from the grave and have her answer them. "This is about your mom."

"It's too late for me," Cyrus says. "But for a lot of people, it could be a lifeline."

I recognize the song. It's Mama Cass singing "Dream a Little Dream."

"I understand that this is important to you, Cyrus, but surely you can see that preventing people from grieving might also be dangerous." I turn to Jules. "Jules, come on, you can't let him do this."

Jules shakes his head. "Technology allows us to stop doing the things we no longer wish to do. Like hailing a taxi on the street or sending faxes. Nobody wants to confront death. And now we don't have to."

"I don't think death is optional."

"But it could be."

I want to bang my head against the wall.

"We have a board meeting in two weeks," Cyrus says. "I hope you'll agree that presenting a united front is the best approach."

Cyrus will not change his mind. The young man who lost his mother will not be swayed. He's going to take it to a vote, and I'm going to have to decide where I live: in peace with my husband or alone with my conscience.

I take the subway uptown to get some advice from Mira. She and Ahmed started dating in high school, got married young, waited for a long time for Gitanjali, and through it all, I still see them laughing at each other's jokes.

"Having a kid is like throwing a hand grenade into your marriage. So we are not exactly loved up at the moment. But the small things make a huge difference—last week I actually slept through the night and when I woke up and I was like, 'Damn, I am so nice when I'm not tired.'"

I feel guilty. I've been so obsessed with my own life that I've hardly stepped in to help her. "I'm a shitty sister," I say. "It's just . . . the whole thing is getting away from me." I tell her about Cyrus and Marco, how I feel like everyone is ganging up against me.

Mira sighs. She slides her hand across the table and squeezes my shoulder. "Do you think Stevie Wonder changed diapers?" she says.

"Why do all your stories involve poo?"

"Because they do. He has nine children. Do you think he changed their diapers? Do you think he stayed up at night and rocked them to sleep? Do you think he walked them to school in the morning and went to the parent-teacher meetings and cleaned out the crusty bottom of their backpacks?"

"No."

"And would you want him to?"

I can't pretend anymore that I don't know what she's talking about. "No."

"No. You would want him to write 'My Cherie Amour.'"

The world would be a dark place without that song. "Yes."

"Someone else had to do all of that."

"You're telling me that all greatness happens on the backs of other people."

"Yes, that is what I am telling you."

"This is the worst thing I've ever heard." It's not news to me, but it's the first time someone has spelled it out this way, like she's telling me the story of my own life, which is not just my story but a really, really old story that has been playing out for centuries.

"Let me tell you something," she says. "Last week Ahmed went to a conference for three days in some small town in Louisiana. There's a hospital, a Walmart, and a separate gun store even though they also sell guns at the Walmart. That's it. He shows up and he's the first brown person they have ever seen. I mean, the mayor of this town has actually banned CNN, so all they watch is Fox News.

"So Ahmed just puts his head down, goes to work, comes back, and goes to the gym. Every day he's working out like a maniac, and then after the workout, he's going to the sauna. One day he's in there when this huge white guy comes in. The guy is holding an empty glass. He sits down next to Ahmed, and he holds the glass with one hand, and he points the finger of his other hand down at the glass. And then he starts to sweat. He's sweating like a slab of cheese on a hot day. The sweat pours down his body and down his arms, and he's still pointing at the glass he's holding, which is filling with sweat. And in, like, two minutes, the glass is full. And do you know what he does?"

"What?"

"He throws that shit on the ground. It splashes up, and drops of it hit Ahmed in the face."

"And Ahmed is just sitting there?"

"That's what I asked. I was like, 'Dude, why didn't you get out of there,' and Ahmed said he hadn't been that relaxed in months, and I was like, 'Fair enough.' So finally, Ahmed gets up the guts to say, 'Please, would you mind not doing that?' And do you know what the guy says?"

"What?"

"He said, 'I hate Hillary.'"

Mira starts to laugh, and I follow. "Shit," I say. "Really?"

"Swear to God," she says. "I could not make that up. This is the world we live in."

"Guess it puts things into perspective."

"So the question is, are you Stevie Wonder, or are you the person who gave him all the time in the world to become a legend?"

Cyrus begins as only Cyrus can.

He puts up a slide of a white telephone booth in a meadow

overlooking the sea. "This is Otsuchi, in northern Japan. When the tsunami hit this town in 2011, ten percent of its population was killed. One of the local residents set up this phone booth to talk to his cousin, who had disappeared in the tsunami and was never found."

Inside the phone booth sits an old rotary phone.

"The phone booth has become a place of pilgrimage. It doesn't connect to anything, yet thousands of people come here every day. It's called the Phone of the Wind, because people's voices, their messages to the dead, are carried through the air."

Now he brings up a slide of the death messaging app.

"AfterLight uses Asha's algorithm, the same one that powers WAI, to allow users to continue their conversations with their loved ones who have passed away. With AI and data gathered from the platform, it creates an authentic simulation of their online voices."

He doesn't present a sample of the tech. He doesn't need to. Everyone is sitting silently, imagining what would happen if they could suddenly bring a dead person to life.

Craig looks tearful, but I can't tell if it's because of what Cyrus is saying or because he's coming to an understanding of how much money this thing is going to make him. He gets up, walks over to Cyrus, and puts out his hand. Cyrus shakes it. They gaze at each other solemnly.

Then Gaby says, "With all due respect, Cyrus, this is not a good idea."

Cyrus looks genuinely confused. "Why not?"

"Because the tech can easily get out of control," I say.

"And because it seems wrong," Gaby says. "Asha warned us months ago about Marco, and this is the evidence."

"We have rigorous principles of consent around this thing," Cyrus says. "First of all, the person has to agree to it while they're still alive. This means, in the case of accidental death, the Obit.ly tech can't be used.

"Then each person in their network has a choice. Do they want to hear from their departed loved one? If so, under what circumstances? How frequently? And of course, they can cancel their subscription at any time."

I say I don't think that's enough. "If something goes wrong, the stakes are too high."

"What we do can go wrong at any time," Cyrus insists. "People have agreed to allow us into the most intimate parts of their lives."

"Yes, and we cannot abuse that trust."

"No one is abusing anyone's trust," Craig groans, waving his hand as if I'm turning something super-casual into something boringly complicated.

I'm not sure when I decide to dig in, but I find myself saying, "You can't release this. I will vote against it."

Craig leans back in his chair. "Then you will be removed from the board of this company."

"Hold on," Cyrus says. "You can't do that."

"Read the articles of association, man. I can call it to a vote. Majority wins."

Everyone stops moving. We're a canvas, captured in time by an artist, titled *The Fun Is Over*.

"I don't think Asha's a value add anymore," Craig says.

Cyrus takes a deep breath. "If she goes, I go."

"Cyrus, you're not going to quit. First of all, your contract says you have to give us twelve months' notice. And anyway, this is your flock. You're not getting out."

My head is spinning. I start talking without really hearing myself. "I don't want to—break us apart. If it comes to that, I'll quit."

"Oh, hell no," Gaby says. "The entire management team will leave. Jules and I will be out of here in five minutes, and you'll be left with an empty office and a CEO with a broken heart."

I throw Gaby a grateful look, but through all the noise in my head, I know he's bluffing. Jules wouldn't leave Cyrus, and Gaby won't leave Jules. There are murmurs around the table, people trying to step in to see if they can broker a truce. Rupert is talking to Jules, who is whispering something to Gaby. I stare and stare at Cyrus to check if he's trying to tell me something, to see if his hand is reaching out across the table to hold mine. Last night, after we played cribbage and he won for the thousandth time, I felt the weight of his arm across my shoulders and realized we hadn't argued about anything in weeks. We had both imagined that I had capitulated. That I had agreed to let him be the boss, to make the rules, and that I would be a good solider who follows orders and shuts up when she needs to.

"I'm not suggesting we fire her," Craig says.

"I'm sitting right here," I say. "Why don't you address yourself to me?"

"Because you're not being a team player, Asha."

"Me? I built this team."

"Craig, we should take this off-line," Cyrus says.

Craig exhales loudly. "You're right, I'm sorry. The red-eye messed up my circadian rhythms, and I'm all over the place. Asha, I apologize. Let's discuss this later when things are less heated."

Somehow the idea of accepting an apology from Crazy Craig is the thing that lights me up. "Fuck you, Crazy Craig," I say. "And fuck you, Cyrus, and fuck you, Jules and Rupert and all you other dicks. I quit."

▸

I go home and spend so long in the bath that my feet come out looking fifty years older than the rest of me. I hear Cyrus turning the lock and I pad to the door in my bathrobe and the first thing he does is hug me for a really long time. For hours I've been imagining how our conversation will play out. He'll say I shouldn't have told everyone to fuck off and I will agree and say sorry and then we'll quickly switch to strategizing a way to get out from under Craig. Maybe we'll even make some jokes about being older and WAIser. *Am I still me?* he'll ask me, and I'll tell him, *Yes, of course. You're still you.* We'll make up and take the weekend off. I believe with all my heart that this is what is about to happen.

But of course it doesn't.

"When we started WAI," Cyrus says, "you told me I had to think of it as a universe with its own rules, its own systems, and that sometimes it would take on a life of its own and I had to accept that."

We are in our kitchen. Cyrus is leaning against the island, and I am sitting on a barstool in my bathrobe and trying to push down the flicker of panic that is crawling up my legs and bursting into flames around my chest.

"I do remember saying that."

He pulls out a drawer from the freezer and removes a box of mochi ice cream. He arranges the half-dozen spheres on a plate and puts the plate between us. "We are going to finish this conversation by the time these things melt," he says. Cyrus and I have always been obsessed with these little Japanese treats. We are supposed to wait five minutes, but neither of us has ever been able to resist biting into them when the ice cream is still hard. I am encouraged by the inside joke, but my stomach is churning.

"Craig is right," Cyrus says. "I am contractually obligated to remain CEO of WAI unless I tender my resignation, and when I do, I have to give the board twelve months' notice."

"I can't do it with Craig. I won't."

"Jules and I looked into it, and there's no way to remove Craig unless someone buys out his shares, and we can't force him to sell."

I can see little beads of sweat forming on the surface of the mochi.

"Asha, please don't resign from the board. Please. I need you."

"There must be a way for things to go back to being the way they were."

"It's too late for that. You know that as well as I do."

I have an idea which cheers me up. "Let's just start over," I say. "We can come up with another idea, something new, and this time we'll know exactly how to play it."

"Look, if you want, I'll resign, and so will Jules and Gaby, and we'll blow the whole thing up. But we built WAI, and if it's going to survive, we need to stick together even when it's not pretty."

"You and me first, that's what we said, Cyrus."

"That is absolutely what we said. But it would be heartbreaking—for both of us—if we lost the company."

He's right, of course. I don't want to abandon WAI any more than he does. "I will consider staying on the board. Even with Craig. But you have to get rid of Marco."

Cyrus pushes back against the counter. "Dammit, Asha, you're like a dog with a bone."

I want to say, *So now I'm your fucking dog?* But I know he didn't mean it that way. "Then I'm done."

He sighs, a deep, resigned sigh. "You're wrong about Marco. You're wrong and you're going to regret it." He shakes his head. "I just can't agree with you, Asha. I could patronize you and say yes, maybe you're right, but in this case you just aren't."

He pushes the plate of mochi toward me and we each take one. "You will always be a founder of this company. No one can take that away from you," he says, as if I'm about to die and need to be reminded of my legacy.

"I'm not quitting, I'm just not going to be on the board." As soon as the words come out of my mouth, I regret them. I'm about to tell Cyrus that, but he's biting into his mochi and I can see from the set of his mouth that even though he begged me not to quit, he's relieved now that it's done. He relaxes, lets out a little sigh of pleasure as he swallows. I bite into mine. The creamy green-tea flavor floods my mouth. "Oh my God," I say. "Why didn't we always wait? It tastes so much better this way."

I resign from the board. In my place, Cyrus appoints Yvonne Caplan, an ethics professor from Harvard. Apparently, she's a rising star among philosophers. Once a month, I bore holes into the glass walls of the boardroom and see her sitting in my seat, a petite woman with cropped brown hair, her hands folded on her lap. Occasionally, she nods. I could reprogram the camera in that room to live-feed into my computer, but I don't—I know they will hardly give her time to speak, that Craig is panting down the line, that Cyrus is telling everyone how utterly perfect everything is because two hundred and fifty thousand people get married using WAI rituals every week, and now, because of Marco, we can do even more to shepherd humans through their short time on the planet, providing them with community, spirituality, a place to turn when life begins to feel devoid of meaning, and who is little Yvonne Caplan to dispute any of that?

In many ways, things are exactly as they always were. Ren and I design things and we code things and we run our team like Santa's Workshop and the sun swathes the Manhattan skyscrapers in gold dust. In the meantime, I am no Sheryl Sandberg, but people are starting to notice me. "The Brains Behind WAI" is an article that does the rounds. Then I get an invitation to headline the Girls Who Boss Festival, and a few weeks after that, I walk past a woman wearing a T-shirt with my face printed on it. MY FACE. Oh, it's grainy and screen-printed and also antiqued, but it's me. And the caption says, WAISER. I am super-happy about this, even though when I tell Jules and Gaby, I pretend like it's no big deal.

I haven't forgiven Jules for voting against me at the board meeting, but I should've known better than to hope he might break ranks with Cyrus. Cyrus has always been, and will always be, first for Jules. Gaby must know too, and they must have reached some kind of agreement about it. I haven't decided yet whether it's that Cyrus let me down or that I just staked too much on Marco's mania. I'm not angry, or at least I don't experience it as anger. I'm caught somewhere in between, maybe not yet ready to decide whether I've been betrayed or merely sidelined. I do know one thing: whatever anyone else did to me, I was the one who let it all come to this, I was the one who put myself on the wrong side of that glass wall. I'm not sure if I can ever forgive myself for that.

▸

Cyrus and I are on a date. Someone—a tech guru—is being given an award. I can't remember exactly who it is, but Cyrus has to show up to a fancy dinner, and a few months earlier when we were playing Should We Go to This? I agreed to go too. I am wearing a dress. I am wearing very tall shoes. And makeup. I feel shiny and beautiful.

Cyrus is wearing a tux. He is magnificent.

We are seated at the front of the room at a large round table, and as is often the way with these things, they thought it would be clever to split Cyrus and me up, so I'm sitting between two white men in tuxes, one old, the other even older, and Cyrus is sandwiched between two women, one showing cleavage and one in a demure off-the-shoulder dress. All evening, through caviar and blini and rillettes and lamb chops and tarte au citron, Cyrus and I text each other.

How's it going?

> **Yeah good.**

How are your neighbors?

> **Can I tell them how much I hate capitalism?**

No, I don't think so.

> **Are you crushing on the woman beside you?**

Who, Pamela? No.

Cyrus knows everyone. Pamela runs a seed fund, and Celeste, on his other side, is the ex-wife of Dennis, who runs an online gaming startup. People get out of their seats and come up to Cyrus and say things they think are funny, like, "Any chance you can give me a heads-up when the apocalypse is going to hit?"

I mostly don't hate drinking champagne and going to dinners

where the interior decor consists of portraits of people who probably murdered my ancestors. The reason I don't hate it is because Cyrus and I have so much fun ridiculing everyone that it's worth it just for the anthropology, and for the reminder that we share the same view of the world.

How many of these men are on their second wives? I text Cyrus.

At our table, he replies, **I'd say about 70 percent.**

The post-IPO wife is the butt of many of our jokes.

We'd been tetchy when that first lawyer brought it up (*Your odds aren't good!*), but now that Cyrus knows more of these people, we realize Barry wasn't singling us out, because divorce after great success is actually a trend. Not a dirty little secret but like a totally sanctioned and okay thing that men do once they hit the big time.

This is only one of the many qualities we dislike about all the other people who do what we do. Other things we don't like: the sanctimonious way they talk about how much of their money they give away. Their insistence that they are on the right side of politics, even if they support 45, because what they are doing—upending the order of things—is, by its very nature, progressive. Change is everything. If you transform the way people order their pizza or the way they pay their bills or the way they lose weight, you must be doing some good in the world. For that, you deserve money, and lower taxes, and even a wife with a better ass.

Since I resigned from the board, Cyrus has been sweeter to me than ever. He is at pains to let me know how much he loves me, how much he wants me. He passes me little handwritten notes when I turn up at the office. I try to enjoy it, but I suspect it's one big consolation prize when what I actually deserve is a seat at the table. But I never dwell on this thought for very long.

I want to go home, I text Cyrus after the petits fours and the bad coffee.

He comes around to my side of the table, leans down, and kisses the top of my head, and then he says to the old and older men on either side of me, "If you'll excuse us, Ned and Jerome, I'd like my wife all to myself now."

In the taxi home, we make out furiously and then I tell Cyrus I've been thinking more about the mentorship program. We'll launch it at WAI and then get other companies to sign up. When women are hired, they will be paired with someone senior, someone whose job it is to help them cut through all the invisible walls that might hold them back. I'm thinking of calling it Sister Outsider, after Mira's favorite book. "I love it," Cyrus says. "You have my full support." We go home and finish what we started in the taxi and then we drift off into a sweet, spooning sleep.

A few weeks later, I am headlining the Girls Who Boss Festival. My name is printed all over the posters along with a photo of me looking nerdy yet sexy. In the brochure I am described as *the visionary co-founder of WAI.* I'm surprised by how much it pleases me that this word, normally attached to Cyrus, belongs to me too. This morning, when I was looking through my closet, I picked out a jumpsuit, remembering one time it took Cyrus an entire hour of fumbling to get it off me, how I just lay there and laughed and let him keep trying.

When the day arrives, I am informed that Cyrus has made the cover of a well-known tech magazine. The story has been in the works for weeks, a crew coming to the office with recording devices and cameras. They've interviewed Jules and me extensively, talked to everyone at the office, and flown themselves out to California to interview Crazy Craig. They've even tracked down the first wedding Cyrus ever officiated. The couple, Gillian and Michael Rushmore-Smith, live in Boulder, Colorado, and run a no-waste grocery store where you bring your own containers. For them, Cyrus designed something called a Wetting: their guests brought water from all four corners of the country and anointed the couple, after which they all jumped into the Boulder Reservoir. They are still very happy together.

The story is coming out in print tomorrow, but it's online today. IS THIS MAN THE NEW MESSIAH? the headline says. I'm in a tent in the middle of Washington Square Park, which has been rented out for the festival. In the greenroom, there are red fabric armchairs and plastic flutes of champagne. A young man with a beard attempts to attach my microphone, but I have no waistband for him to clip it to. I'm thinking of a book I read recently, about how seatbelts and kitchen counters and spacesuits are all designed for men. "This contraption is made for a person wearing pants," I say. The bearded young man nods solemnly. His face smells like CBD oil. I really, really hate him.

I try not to, but I can't help reading the article about Cyrus. I see a photo of Cyrus against a dark blue background, his hair draped across his shoulders. The implication is not that Cyrus is a messiah, it's that he is *the* Messiah: the Jesus, Abraham, and Mohammed for our age. I scroll through. More photos. Cyrus looking up at the sky. Cyrus with his arms out in the middle of a field. The organizer calls my name and I am nudged onto the stage. When I look out into the audience, I see a large crowd of hopeful women staring back at me. I attempt a confident wave. Destiny is onstage too—the organizers heard we were friends and they've paired us up. I'm happy to see her and trying not to think about the forty-five hundred words all about my husband, the Second Coming.

"Welcome, Asha Ray, we are delighted to have you here," the moderator says. She's the same woman who interviewed Manishala Brown all those months ago, a kind of Smart Barbie, bleached-blond hair, big smile, oversize glasses. Right now she's in millennial-pink everything and holding on to a set of index cards with her gleaming manicure. She introduces me, pointing out all my excellent accomplishments: "Your platform needs no introduction. Many of us have become frequent users of WAI. Tell us, how did you and your co-founder Cyrus Jones come up with the concept?"

"WAI was totally Asha's idea," Destiny says. "She's a genius, plain and simple. For the rest of us, things aren't as straightforward."

I shoot her a grateful smile. "Destiny is being overly generous. I'm here because my friends and I decided to take a chance on a crazy idea," I say. "Cyrus, Julian Cabot, and I were just experimenting with the idea of using AI to give people a different social platform— we never thought we'd end up here."

Pink Fingernails asks a few more questions about how we got started. I tell her about the s'mores, about working long nights at Julian's house, about dropping out of Dr. Stein's lab. Then she flips to a new index card. "And do you personally come from a business background? Are your parents entrepreneurs?"

"They are, actually. They came over here from Bangladesh in their twenties, right out of college. And now they run a small chain of pharmacies."

"What a sweet story. So I guess you're used to mixing business with family life? For those of you in our audience who don't know, Asha and her co-founder Cyrus Jones are married."

There's a small rumble in the audience, and then a few people clap. "Woo-hoo!" someone shouts.

"So which came first, the marriage or the business?"

"The marriage, actually," I say. "But the business followed shortly after. It's sometimes hard to tell the two apart now."

More laughter and applause. I'm starting to enjoy myself, but then I feel my phone buzzing in my handbag and I remember Cyrus's article.

"Your office is in an unusual setting, isn't it?"

"We beta-launched the product, and the team at Utopia invited us to join them. That was three years ago, and we're still headquartered there."

"What is Utopia like? I think some of our audience members are pretty curious."

Destiny winks. "What happens at Utopia stays at Utopia."

I gesture to her. "It's been great to have a friend to share the experience with."

I get a few more questions about Utopia, which I dodge, all the while resisting the urge to steal a glimpse at my phone. Then the conversation circles back to Cyrus.

"Asha, tell us about the challenges of working with someone and living with him at the same time."

"Well, there's not a lot of work-life balance," I say. "But we like it that way. We're committed to WAI and we're committed to each other." I knit my hands together. "It's an integrated whole. Like our platform." I smile, wishing this line of questioning would end.

Satisfied, she moves on to Destiny. Destiny entertains the crowd with a graphic description of how she came up with the categories for Consentify. "The anus is a very contentious area," she says. "People want to be touched there, but they don't want to admit wanting to be touched there. So we had to deal with it quite delicately."

After that point, no one is interested in me anymore. The audience is invited to participate, and Destiny is showered with questions.

"*What happens when people consent to being touched, does the consent expire after a certain period of time?*"

"*What if you are in the middle of sex and you end up doing something you didn't explicitly consent to?*"

"*Do men hate it?*"

There is a lot of laughter and whooping.

"Any more questions?" the moderator asks.

Someone in the back raises a hand. "My boyfriend and I are about to become co-founders. Do you have any advice for us about how we can keep our relationship and our business together at the same time?"

I decide to play it for laughs. "When Cyrus and I first started WAI, our lawyer told us our marriage wouldn't survive, so we fired him."

"Do you feel like people give Cyrus more credit than they give you?"

"No," I say, shaking my head as if to mean *Why would you say that?* when really, I'm thinking, *Yes, yes, of course, what planet do you think we live on?*

"Not a lot of people know that you built the platform," she says. "Does that bother you?"

The blood rushes to my face. "Not at all," I say, attempting to cover up the fact that it bothers me like a mosquito bite on my eyelid. "Cyrus was and remains the inspiration for the algorithm. It's his mind, his way of connecting ideas."

The moderator says, "I think what our guest is trying to say is, do you feel like maybe he's hogging the limelight? He does talk about you a lot in this article that just came out, doesn't he? About how crazy he is about you. But not as much about how you built the tech."

"We don't want to be defined by the men in our lives," Destiny announces. "If there's a tiny amount of wisdom that Asha and I can impart, that would be it."

Afterward, Destiny and I make the minimum amount of small talk, get a handful of business cards shoved into our palms, and we're out of there and in a West Village café by nine, sharing a plate of truffle fries.

"I could read it so you don't have to?" she offers, but I'm already halfway through. I start to read aloud. "'I had this vision for creating a platform that would help people to connect and coalesce around the things that mattered most to them. It was a natural extension of what I'd been doing for years. People used to call me a humanist spirit guide— I guess that's what I'm bringing to WAI now, just on a larger stage.'

"He doesn't even mention us. Doesn't say anything about how Jules and I dragged him kicking and screaming into this. *I* wanted to create a platform. Cyrus just wanted to baptize cats."

"To be fair, the Cat Baptism is one of the most shared rituals," Destiny says, trying to lighten the tone. "Eight hundred thousand videos and counting."

I keep going. "'I'm attracted to the solitary life, Jones says. You can imagine him in a monastery, although he'd have to cut off that halo around his head. In addition to creating a social network that millions of people are turning to for meaning and community, he is also taking care of his employees—he has just kicked off a mentorship program to give the women on his team the support they need to thrive in their roles.'"

Destiny tells me to stop reading. "It's just bullshit."

I take a shaky deep breath. "That's my mentorship program," I whisper.

"Cyrus is telling them what he wants to hear. You and I both know that."

I'm stammering now, but I keep going. "'He's otherworldly but handsome in an almost comical way. His sentences are long, and when you're in the middle of one, you wonder, where is this going? But he always manages to bring whatever he's saying to a satisfying conclusion. Everything he says is mysterious and somehow obvious at the same time.'"

At least this one is funny. I allow Destiny to laugh briefly.

I get to the last line. "'I have to say, I'm developing something of a crush.'"

"Oh, for God's sake, another woman in love with Cyrus. Take a number, sister." Destiny leans over, reads the byline. "George Milos. Guess Cyrus appeals to all genders."

As we get up to leave, she says, "I don't think Cyrus is a bad person. He's just basking in a sea of adoration, and it makes him think more of himself than he should."

"Where does that leave me?"

"You have a tough gig. No one wants to be married to the guy everyone thinks is going to save the world."

As I make my way home, it starts to snow. I've been trying not to cry this whole time, but now I let it happen, and the sting in my eyes mixes with the snow falling on my cheeks and makes my face burn hot. By the time I get to the apartment, I am sobbing. I don't even try to hide it from the doorman, who turns his back discreetly as I get in the elevator.

Cyrus is home. I can tell from the way his shoes are lined up neatly on the shoe rack, his backpack on the hook where I have begged him to hang it so many times, that he's been waiting for me and that he knows exactly how I have responded to his interview.

"It was edited all wrong," he says. "I've already spoken with them."

I throw my coat on the floor. "What are they going to do? Issue a correction? 'In a recent issue of our magazine, we implied that Cyrus Jones is the sole visionary behind WAI when, in fact, he couldn't have done it without his wife'?"

My voice has risen. Cyrus approaches me, but I hold my arm away from my body so he can't come any closer. I wipe my face roughly with the back of my sleeve and try to steady myself. "I could've forgiven you for taking me off the board. I told myself it was fine, that you were cornered and didn't have a choice."

"I didn't take you off the board, you quit."

"Because you chose Marco and Craig over me."

"You made me choose—you didn't have to. You didn't have to make it personal."

Cyrus sits down on the sofa, but I stay standing, holding my back as straight as I can, as if this will give me some purchase on the situation. "I hate who you are in this," I say, gesturing to my phone. "My mentorship program, Cy—did you have to take that from me too? It was such a tiny thing—you couldn't let me keep it?"

He shakes his head. "It's not me, it's just a persona."

"So you did it on purpose."

"I spent the whole time telling him how much I love you."

"Yeah, so everyone can be like, 'Ooh, she has the best husband in the world.'"

"What else did you want me to say?"

The thought comes out before I can really register it. "The truth. Which is that you're pimping something your wife invented and peddling it as your own."

I've drawn blood. Cyrus's face closes. "So that's what you think. That I stole something from you."

I circle around and sit across from him. "I don't think you stole it,"

I say, my voice softening. "I think I let it be yours and you let me be sidelined. You diminished me and I allowed it to happen."

He pauses for a moment and I think maybe we can bring it back. *The next time he apologizes*, I think, *I'll relent.* "It's Hegelian," he says.

I try to load my silence with as much of a fuck-you as I can manage.

"You and I are in a dialectic; we created this situation together. I'm as much a product of you as you are of me."

"Hegel? Really? You're going to hit me with Hegel?"

"I never wanted any of this in the first place. I was perfectly happy living my medium-size life when you came along and forced me to become Cyrus the Great. And now you resent me."

"That's bullshit and you know it. You enjoyed every minute of it."

"I didn't have a choice. The two people I love most in the world are telling me to do something, and I have to go along with it because if you left me, I'd have nothing."

"Don't act like we forced you to do it, Cyrus. That we somehow threatened you." I can feel myself going to a place from which it will be impossible to return. But it's too late; I am already there. "And anyway, Jules would never leave you."

"But you would?"

In that split second, I make up my mind. "You've allowed yourself to become someone I no longer respect. You can blame me or tell me it's Hegelian all you want, but it's who you are now. And I'm not playing anymore, Cy. You're going to have to go the rest of the way on your own."

Cyrus moves very slowly. He puts on his shoes. He winds his scarf around his neck. He shrugs into his coat. And then he's gone into the snow and the night, a trail of unsaid words following silently behind him like a clutch of shadows.

Fifteen

THE END

It's the start of a new year. Rory's Christmas tree, the one he grew in his lab, has come down, and there's the smell of fresh paint on the walls, and Tenth Avenue is dusted with snow, and we are in the boardroom because Li Ann has called us to a meeting. Everyone's here: Destiny, the founder of Freud, the twins from No Touch, Rory, and of course, Jules and me and Cyrus and Marco.

When I arrived at Utopia that first day, still sweaty from the bus ride, no idea why I'd been summoned, Li Ann had told me that she was preparing for the apocalypse. The afterworld, she called it. I was inspired and possibly a little bemused by the idea, and although I showed up and built our platform and talked often about how we were going to deal with the end of the world, I didn't for a second imagine I would see it in my lifetime.

Well, according to Li Ann, it's here.

She says words like "pandemic," "virus," "death rate," and "vaccine." I try to thread it all together. There is a virus. It has a high death rate. It will cause a pandemic. And there is no vaccine.

"And no cure," Rory adds.

Li Ann is calmly ordering everyone around, telling each one of us in turn what our role in this new reality will be. It's comforting to have someone in charge, making it seem like we have some control over what's about to happen.

"WAI, you're in charge of ritual, community, and continuity.

"Consentify, Freud, No Touch—togetherness will never be the same—think about that and start strategizing.

"Obit.ly, you're going to shepherd people to their end.

"And AfterLight—a lot of people aren't going to be able to say goodbye. Maybe you can provide some solace."

I can feel the smile creeping across Marco's face. The world is going to shit, and my mind is turning to Marco, but I can't help it because that means he was right. And if he was right, then Cyrus and I have no chance.

It's the apocalypse and all I can think about is my broken heart, and how desperately I want to be near Cyrus.

Julia and Julia do a presentation called Fingerless Friendship in which they suggest we no longer shake hands or get within six feet of people we don't know.

"No one has died from this disease yet," Rory tells us. "So you might think we're being paranoid. But I've been studying these things, and you have to trust me, there is a very strong chance that it's going to kill tens of thousands, possibly millions, of people. Try not to become a statistic."

We file out, stunned, but knowing better than to doubt Li Ann and Rory.

Jules and Cyrus are waiting for me on the stairs. "Let's meet in my office," Cyrus says somberly. "We should prepare a statement for the team."

Every time I hear his voice, my stomach lurches. "Sure," I reply, trying to sound normal. These days, at least 25 percent of my energy goes into sounding normal.

I have to. We still work together. All day we pass each other on the stairs and on our way to the bathroom, and we have meetings and briefings and people to hire and a customer base to please. And then, at the end of every day, we go home to separate places.

I don't know where he goes. I don't like the asymmetry of him knowing where I live and me knowing nothing about his life, but he doesn't tell me and I'm too proud to ask.

We gather around the table in Cyrus's office, and I try not to focus on every little thing that has changed since we broke up, like the reorganized books on the shelf, and the subtle scent of incense that burned off hours ago—was he here last night?—and the new pen he's holding, something too small for his hand.

Jules and I prepare the statement. Cyrus and I avoid looking straight at each other, but otherwise he's careful to be super-nice to me, and I'm careful to be, well, normal.

He's still wearing his wedding ring. Small mercies. I distract myself by doing a few calculations of what would happen to the platform if we suddenly got a surge of users for AfterLight.

"Jules," Cyrus says, "can you write to the board and tell them we'll be suspending all membership dues until this thing passes? We're all agreed, right, that it would be wrong to benefit in any way?"

Jules and I nod. Craig won't mind. By the time this is over, so many people are going to be hooked on AfterLight that we can more than make up the difference.

"I'm going to put some more devs behind Obit.ly," I volunteer. "Make sure the security is extra-tight."

"I'll do a special WAICast," Cyrus says.

We run through the details, then get up to go. We have to start planning, call our families. Cyrus asks to speak with me for a moment, and my breath stops in my chest. Will he fall on his knees and beg me to forgive him?

But no.

I can't help myself, so I say, "I guess Marco called it. He said bad things were coming."

Cyrus nods. I look at him and I realize what he wants. He wants me to tell him he's right, that AfterLight is going to give something real and important to people in the coming months. He wants me to apologize and ask for things to go back to the way they were. Every cell in my body bellows to be reunited with Cyrus. Can I change my mind to get what I want so very badly? I ask myself what I would do if something happened to Mira. Would I want a little glimmer of her to remain?

Of course I would. But that is precisely why we shouldn't do it. "Just because the world is ending doesn't mean it's no longer wrong," I say.

Cyrus's face softens and hardens. He is that very worst thing, an intimate who is also a stranger. My legs go all watery.

"The difference between us," he tells me, "is that I have lost someone and you have not."

He puts the cap back on his little pen. I am dismissed; he is the boss, after all.

I can't tell anyone my heart is broken, because if I did, I would have to admit that Cyrus isn't coming back. I haven't even had the guts to tell my parents. So on the days when I wake up with puffy eyes and feel like my stomach collided with a kettlebell, I ignore it. And when I catch sight of Cyrus, when I search his face for something, some sign that he regrets leaving me as much as I regret his leaving, I tell myself it's just habit; after all, I've spent my whole life in love with this man.

I veer between remorse and self-righteous anger. I was right to stand my ground. He owes me an apology, and so much more, an admission that all of this has gotten to his head and that he's changed, and he needs to ask me whether I can live with this new person who wants to take over the world. But I also said some terrible things, things that keep going around and around in my mind. And I miss him. God, do I miss him.

I drink, but I'm still too much of a control freak to drink enough to numb myself. I borrow one of Li Ann's marijuana sticks and spend twenty-four hours eating the entire contents of my fridge. Destiny invites me over and takes me out as much as any friend can reasonably be expected to, but nothing can fill the Cyrus-shaped hole in my life.

What Li Ann has told us is coming to pass. Within a few weeks, death ritual requests are up 22 percent on the WAI platform, and Rory has been hired by the CDC to start mapping the virus's genetic code. The mood at the office is somber as we start making plans for people to work remotely, and even Jules is solemn as he leads the morning team meetings; there is no more singing or cheering, just a growing awareness of what's to come.

The constant knots of people standing outside the entrance to Utopia are making Li Ann anxious. "They're creating a viral load," she explains. "You have to get rid of them." But the situation is making Cyrus more of a symbol than ever. The fans carry signs. WAI IS THE WAY. FIND YOUR WAI. WE ARE THE WAI. We've gotten to know some of them. I wave to Rick, a tall, waifish man with silver dreadlocks; Trinity, who arrives with a different dog every week; Stephen, a bright-eyed young man who showers us with questions about Hindu scripture as we pass by. Cyrus stops and talks to everyone, especially Stephen, with whom he exchanges detailed views about Krishna, Ram, and the Bhagavad Gita; on especially cold days, he goes down and serves everyone hot chocolate in paper cups. But he is far from the humble, approachable man he seems to be. Up in his glass-walled office, he has charts and graphs showing the exponential growth of WAI. All his plans, his plotting with Craig and Marco, are coming to pass. With the help of Obit.ly and AfterLight, WAI has the potential to become the biggest social media platform in the world.

Jules tells me that Cyrus was destined to become this way, WAI or no WAI. We are on the roof of Utopia, where Rory has set up a low-watering greenhouse. There is a narrow path through the foliage, but otherwise every inch of the space is filled with his genetically modified, high-nutrient Popeye leaf. He's got it tasting great now, sort of like kale but without the hard-core chewing requirements of kale. And it grows everywhere—all you have to do is scatter a few seeds and water it sporadically. I have some at home I haven't managed to kill yet.

"You're telling me he was always like this?" I ask Jules.

"Not exactly. He didn't have millions of people telling him what a genius he was. But he was always entitled as fuck."

"Why have you put up with him? All these years?"

"You've met my family, Asha."

I have settled on a story that I can live with. I love Cyrus, but we are no longer together because I turned him into a terrible person. I didn't do it alone, but it has happened, and it has happened because of me and because of WAI. Cyrus, my sweet, mellow, not-priest has turned into a shallow, narcissistic man-child. This way I can blame Cyrus (for becoming a terrible person) while taking some responsibility (for making it super-easy for him to become a terrible person).

Many times I try to trace back to the moment when Cyrus morphed into his current form. Was it when people started camping outside our offices? Was it when multiple "Cyrus Is the Messiah" fan sites popped up online, something that caused Jules and me and Destiny to laugh and Cyrus to scroll for hours, reading what people were saying about him?

Right now Cyrus is in Washington, DC, giving a TED Talk entitled "Death: A Manual." There are currently several hundred thousand people all over the world waiting for him to tell them how to die. After the TED Talk there will be interviews, and after the interviews someone will transcribe the talk, and then there will probably be a book.

"How's the warning system?" Jules asks.

"For WAI or for the world?"

"The world is fucked anyway."

Jules is asking about the risk register that Ren and I have devised. It aggregates all the rituals produced by the platform and gives us a sense of where things are at, how heated up the community is. Elections usually raise the risk profile, as do major environmental disasters, like cyclones or the hurricane that caused one of the Hudson

Yards buildings to close down last year. And this new thing, which is about to be declared a pandemic. "I would say we're somewhere on the orange to dark orange spectrum."

"How many death ritual groups are there?"

I check the latest stats on my phone. "Twenty-three thousand."

"Any particularly weird ones?"

"They're all weird. I mean, take your pick. The Cremation Club. The Ship Burial Society. There's one guy who keeps asking questions about sati."

"What is that?"

"It's when a woman is burned alive on her husband's funeral pyre."

"Are you okay?" Jules asks, as if I am having thoughts of immolating myself. He tears off a piece of a Popeye plant and rubs it between his fingers. "It's been over a month—I thought you guys would be back together by now."

"Yeah, I guess I thought so too." I don't say more. Things between Jules and me haven't been the same since that fateful board meeting. And it takes all the strength in my bones not to ask him where Cyrus is and where Cyrus sleeps.

Someday I know I'm going to ask myself what happened. How I put all my chips on this particular bet and allowed my life to be subsumed by WAI. And I will tell myself this: because it was the purest form of togetherness. Me and Cyrus, waking up every morning with the same purpose, walking through those doors together, dreaming the same dreams, working for the same thing—that was my joy. All the aloneness I ever felt, every dark sad thing I had inherited, disappeared in its bright light. And once I had done it, once I had fit together with Cyrus and put my thinking and my mathematics and my body's wants all in one place, its power was so great that it was impossible to imagine taking apart even one small piece of it.

So when a piece broke off, the whole came crashing down.

I had always been ambivalent about how much I wanted to keep the work me and the me me apart. I wanted everyone to know Cyrus was my husband, but I also wanted them to recognize me and my brain-bending genius. I wanted to be a coder and I wanted to be his wife and I wanted to be his partner, but I also wanted to rule just the way he did, without a thought, without effort, as if I had been born to it.

For a while, it worked. We made something magnificent. We disrupted the very thing that was seemingly fixed—the way people handled the most intimate moments of their lives. We gave them something they didn't even know they wanted, and once we'd given it to them, nothing was ever the same again.

We were revolutionaries. We were radicals. We had upended the order of things.

When people asked me and Cyrus and Jules about our friendship (had it survived the business, or had we changed, like a band who couldn't stay together after four consecutive triple-platinum hits?), Cyrus made much of how close we all were. "We're like a family," he would say.

Except Cyrus and I *were* family. We had stood up in front of that woman in the pantsuit and we had said things. And try as we might, we found it impossible to keep our family together when the rest of it shattered. It was all just too connected.

"You know I love you," Jules says.

"I know. You just love him more."

Jules doesn't reply to that. "It's okay, I don't mind," I tell him, even though I do. Jules has no family; Cyrus is it, and that was always going to matter more than anything else.

Then he says, "Gaby and I are getting married."

I hug him and then I burst into tears. "That's amazing. No, don't do that—don't look sorry. It's great. Marriage is great. Maybe just don't start a business together." My sobbing turns to laughter.

"I'm really happy," he says. "Even though the world is ending, I'm really fucking happy."

We link arms and dance among the Popeye plants.

When he gets back from Washington, Cyrus suggests that maybe he should come over and get a few things from the apartment. I feel a knife going into my heart. Why does he need his stuff? Is he going to wear that blue suit to dinner with some other person? Is he going to read aloud from his paperback of *Ulysses*, the one with the taped-together spine, to someone else? I don't ask him what it means and he doesn't tell me.

He arranges to come over on a Saturday afternoon, and I make plans to see an osteopath and to have lunch with Destiny at her place in Long Island City. I want to be in a totally different borough. "What if he lives in Queens now?" Destiny says when I call to ask if I can drop by. Then she says, "I don't think he lives in Queens. He probably lives in a Zendo downtown."

On the subway I notice a woman wearing a mask. It's fogging up her glasses, but she keeps it on the whole way to Long Island City. I try not to touch anything while also trying not to obsess about Marco and how fucking smug this is making him.

Before I ring Destiny's doorbell, I practice a cheerful but not too fake smile.

"How was Cheryl?" she asks, handing me a small cup.

"She cracked my back like it was a Rice Krispie treat," I say. I take a sip. It's warm sake. She settles me on the sofa, puts the carafe of sake by my elbow, and starts to make lunch.

Right now, as Destiny tosses a salad, Cyrus is opening and closing the doors to his side of the closet and putting his sneakers in a box and looking for a notebook he thinks might be in the sideboard. I'm putting kale and pine nuts in my mouth, and with every chew, there is less of Cyrus in the apartment, less of Cyrus in my life, less of his smell, less of his loose change and his socks stuffed between the sofa cushions, less of his voice on the other side of the bathroom door, asking when I'll be done even though there are two other bathrooms in the apartment.

There is an East River between us now, and it's possible that soon we won't even be married. Marco has informed us that Wuhan is under lockdown and that it's only a matter of time before the virus strikes New York. I realize I've never really believed in the apocalypse. It was a distant possibility, one that we might even avoid if people like me used our brains enough. I thought that's why we were here, at Utopia, why we had doctors and climate scientists and AI and tech. And I certainly didn't imagine I would have to face it without Cyrus. I had assumed that Cyrus would be beside me to answer the big questions. Mine was the realm of ones and zeros, not the space of the unknowable—that was all his, and without his sure, calm voice, I am adrift. I'm just like everyone else: my imagination fails me.

"Do you want to sleep over?" Destiny asks. Her apartment is high up on the twenty-third floor. It looks east, not toward Manhattan but away from it. It's what she wanted. The sun on her face and the city at her back. She and Ren found it around the same time Cyrus and I bought the loft. They moved in together as friends, and somewhere along the way, I think, they've become more than that. They don't say and I never ask; I just assume it's the way she wants it, a kind of accidental blurring of roles. Nothing dramatic. No sacred rituals.

I'm tipsy now and full of raw greens, so I think about taking the guest room for the night. I could put off returning to the loft and finding empty corners and realizing there were things that were Cyrus's that I assumed were mine. Gaps in the bookshelf. Little absences that will hurt even though I've made a huge effort to numb myself to a lot of things related to Cyrus.

Queens is out in front of me, industrial, squat, squares of green where someone has thought to put a park. I wonder if I too can turn my back on the city, on WAI. But I know I can't. Jules and I have talked about it. I know he's been approached by headhunters, that Gaby has encouraged him to leave WAI and branch out on his own. But we are bound together, and to Cyrus, by the thing we have created together. The truth is, I wouldn't know what or who we would be without it.

I decide to go home after all. Destiny takes the elevator down with me. "I'll see you tomorrow," she says.

Tomorrow is Sunday. "Why? What are we doing?"

"It's pizza-bagel appreciation day. I'll bring the bagels."

"Okay." I give her a grateful hug, even though Li Ann has told us to stop hugging.

The Midtown Tunnel takes me home. When I'm there, I press buttons on the alarm system. The apartment is dark when I enter, so I say, "Lights on." And then I say, "Lights dimmer." And the metal-framed windows come into view. Very slowly, I turn my head this way and that.

The boxes are gone, and so is the watercolor that Jules gave us when we first moved in, which I assured Cyrus, before he had a chance to ask, would be his. Other than that, there is a generalized sense of emptiness, a vague feeling that the space is hollow. Nothing I can quite put my finger on. I tell the TV to turn on Netflix, and I browse through a bunch of options until I retreat to *Anne with an E*, which is what I watch every night when I am alone. And then I fall asleep in front of the green hills of Prince Edward Island.

Later that week, Ren and I are reengineering the messaging service. Cyrus wants to turn it into a stand-alone app, and we have a few developers building a prototype. When I check the time, it's past midnight, and I resign myself to staying over. I do that a lot these days; with the apartment empty, it's a relief to have somewhere else to be. I'm just about to head to the nap room when the fire alarm goes off. At first no one notices—we all just assume it's a drill—but after about a minute, people start to take off their headphones and shuffle over to the staircase.

Li Ann appears. She's holding a mini fire extinguisher in one hand and a hardcover of Michelle Obama's *Becoming* in the other. "Why are you all still here? Let's go."

"Is it a real fire?" someone asks.

"Of course it's real. Come on, everyone out." The devs grab their things and disappear down the stairs. "You stay," she tells me. I put my hands over my ears. Finally, the alarm stops.

"There's a man on the roof," Li Ann says. "He's got a can of gasoline and a lighter. Says he's going to set himself on fire."

In the minute it takes me to assemble this image in my mind, Jules and Gaby appear and the fire alarm starts ringing again.

I lean close to Li Ann and ask, "Is this guy—is he one of ours?"

She puts her hand on my elbow. "We don't know yet."

My breathing becomes jagged and loud. "Have you called 911?"

"They're on their way. They told us to evacuate."

There's no way I'm leaving if someone who uses our platform is about to set himself on fire. "But we can't."

"I know. There's a panic room. We can go there."

"There's a panic room? Why is there a panic room?"

She makes an irritated gesture which I think means *Why wouldn't there be a panic room?* and leads us to the back staircase, down four flights, and then past the hydrotherapy pool and Rory's lab. The siren continues to rise and rise. Finally, after we go through a maze of corridors, Li Ann taps her keycard and a heavy door slides open. Inside, it looks like a basement living room—there's a sofa, a rug, a mini fridge, a television, and three desktop computers. The computers look like they're a few years old, but otherwise everything is clean and new, and there's even a little basket of snacks on top of the fridge.

Ren and I immediately get the computers online. No one speaks. Gaby makes coffee, and Jules makes the room shrink by pacing back and forth. Li Ann switches on the television. I wonder, for the millionth time, where Cyrus is. We have to tell him.

"Julian, can you call Cyrus?" I ask. I can't bear to hear his voice right now.

Jules tries Cyrus. There's no reply. I get on the phone with Charlie, our lawyer. We flip to the news, and so far we aren't in it, but just as I'm about to tell Charlie everything, the story breaks. I hear the reporter saying, ". . . young man has posted a message on the WAI platform saying his wife, who died of leukemia last year, has asked to be reunited with him."

Ren has been sifting through the users. He tells everyone who it is.

"Stephen?" Jules says. "The guy who's been hanging out on the sidewalk?"

Ren turns his screen toward me, and I see that Stephen has asked the platform for a sati ritual three times, and that the platform has turned him down. Stephen's profile picture is a man on a beach with his arm around his wife. He has bright green eyes and a big smile.

The Stephen at the door is the same Stephen who asked the platform for the sati ritual. And when the WAI platform said no, Stephen opened an account with AfterLight and asked to speak with his wife. The news is still on, and the reporter is saying something about the virus, how it's hit the East Coast and that there is going to be a concentration of cases in New York. Everything seems to be falling apart at once.

"We have to delete his account."

"Already done," Ren says.

Charlie is still on the phone. "Decide how you're going to respond. I'm sending Tina Vardalis to your office, and I need you to do exactly what she tells you. She handles these kinds of things." I want to ask her if a man threatening to set himself on fire because an app sent him text messages from his dead wife is one of these things, but I already know the answer.

I turn to Jules. "Did you get ahold of Cyrus?"

Jules has stopped pacing. He's on the sofa with his head in his hands. Gaby is stroking his back. "No."

"Ren and I are going to disable AfterLight—do you agree?"

"I don't care. Do whatever." Then he says, "Actually, turn the whole thing off. Obit.ly too."

I turn off Obit.ly and Afterlight. No one is hearing from dead people anymore.

On the television, there is a grainy image of Stephen on the roof of Utopia. A small figure with his arms outstretched, as if he expects to take flight.

I ask Jules to keep calling Cyrus until he answers. Li Ann tells us that the fire brigade has arrived and that someone is trying to get Stephen to put down his lighter.

I remember whose fault this is. "Where the fuck is Marco?"

"I tried. His phone is off."

"Fuck that. Fuck him."

"Asha," Jules says, "I'm sorry. I'm so sorry."

"We don't have time to do this now. Let's just try to fix it— you need to figure out what you're going to say to the team." Ren and I are going through all the chatter on the platform. As the news breaks, people start messaging one another about Stephen. I think maybe we need to get Cyrus online to calm everyone down. Where the hell is Cyrus?

There is a knock on the door. It's Tina. She's impeccably coiffed and wearing a white suit as if it's a decent hour. She introduces herself, sits down beside me, and starts taking notes. "Asha, right? Tell me what's going on."

I start to tell her. "We have this service—it uses AI to send messages from people even after they're dead. This guy Stephen—he was talking—thought he was talking—to his wife."

She's looking at me like *What kind of fucked-up Internet Frankenstein did you make, sister?*

"Then I guess somehow he got the message—not from us, I mean, not directly—that she wanted him to join her." I show her the conversation between Stephen and his wife.

How could you leave me?

I never left you. I'm right here.

"And now he's up on the roof?"

"He's going to set himself on fire." I explain sati to Tina: "It's an ancient Hindu ritual. Women sit on the funeral pyres of their husbands so they can be together in their next life. It's the ultimate sacrifice."

She inhales sharply. "I deal in worst-case scenarios. So, just for the sake of argument, we have to assume he's going to do it, and I need you all to be prepared. Can you reach out to your members now, maybe post a message on the site? Something along the lines of *We are deeply concerned with the well-being of a member of our community, we have representatives on standby for anyone who is feeling vulnerable*, et cetera, et cetera?"

Ren is taking notes. He suggests we ask the team members in Hong Kong, who are already awake, to get a help line together.

"I'm assuming you've dealt with all the technical issues," Tina says.

"We've shut down the relevant parts of the platform."

"You need to tell them why. You need to explain without taking responsibility for the whole thing."

We are *responsible*, I want to say. My phone rings; it's Mira. I don't answer, but I text: **I am safe, don't worry. Tell Ammoo**.

The image on the TV screen is static. SOCIAL MEDIA PROMPTED YOUNG MAN TO ATTEMPT SUICIDE, the headline reads. "Just a minute," the correspondent says, "I think Cyrus Jones, CEO of WAI, is here to talk to Stephen. He's being led through the police barrier by an officer."

Cyrus is here? The camera shows him being led to the entrance of Utopia. Then a few minutes later it cuts to the scene on the roof, and I see him in a corner of the frame. Stephen raises his arms up and down. The camera tries to zoom in, but he's too small and grainy to make out much beyond an outline.

The image changes, and now we're in the studio with the newscasters. "We have a social psychologist and expert on social media here to comment on the situation. Dr. Sharma, you've spoken publicly before about the dangers of these types of websites. Is this the result of being overly dependent on the internet for the kinds of social connections we used to enjoy in person?"

"This platform claimed to be more responsible," Dr. Sharma says. "They were quick to ban people who went against their values or shared content that was harmful. They were overtly progressive—the Woodstock of the internet, we were told. But at the end of the day, they're all the same—the whole sector needs to be regulated."

The presenter nods, citing all the ways we had sold people a fantasy. I don't know what bothers me more, the suggestion that we're like everyone else, or that we tried to be different but failed.

They go back and forth for a while, and when Dr. Sharma runs out of things to say, they cut back to Cyrus and Stephen. There's a photo montage of Cyrus—Cyrus being greeted by a raptuous crowd, Cyrus shaking hands with Bill Gates, radiating his confident CEO smile, Cyrus glowing as if he's been dipped in caramel. Then, for a little while, the virus story takes over. Pictures from Wuhan, where the streets are empty and everyone is under lockdown. Time moves slowly and it's two a.m., then three. Jules and Gaby sit quietly on the sofa, their eyes glued to the TV, while Ren and I monitor the platform. Suddenly, the broadcast ends and cuts to commercial.

I have this sick feeling in the pit of my stomach. "I think he's done it."

Li Ann turns up the volume on the television. "I'm very sorry to report that Stephen Grant, the thirty-two-year-old man from Bridgeport, Connecticut, who's been standing on the roof of Utopia, a co-working space in Chelsea . . . I'm sorry to say we have just learned that Stephen has ended his life. We go live now. Chris, tell us what happened there in the last tragic minutes."

Chris, the newscaster, is on the sidewalk across the street from Utopia. "Well, Dan, the scene here is heartbreaking. It seems that the CEO of the social media platform, WAI, was trying to talk Stephen out of his actions, but ultimately, Cyrus Jones was unable to persuade the young man to come down, and as you know, Dan, he took matters into his own hands."

I feel a ripple, a tear in the membrane that surrounds us; everything is muffled and strange. Jules is crying softly in a corner. Ren has stopped typing and is sitting with his hands folded in front of his computer. Tina has brought me a glass of water, and I drink it. "How do we— How do we know Cyrus is okay?"

"There are a lot of firefighters up there," Li Ann says. "They'll take care of him."

I'm suddenly very tired. I want to close my eyes and sleep through the next few hours, but Tina won't let me; she's nudging me, giving me things to do. "One of you has to start getting on top of the story. You decide who. I've got all the networks lined up for interviews. Asha, maybe you want to go on *Today*, and send Julian to some of the afternoon shows. I'll have my team make a schedule with talking points."

Ren is back at the computer; Li Ann is breaking open a bag of peanuts. She looks up, meets my eyes, and gives me a short nod. "Okay, Tina," I say. "I'll do the interviews. I'm not sure if Cyrus will be up for talking, but it's probably better if he addresses the community directly."

"You're keeping coolheaded," Tina says. "I respect that."

"This is my company," I say. "I built it with my own hands."

Dawn is cracking open over New York. The building is safe, the firefighters have said. We can't go to the roof, but we can return to our desks. There's a stretch of Tenth Avenue that's cordoned off, but here on the fourth floor, it's like nothing ever happened. Jules, Ren, Gaby, and I are waiting for Cyrus to come down. He's being supported, one of the firefighters tells us. "But is he okay?" I ask. "Did he—did he get hurt?"

"No," the firefighter tells me. "He's just in shock."

We wait in silence. Every once in a while Jules gets up, walks around the room, and sits back down. Our teacups clutter the surfaces. Eventually, Cyrus comes in, walking very slowly. I wonder if he is hurt, but he shifts his weight and I realize it's not an injury, at least not one I can see.

Our eyes meet, and before I know it, I'm crossing the room and wrapping my arms around him, telling him it's okay, that it wasn't his fault, that he did everything he could. Jules reaches for us and we all hold each other for a long time. Cyrus is crying softly. "It wasn't your fault," I tell him. "You did everything you could. And I'm sorry too, Cy, I'm sorry for what I said. I'm so sorry."

Tina texts to say the car is waiting and I should come down. I hesitate; I want to stay in this huddle a bit longer and make sure Cyrus is okay. Maybe even have my own little breakdown. But I have to go; I have a job to do. I put the speech into Cyrus's hand and explain that he has to tell the community what has happened. And then I tell him to go home and wait for me. I'll be there as soon as I can, I say. And then he kisses me, a soft, tearful kiss.

Gaby walks me through the building and down the stairs. "I don't care that I was right," I say as soon as we are out of earshot.

"I know," he tells me. "It doesn't matter." He's holding my coat. I realize I've never really thanked him for standing up for me at the board meeting. I stop, steady myself against the banister, and try to summon the words. "Gaby, I wanted to say, all those times when

Cyrus, when everyone thought I was crazy—" My arms are shaking. I lean against Gaby for a moment and he holds me there, the wool of his suit soft and scratchy against my cheek. I give myself a few seconds, then I straighten up, he hands me my coat, and I make my way out of the building.

Tina has worked out a plan. Cyrus is going to announce a sweeping set of changes to the way things work, including shutting down Obit.ly. Then he's going to promise to do a better job of noticing when someone in our community is facing a crisis, and it's up to me and Ren to work out how the algorithm is going to identify people who might be at risk. I'll be at the NBC studio while Cyrus makes his WAICast, and then I get to answer questions on live TV.

At the studio, while they're doing my hair and brushing things onto my face and the producer is hovering with headphones and a clipboard, I'm thinking about what Cyrus might have seen on that rooftop. Whether he was able to get close enough to talk to Stephen, if Stephen turned around and met his eye, if they exchanged any words, if Cyrus came close to convincing him to stop, or if he was too late all along, every desperate word futile against the crime he had already committed.

The studio lights are ablaze in my eyes, and there's a person in my ear who's going to tell me when to go on. Directly in front of me, I can see what the television audience is seeing, which is a live feed of Cyrus's announcement.

Instead of the serene gaze that has greeted his audience every weekday, he looks out with cloudy eyes.

"Over the last three years," he begins, "our community has grown from hundreds to the tens of millions. We have developed long-lasting bonds that are based on the fundamental premise that the big moral questions of our lives remain unanswered, and that to ask these questions, of ourselves and of each other, is what brings us together as human beings.

"Last night I failed you as the steward of our community. I always said that I was only here as one of you, a person who has the same basic need for spiritual sustenance as everyone else. And yet I took on the responsibility of leading this organization, for making decisions that would affect all of you. A few months ago, I made the decision to integrate Obit.ly and WAI. I thought both platforms used the best of technology—that is, the ability to replicate our humanness into new and groundbreaking forms—to give us something that was previously unthinkable. But unthinkable things should sometimes remain in the realm of the imagination: ideas we consider and dream of but resist the urge to bring into being."

I know this speech by heart; I helped write it an hour ago. But now Cyrus hesitates. He looks down, pauses for a long moment, and goes off-script.

"There was one person on my team who warned me against the dangers of Obit.ly's messaging service. Her name is Asha Ray and she is my co-founder and my wife. She fought hard to make me and the others on our team see that we were out of our depth, and that this new path was unsafe for our community. Unfortunately, I did not listen. Our disagreement on this matter led to a rift between us, as colleagues, friends, and partners. I thought we were parting ways on ideological grounds, but really, it was my shortsightedness, my inability to see that she was fundamentally right and I was wrong. I gave up my life's greatest gift—my closest human connection—

because I was unable to see the higher truth in another person's vision."

At this point, his voice, quivering but steady, breaks. "For this reason, I am stepping down as CEO of WAI, effective immediately. I am announcing this to you, my friends and fellow travelers, first. My team and my board are hearing of it now for the first time. And I would like to say to my wife, Asha, that I can think of no better person to run the company from this day forward. Our future—not just as a company but as a human collective—is in question. We have challenges ahead that none of us could have foreseen. I hope sincerely that Asha will be the one to guide you through these challenging times, and that you, my friends, will embrace her as you did me."

I'm trying to get my head around what I've just heard. The screen that was previously displaying Cyrus's face is now reflecting what the viewers are seeing, which is me, perched on a stool, with improbably shiny cheekbones and a blowout that could hang at the MoMA.

Someone is talking to me. "Wow, Asha, what an announcement. Did you expect this at all?"

I open my mouth, but nothing comes out.

"Let's give Asha here a moment to absorb the news. She's just been invited to run WAI, a major social media platform that people say might soon become a rival to the establishment. Asha, did you ever imagine you would become CEO yourself?"

I try to assemble the random assortment of words that are flying around inside my head. "It wasn't something I ever expected to do. WAI was born on my laptop, an idea that I had when I met the extraordinary man you just heard from."

"And what happened then?"

"We all just agreed that Cyrus would run it. He was the one who had the rituals in his head, and once we launched, he was the person everyone looked up to."

"He certainly is a charismatic man. And if you decide to become CEO, what do you think you might change, especially in light of last night's tragic events?"

"We are all going to have to do a lot of soul-searching," I say. "Not just us at WAI but at all the tech companies. We have influence across every aspect of human life now. We have to take better care of our communities."

"Before we finish, I know our listeners out there are wondering— are you and Cyrus Jones going to remain a couple?"

I feel the tug of the fake lashes that are glued to my eyelids. "This project was a partnership from the start," I say. "It will always be that."

I'm led offstage. By the time Tina and I exit the building, there are cameras and microphones in our way. Tina takes a pair of sunglasses out of her bag and I put them on, and it's like a wall has gone up between me and the world. "You did great," she whispers, then she ushers me forward, where a car door is held open.

Jules is waiting for me inside the car. We drive downtown, the traffic still light at this early hour. He takes my hand. "We fired Marco," he says. "Charlie made him sign everything over to us, so we can do whatever we want with the tech."

"Burn it," I say. Then I say, "A lot of people loved AfterLight, didn't they?"

"It's possible that we were trying to do something important. But it doesn't matter now. It was too dangerous." He is still holding my hand. "Cyrus is right, you know. It should be you. It should always have been you."

"What's going to happen?" I ask him.

"Come stay with us," Jules says. "Gaby will cook, and we can sing duets and drive him crazy."

I smile, grateful, and tell him I'll think about it. But I feel like he's talking about a totally different group of people. Not ones who just killed a man because they couldn't stop what they were doing for long enough to consider the consequences.

Cyrus is curled on top of the blankets. He's wearing his coat, but he's taken off his shoes, which lie in a pile along with his hat, gloves, and scarf. He's asleep; he doesn't stir even as I lean over and lightly kiss the top of his head. I want to wake him up right away, but I also need a moment to take it all in. Cyrus, in our bed. Home.

I pace the apartment. Then I make myself sit down and reply to the frantic messages from my parents, and I send about a dozen emails to people who need to know that things are under control. My fingers are shaky on the keyboard, but inside I am strangely calm, working through the messages, saying what I have to say, reassuring, in control. Then I wander around the apartment again and eat an egg I boiled yesterday.

I pad up the stairs and find that Cyrus hasn't moved, he's still lying there on his side with his face pressed against the pillow and his hands between his knees. I get into bed beside him, and he stirs, removes his coat, and gets under the blanket with me. I nudge closer until I can feel the heat of his body radiating toward me, till I can smell his exhaled breath, which is so familiar it makes my own breath stop in my chest. He stirs, and then we are kissing, softly but urgently. Our bodies edge closer, our hands reaching toward each other. He mumbles tenderly to me, I hear him saying he loves me. He dips his head and grazes my neck with his lips, and then he unbuttons my shirt and everything is hazy and dreamlike, the want growing inside me as he shifts his body and presses on top of me. Cyrus. The tender yield of his skin, the rhythm and weight of his body, so familiar. I keep my eyes closed and let out a small cry. Cyrus.

We sleep. I wake up and it's dusk, and there are about a hundred messages on my phone, so I turn it off. I put my hand on Cyrus's face and he stirs, opens his eyes.

"I used my key. I hope you don't mind." And then: "I love you so much, Asha."

"I love you too."

"I killed Stephen."

"You didn't."

"He wanted to stop, I know he did. He just didn't give me enough time. We were talking about his wife, how they had gone all the way to this little town in Kerala to get married. That's the first time he had asked the platform for a ritual, and it had sent him halfway across the world. And he talked about how his wife had said that she felt her soul belonged in India even though she had never left Connecticut. He told me all of that. He talked and talked. But then, when I begged him to come down, when I said, 'Put the lighter down and you can tell me the rest,' this other look came over him, as if he was being taken over by something else, and he just turned around and then he was on fire."

Cyrus is crying now. "I ran toward him, but he had poured the gasoline everywhere and I couldn't reach him. I couldn't even get close." I feel him shake and I tighten my arms around him.

"It's okay," I say. I rub his back. I keep talking, soothing, reassuring.

"We were supposed to do good," he says. "We were supposed to be good."

"I know." What I think is, *We could have been good.* I feel a hollowness spreading through me, and then I can't bear to be so near him. I get up, move to the armchair across the bed.

"The worst thing is, I ruined us," Cyrus says to the ceiling.

"It took both of us to do that. You can't take credit for everything."

He manages a laugh. "Will you forgive me, Asha?"

"Of course I will. I do."

He crosses the room, kneels in front of me. "I'm so sorry. I will make it up to you. When I come back, we'll start over, I promise."

"Come back? Where are you going?"

"I can't stay here," he says. "I need to think. I need to try to figure some things out. How I got to this place. Something happened to me and I need to fix it. There's an ashram in Mysore."

I have a sudden image of him flying to India and eating cratefuls of mangoes. "Cyrus, there's a weird virus out there and we almost blew up our company. You're really going to leave me here to clean up your mess while you fuck off to the beach?"

"Don't be angry, Asha."

The blood rushes to my cheeks. I am angry. I am so, so angry. "Dammit, Cyrus."

"Let's not fight, okay? I screwed up. Even though you gave me every chance to not screw up, I still went ahead and did it."

"I can't tell if you're really apologizing or just feeling sorry for yourself."

"You have to decide that."

I look Cyrus straight in the eyes and it all comes rushing out of me. "Okay, then, let me tell you: you fucked up. You fucked up in the most profound sense. Not only that, you got everyone around us to believe that I was being paranoid when I was the only one who had my head screwed on straight. Marco is deeply damaged, anyone could see that, but you blew smoke in people's eyes and they didn't have the balls to call you on it. Not even Jules."

"Don't blame Jules."

Now that I've started, I can't stop. "Oh, I don't. I blame you. The only thing that's not your fault is the way people follow you, the way they believe in you even when you make mistakes. That is not your fault, that's just the way you were made. But the rest of it—the rest of it belongs to you. And I need to take responsibility for the fact that I just went ahead and let you. I let you take charge, make all the decisions, as if you were the only one whose opinion mattered."

And there it was. Sure, Cyrus displayed some epically bad judgment. But I gave him that power over me. I gave him all the privilege in the world so he could turn around and mess me up. *It wasn't your fault, Cyrus, it was mine. I bigged you up and smalled me down. I shone the light on you. I carried the water and let you drink.* Every injustice was authored by me, every wound nudged by my hand, even if he bore the knife. I opened my shirt and he cut me.

He pauses for a long time, allowing my words to circle around us. "We're not going to make it, are we?"

Cyrus does not need me to answer. He has always been able to look inside me, and now he can see it on my face, that though I may still love him and that the feeling of him, so close to me now, is enough to make my insides melt, too much has happened for us to be together.

He takes my hand and I let him. "I've lost the right to ask you to change your mind. Maybe once I've done some hard work, I'll begin to deserve you. You can decide."

"What happens to WAI?"

"That's up to you."

"When all of this went down last night, my first thought was we've worked too hard, we've done too much, to let it go. But maybe we have to shut it down, Cy. We killed someone. We can't just go on."

"You'll fix it. You know what to do."

I say the one thing that is still hovering between us. "Marco and Rory—all that talk about the apocalypse, the end of the world— it's happening."

Cyrus nods. "But I was still wrong."

"I'm scared, Cy." There, I've said it. The truth is, I'm afraid to face the world without Cyrus. But once the words are out of my mouth, they lose some of their power, and Cyrus tells me not to be afraid, because though he wishes desperately for us never to be apart again, I am strong, and I don't need anyone to see me through this. Not even him.

The moment I hear the door close, I want to run after him and tell him to come back, tell him it'll be okay, that I will take care of everything: him, the company, our marriage. The world is no longer a safe place—where will he go? He should be here. I should let him stay. But I give myself the gift of not doing that. Instead, I allow him to make his way downstairs, to walk out of the building and onto the street.

What would happen, I wonder, if we could return to that other time, the time where we drifted without purpose? Making s'mores in a fireplace. Sleeping under a sloping roof, our limbs entwined. Perhaps that time is over forever—not just because of what we have done but also because it was just a moment, and that moment has passed; the world has moved on, and perhaps those kinds of casual pleasures are gone forever. Perhaps, in the aftermath, Cyrus and I will tether ourselves together in a new way, with rules written in light of the ones we've already made and broken. Maybe our promises will be different this time.

I linger for a few more beats on the sensation of Cyrus, of holding Cyrus, pressing my face into his neck, his smell like rubbing a leaf against my hand.

And then I turn my attention to the thing we have broken. How I will fix it. Whether there is a way to fix it at all. I think about what will happen when I turn up at the office in a few minutes, whom I will talk to first, whether I will sit behind Cyrus's desk or remain where I've always been, leading from the middle. I wonder if our users will take me seriously, if they will forgive me for what happened to Stephen, or if they'll turn against the platform and shut us down. And I wonder about Rupert and Craig, whether they will let me run the company and if they will ever listen to what I have to say. More than anything, I wonder if it all will have been worth it. All that time trying to anticipate what people want and how to give it to them, how to answer their collective need for connection, while keeping sight of my own human self. And even if I solve that, will there be any point to it if the world as we know it collapses around us? I think of the question Li Ann asked me from the start, about what we will do when all the things that are familiar are gone, when the scaffolding of our lives comes apart and leaves us with the terrifying opportunity to start over. I would usually turn to Cyrus to answer these big questions, but it's up to me now. All of this is ahead, in the minutes and hours and days before me. I gather my coat and lace up my shoes, close the door behind me, and move toward a future—uncertain and unknown—and of my own making.

Acknowledgments

My thanks, first and foremost, to Roland, for being the kind of real-life romantic hero I can only hope to capture in writing, and to Rumi and Roxy for helping me find my funny bone. I love you all so much.

Thank you to Sarah Chalfant, Alba Ziegler-Bailey, and all my friends at The Wylie Agency for more than a decade of support, cheerleading, encouragement, tear wiping, and for humoring me when I tried to publish this book under a pseudonym because I was worried it wasn't serious enough. Sarah, you are the best agent and friend a girl could ask for, and I will always be grateful for whatever stars conspired to bring you into my life. My love, also, to Daisy and Clementine, for letting me watch you both grow into such beautiful, opinionated young women.

My gratitude to Jamie Byng for publishing all my books with the enthusiasm and spirit of adventure that only he can summon, and for setting me up on the world's best publishing blind date with Nan Graham and Kara Watson at Scribner. Thanks also to Jenny Fry, for many dumplings and much encouragement over the years, to Ellah Wakatama for superb editorial guidance, and to Francis Bickmore, Alice Shortland, Lucy Zhou, Gill Heeley, Aa'Ishah Hawton, and all the magicians at Canongate. Thank you to Nan Graham for taking a chance on Rose Lanam. To Kara Watson: making you LOL over

ACKNOWLEDGMENTS

email has become an important life mission. Thank you for reading countless drafts and for your insightful, intelligent, gracious editing.

Thank you to Jason Richman, Addison Duffy, and A. J. Leone at UTA for sending Asha's story into the world.

Many thanks to the entire ROLI crew—team, board, investors—especially Corey Harrower and Sarah Kosar—for letting me be your resident anthropologist. Thank you to Joe Treasure for always giving me a safe place to send writing I'm too embarrassed to show anyone else. Thank you to Michael Puett for reading an early draft and giving me the kind of enthusiastic support that has buoyed me through many moments of doubt, and thank you to David Grewal and Daniela Cammack for getting married in Cambridge City Hall. Thank you to Inshra Russell for brilliant website design.

To my people: Bee Rowlatt, Maha Khan Phillips, KS, Anya Serota, Leesa Gazi, Nazia Du Bois, Sohini Alam, Rohini Alam, Sawsan Eskander, Alexandra Pringle, Nataleigh Rene, Kate Enright, and Rachel Holmes—you are the feminist cavalry of my dreams.

And finally, thank you to my sister, who is exactly Asha's age and remains my inspiration for all things sassy, cool, and DGAF. And to my truly excellent parents, for a lifetime of love and encouragement. May we never be parted again as we have been in the Age of Covid.